Passion Unmasked

The drunken oaf's voice boomed again. "I'll see your face before the night's done, you jade!"

Her masked rescuer pushed Livvy gently against one of the pillars lining the ballroom. Shielding her with his body, he pressed her head to his shoulder and draped his cloak around her. Her heart galloped as his muscular form pressed against hers, at first in fear. Then, as he did nothing more, heat flowed through her, stoked by his ragged breathing, his unmistakable reaction to their closeness. It was wonderful and terrifying. And all he did was hide her under his cloak, his body subtly vibrating with restraint. Then he shifted. "I think . . . he is gone," he whispered.

She looked up at him, but it was too dark to see his eyes. The heat rose again inside her, like a madness. Recklessly she stretched upward, on tiptoes, and raised her face to him. His kiss was shockingly sweet: shy, hesitant, as he pressed his lips almost chastely to hers and stilled his body. Dreamily, she succumbed to pleasure; she parted her lips and kissed him back. . . .

Lady Dearing's Masquerade

Elena Greene

A SIGNET BOOK

SIGNET
Published by New American Library, a division of
Penguin Group (USA) Inc., 375 Hudson Street,
New York, New York 10014, USA
Penguin Group (Canada), 90 Eglinton Avenue East, Suite 700, Toronto,
Ontario M4P 2Y3, Canada (a division of Pearson Penguin Canada Inc.)
Penguin Books Ltd., 80 Strand, London WC2R 0RL, England
Penguin Ireland, 25 St. Stephen's Green, Dublin 2,
Ireland (a division of Penguin Books Ltd.)
Penguin Group (Australia), 250 Camberwell Road, Camberwell, Victoria 3124,
Australia (a division of Pearson Australia Group Pty. Ltd.)
Penguin Books India Pvt. Ltd., 11 Community Centre, Panchsheel Park,
New Delhi - 110 017, India
Penguin Group (NZ), cnr Airborne and Rosedale Roads, Albany,
Auckland 1310, New Zealand (a division of Pearson New Zealand Ltd.)
Penguin Books (South Africa) (Pty.) Ltd., 24 Sturdee Avenue,
Rosebank, Johannesburg 2196, South Africa

Penguin Books Ltd., Registered Offices:
80 Strand, London WC2R 0RL, England

First published by Signet, an imprint of New American Library,
a division of Penguin Group (USA) Inc.

First Printing, September 2005
10 9 8 7 6 5 4 3 2 1

PUBLISHER'S NOTE
This is a work of fiction. Names, characters, places, and incidents either are
the product of the author's imagination or are used fictitiously, and any resemblance to actual persons, living or dead, business establishments, events, or
locales is entirely coincidental.

The publisher does not have any control over and does not assume any
responsibility for author or third-party Web sites or their content.

To Teri and Kathleen

Prologue

*H*eart pounding, Livvy stared down at the elegantly engraved ticket in her hand. Dare she indulge this whim?

Ladies of Quality did not attend public masquerades. Except, perhaps, for a lark, or to meet a lover. She was not seeking a lover, but a lark . . . a lark was just what she deserved. She'd already spent a glorious week reveling in London's theatre, the opera, shopping, and even picking up the broken threads of friendships begun over ten years ago. Some of those morning calls she'd paid had even resulted in invitations.

The thought made her pause.

Though she had no ambition for anything but the most minor role in society, and certainly no desire to remarry, she had no wish to cause a scandal either.

The sound of the orchestra playing a quadrille seduced her ears, set her feet to tapping. It fed the reckless mood that had stolen over her since she'd donned her costume. She did not feel like herself, and the sensation was intoxicating.

Who could possibly recognize her?

She glanced down at her costume. How she and
Alice, her maid, had laughed over the black wig, the
golden headpiece and matching mask, the golden asps
that encircled her upper arms, the flowing white gown
that bared one shoulder. Drat! Livvy quickly pulled the
bodice up a fraction of an inch to hide her distinctive
little birthmark, shaped rather like a musical note.

There. Now she was Queen Cleopatra. No one
would recognize her as Olivia, Lady Dearing, relict—
what a ghastly term!—of Walter, sixth Baron Dearing
of Dearing Hall, Kent, who'd broken his neck on the
hunting field over a year before.

Eleven years rolled back. It was over.

She was free.

She stepped forward, gave her ticket to the usher
and entered the ballroom. Enormous chandeliers cast
a glow over the dance floor. More chandeliers lit the
upper galleries above, but the boxes at floor level were
dark. She wondered if the rumors about what went
on at these public masquerades were true. But no
harm would come to her if she remained on the dance
floor, and Charles awaited her outside. Her burly footman would know how to deal with anyone who tried
to cross the line.

She lifted her chin and surveyed the scene with
growing fascination. The ballroom swarmed with
pleasure-seekers: some wearing simple masks and
dominoes, others in more fanciful costumes. Fairy
Queens, Turks, Greek gods and goddesses, shepherds
and demons swirled before her. Above, in the gallery,
she saw more joking and flirting merrymakers.

Then her gaze was arrested by a lone figure just
above her.

Tall and powerfully formed, he wore a black cape
that hung open to reveal a skeleton painted over a
black shirt and pantaloons. A hood covered his head
and he wore a mask painted in the semblance of a

skull. His solitude and perfect stillness made a stark contrast to the movement on all sides.

She shivered, and not unpleasantly. How pagan it was: Death among the revelers! A throwback to earlier, more superstitious times. A reminder that life was fleeting and pleasure should be savored.

A moment later, the quadrille came to an end and just as she'd hoped, several gentlemen came her way to solicit her hand to dance. She bestowed the first dance on a young, shy-looking Highwayman, then, careful not to encourage any one partner, on a dashing Spaniard. Feeling suddenly younger than her twenty-nine years, she smiled at the silly compliments they paid her, and even more with the simple joy of dancing.

Walter had despised the pastime.

During the next interval, her gaze was drawn back to the gallery. Death still stood there, but now he conversed with a gaily dressed Harlequin.

So he was flesh and blood after all.

And—she could not help noticing—certainly the finest figure of a man present.

Distracted, she allowed herself to be led back to the floor by a colorfully garbed Grand Turk. Too late she smelled the hateful odor of brandy on his breath; too late she realized that he'd mistaken her for an entirely different class of female. Stilling a sense of panic, she endured his broad hints and the sweaty squeeze of his hands, but when the music ended, she slipped away from his groping arms and darted through a gap in the crowd. Clearly it was time to leave. She'd enjoyed her few dances; there was nothing else worth staying for.

Vaguely disappointed, she stopped beside a pillar to check if the Turk had followed her.

"I see you, my Queen! You shan't escape me so easily!"

Seeing him not far behind, she hurried off again, dodging between knots of curious revelers and amorous couples, making her way toward the entrance and the protection of her footman. She broke into a run, and suddenly cannoned into what seemed like a wall of darkness. The unseen wall swirled, revealing a ghastly skeleton, and she lost her balance.

Black-gloved hands held her in a strong grip. A shriek escaped her throat.

"Please do not be frightened, ma'am. I am perfectly harmless."

His voice, a mellow baritone, warm and dark, struck a chord deep within her. As she regained her balance, he loosened his hold.

There was no need to panic.

"I—I am sorry I screamed," she said, straightening up. "It was just that—your costume was so—startling."

Let him think it was just the costume.

"You are in a hurry; is someone troubling you?" he asked in that same rich and reassuringly sober voice.

Dark eyes gleamed down at her through the eyeholes of Death's mask; below, another opening revealed full, beautifully shaped lips.

Nervously, she glanced back. About twenty feet away the Turk still meandered among the crowd, perhaps seeking new prey.

"The man in the turban?" the stranger asked.

She turned to him and nodded.

"Do you think he would leave you be if we danced together?"

Her breath caught, and she stared up at him. No one would tangle with a tall gentleman in the guise of Death, she decided. If they did, they would soon discover that the painted bones concealed entirely solid and powerful muscles.

But could she trust him?

"Y-yes, I am sure he will," she replied.

"Then I would be honored to lead you out into this set," he said. He released her shoulders and offered her his arm, eyes gleaming, as if he enjoyed coming to her rescue.

He was sober. He was polite. And thoroughly intriguing.

She could not resist.

"Thank you, sir." She laid her hand on his arm.

"I should thank you. You will have to be patient with me. It has been many years since I last danced."

His tone was light, but she wondered . . . had he been in mourning, too?

"It is no great matter." She smiled up at him. "No one will notice a misstep, I'm sure."

They took their places in the set. A moment later, another familiar country-dance began to play, lively, too vigorous for conversation. Livvy once again threw herself into the dance, relieved to see that after a few stumbles, Death fell into the rhythm as well, his cape swirling around him theatrically. Though as large and powerfully built as Walter had been, the stranger was light on his feet. From the grin that peeked through the opening in his mask, she guessed he enjoyed it, too.

Then she realized her bodice had shifted again. When they came to the top of the set, she surreptitiously twitched it back into place.

"I must thank you again for coming to my rescue, sir," she said as they stood awaiting their turn to rejoin the line.

"It was my pleasure. In truth, I had seen you from above and was hoping to ask you for a dance." He cleared his throat. "I hope that Grand Turk did not frighten you too much."

"No, he was merely making a nuisance of himself. My footman awaits me and would have protected me in any case."

"You came alone?"

Livvy paused, knowing how scandalous her behavior must seem. But it was unlikely they would meet again, or that he would recognize her.

She nodded. "And you?"

"I came with my cousin. He has been plaguing me for some time to come with him to one of these affairs. I agreed only to prove I am a hopeless case, beyond the pleasures of dancing."

"Is that why you chose to be the skeleton at the feast? A joke on your poor cousin?" she asked playfully.

"A rather feeble joke, I suppose," he said, looking down at her with an expression that was suddenly intent. Hungry.

"Have you accomplished your aim, then? Proven that you are a hopeless case?"

He stared down, light from the chandeliers again reflecting in his eyes. Brown. No, not brown: a rich mahogany, deep and velvety, fire in their depths.

"Perhaps not."

His voice sent another current of warmth curling through her. A dangerous feeling. One she'd not felt since she was seventeen.

Then it was time for them to rejoin the dance. Livvy did so with a mixture of regret and relief, which only grew as the dance progressed to its inevitable end. She curtsied toward her partner, the warmth he'd kindled strengthening as he swept her a deep bow.

She did not want to feel it. And yet . . .

"I must go now," she said, forcing the words out.

He stared down at her, mouth tightening. In disappointment?

"Must you?" he asked softly. "I would very much enjoy another dance."

"I . . . think I must go."

"At least allow me to escort you to your footman."

She nodded, reluctant to part any sooner than necessary. And she did feel safe with him. As he took her arm once more, she stole a glance toward his profile. He was licking his lips; he was about to speak. Was he going to ask her name, or . . . Lud! She'd read about it so many times in novels. He might be planning to invite her to a late supper. In stories, that always ended in the heroine's seduction and ruin. The authors of those novels did not, perhaps, realize that ruin could take more respectable forms.

In any case it was time to leave.

She sped up, but a moment later the stranger spoke.

"Forgive me if I seem forward," he said, with disarming hesitancy. "But I should very much like to know—"

"Ah, there you are! You shan't run away now!"

Livvy turned to see the Turk coming their way from the opposite end of the ballroom. Her escort glanced back, then took her arm and began to lead her on a crooked path through the milling revelers.

The Turk's loud voice boomed again. "I'll see your face before the night's done, you jade!"

Death steered her ever faster through the crowd, then pushed her gently against one of the pillars that lined the sides of the ballroom. Shielding her with his body, he pressed her head to his shoulder and draped his cloak around her.

Her heart galloped as his muscular form pressed against hers. First in fear, then, as he did nothing more, an old, familiar heat flowed through her, stoked by the sharp intake of his breath, the betrayal of his unmistakable masculine reaction to their closeness.

It was wonderful and terrifying.

And all he did was hold her. He made no attempt to kiss or fondle her, merely hiding her under his cloak, his body subtly vibrating with his restraint. Nothing more. He demanded nothing more.

Desire flushed her body, and she stiffened. She couldn't allow this, didn't want to feel anything like it again. But she didn't wish to run away either. So they stood for long moments, pressed so close that she could barely distinguish his labored breathing from her own, while desire ebbed and flowed with her fears.

Then he shifted. "I think . . . he is gone," he whispered.

She looked up at him, but it was too dark to see his face. His ragged breath spoke of arousal. The heat rose inside her again, like a madness. Recklessly, she stretched upward, on tiptoes and raised her face to him. Another tortured breath, and he lowered his face to hers.

His kiss was shockingly sweet: shy, hesitant, as he pressed his lips almost chastely against hers and stilled his body. As if he guessed what she wanted when she herself had not known. Dreamily, she succumbed to pleasure; she parted her lips and kissed him back, relishing the firm roundness of his lips, the taste of him, the merest hint of wine on his breath.

She gasped as the stranger's tongue curled around hers. Shocked, she submitted to his slow, tentative exploration, sensing she had but to say the word and he would stop. But she didn't wish to stop him. She lifted her arms to embrace him, ventured to flick her tongue against his. A shudder ran through his body; he let out a low groan, yet did nothing but kiss her.

Walter had never kissed her like this; she had not known that anyone *could* kiss so.

Then thoughts of Walter fled. The stranger deepened his kiss; she let out a little moan of pleasure. He pressed against her more closely and she tightened her embrace, whimpering, returning each flutter of his tongue. She felt safe yet lost, feasting yet hungry, helpless with longing for more.

A chill came over her. She froze, then pulled her face away.

She had vowed never to be helpless again.

"I cannot . . . I am sorry. Let me go," she whispered.

For a moment Death continued to press her against the pillar, the rhythm of his breath harsh, his body hard.

"Please," she begged, terror constricting her throat. "Let me go. I should never have come!"

Then he backed away, slowly releasing her. As she slid out from under his cloak, she nearly wept with relief. He was a gentleman after all.

"Forgive me," he said in one shuddering breath. "Please don't be frightened. I won't touch you again if you don't wish, but please let me—"

His eyes were dark, full of desire and remorse; his voice low and caressing. She was touched, but it was wrong to stay. It was terribly wrong of her to have encouraged him.

"I must go," she interrupted before she changed her mind. "Please don't follow me!"

Legs shaking, she ran along the side of the room, vaguely aware of curious glances as she dodged groups of people in garish costumes, bumping into some. She rushed into the sparsely filled entrance hall. Thank God! There was Charles, solid and reliable, coming forward and holding her dark blue evening cloak.

"Is someone causing you trouble, ma'am?" he asked worriedly.

"No, no, but I must leave now." Frantically, she pulled on her cloak and lifted the hood over her head.

Then a mad indecision came over her. She glanced back toward the ballroom. Had the stranger followed her, to make sure she left safely?

"There you are! Promised myself I'd see your face, and more, before the night's through!"

She began to tremble. The Turk was approaching. She'd forgotten him, but now there was no choice but to leave.

"You'll not touch my mistress," said Charles, interposing his formidable mass between Livvy and the oncoming man.

"Leave the lady be!" Death's resonant voice rang through the entrance hall. Livvy peered around Charles and saw the Turk turn to face his antagonist.

"Who the devil are you and how are you going to stop me?" the Turk asked, with all the bravado of a drunkard.

In two swift strides, Death closed the distance between them; in another heartbeat, his fist swung into the Turk's jaw, knocking him to the floor.

A woman screamed. Several persons started toward them.

"We must go, my lady!" said Charles.

Death stood over the Turk's rolling and cursing form, eyes blazing grimly through the holes in his mask.

The Turk staggered to his feet. "Damn you, you doxy!" he shouted, staring at Livvy, then at Charles, then back to Livvy. "I've a notion who you are, and once—"

He lunged toward Death, only to be knocked neatly to the floor again. More screams echoed. A crowd began to form.

"We must go," insisted Charles. Putting an impersonal arm around Livvy, he half-led, half-dragged her away.

She stumbled along, not daring to look back. Death was more than a match for the Turk. There was no need to worry about him, or even to think about him ever again. They'd shared a few dances. A kiss. Anything more was unthinkable. Impossible. And it always would be.

She choked back a sob as Charles helped her into the carriage. This was just a temporary madness. She would laugh about it tomorrow. But as she watched the Pantheon recede through the window, it was all Livvy could do not to cry.

The Morning Intelligencer, *March 10, 1809*

The Author of this column thought himself in- ured to the Licentious Behavior commonly dis- played by Persons attending those most Iniquitous of Entertainments, Masked Balls at the Pantheon Theatre. However, at Yesterday's Ball, even this Author was shocked by the behavior of a certain Lady D— of Kent, a Widow, who was seen sport- ing with Lord A—, a Nobleman known for his Promiscuous Inclinations. It is this Author's re- gretful conviction that Lady D— will continue to welcome Solace for her Loneliness from such Gentlemen who prefer Beauty and a Liberal Character to Modesty and Virtue.

Chapter One

April 15, 1812

"*P*romise me you won't do anything hasty!"

Sir Jeremy Fairhill frowned, listening to Lord Bromhurst's warning as they strode along the plain but scrupulously clean halls of the Foundling Hospital. How could he convey to his friend the sense of urgency he'd felt ever since he'd spoken to the matron?

"I know it seems sudden," he replied. "I said nothing to Mrs. Hill yet, but as soon as she told me about the child I knew it was meant to be."

"Have you thought how it will look?" Bromhurst scowled and came to a halt. Almost as tall as Jeremy and much stouter, with grizzled hair and fierce eyebrows over steely gray eyes, he could seem intimidating to anyone who did not know he bore one of the kindest hearts in England.

"Some people may misconstrue the situation, but—"

"You don't know the half of it! As President of the Board of Governors, I have over four hundred souls to think of—and perhaps more in the future, God willing! I owe it to them to maintain the good name of our institution."

"I understand," said Jeremy soothingly. "But will you at least allow me to broach the matter to the General Committee?"

Bromhurst continued to frown. "I would rather you took some time to think it over. Better yet, sleep on it."

"I shall not change my mind. I owe this to Cecilia, to her memory."

Finally, an opportunity to make things right.

"Oh very well then, we're already late. Talk to the Committee. We'll see what they think."

"Thank you!"

Bromhurst made a harrumphing sound and stomped off. Jeremy followed him. A minute later they entered the Committee Room, simply furnished but graced by the famous painting of *The March to Finchley* that Hogarth himself had donated to the Hospital half a century before. A dozen or so heads turned as Jeremy and his friend entered and made their apologies, then the next hour or so was spent on routine Hospital business. Jeremy forced himself to attend, though the information he'd just learned from Mrs. Hill, the matron, dominated his thoughts.

He'd never felt so sure of fate playing a hand in his life.

Looking about the long table, his heart warmed. Unlike the majority of the hundreds of Governors, who contented themselves with making donations, this group undertook the day-to-day administration of the charity. Consisting of lords, clergy, merchants and professional men, it was one of the most generous and forward-thinking group of men anywhere. They were his friends. They would support him.

The twinkle of a large diamond drew Jeremy's eye to the elaborately tied cravat of Sir Digby Pettleworth, the newest member of the Committee. Well, most of them were his friends.

"Sir Jeremy," said Bromhurst, recalling his attention. "Please present the status for the branch hospital project."

His was the last item on the agenda.

"I have sent about a half-dozen more letters of so-licitation, and received two new pledges this past week," he reported. "If all continues well, we may be in a position to begin the search for a suitable tract of land next year."

"Excellent," said Bromhurst with a hearty smile, echoed by nods and smiles around the room.

They would understand his latest resolve, too.

"I have one other matter to bring forward," said Jeremy, raising his voice slightly.

The group silenced, waiting for him to speak again.

"Earlier today I had occasion to speak to Mrs. Hill. After our business was complete, she reminisced about my wife's visits to the Hospital, and let fall that Lady Fairhill used to take great pleasure in playing with a certain girl. Mary Simms."

He glanced around, noticing arrested expressions on some of the faces around the table.

"On her deathbed," he continued, "my wife begged me to care for someone named Mary, but she did not mention a surname. Her father suggested that she referred to a childhood friend who was in indigent circumstances. Although I helped the young lady toward a good marriage, I never felt satisfied that I fulfilled my wife's wish. But as soon as Mrs. Hill mentioned her, I felt certain that it was Mary Simms she spoke of."

"What did Mrs. Hill say? Is the girl of an age to enter domestic service?" asked the Archbishop.

Jeremy shook his head. "It is of no consequence. I am convinced my wife wanted me to raise Mary as a daughter. As the child we never had."

"That is unheard of," drawled Sir Digby Pet-tleworth, an unpleasant sneer on his sallow face. "No one takes these children to raise as their own."

Jeremy saw a worried frown cross Bromhurst's face.

"Besides," continued Sir Digby, "everyone would say Mary must be your child. How would it look?"

"Malicious individuals might make that construction," said Jeremy, carefully masking his annoyance. "However, if it is made known that I am taking Mary in to fulfill my wife's deathbed wish, I believe no one will be surprised."

A number of the other Governors nodded kindly. Jeremy suppressed a pang at the near-legendary status his marriage to Cecilia held in everyone's minds. At least it would serve him well now, to aid him in fulfilling her last request.

"I'm afraid there is a problem," said Bromhurst, rubbing the side of his nose.

"What is it?" Jeremy asked when Bromhurst hesitated.

"Mrs. Hill did not tell you that Mary is no longer at the Hospital?"

"No, I had not the time to question her. You cannot mean Mary has been apprenticed out already?"

"No, she is not old enough."

Jeremy leaned forward, confused by Bromhurst's reluctance to continue. "Then where is she?"

"At Rosemead Park," said Bromhurst finally.

"Gad! Lady Dearing's home?" Sir Digby exclaimed. "You don't say so! What would one of the foundlings be doing *there*?"

Jeremy flashed a questioning look at Bromhurst.

"It happened several years ago, before you joined the Committee," Bromhurst explained. "Lady Dearing is a widow, and having no children of her own, she wished to take one of the girls to raise. An unusual request, but her friends, Viscount Debenham and his wife, assured me of her character. The matter was discussed by the members of the Committee, and we decided to grant her request."

"You could not have had any idea of the woman's reputation!" said Sir Digby, somehow managing to sound shocked and delighted at once.

The fop had a damned unmanly predilection for gossip.

"What do you mean?" Jeremy asked bluntly.

"I realize that most of you gentlemen do not move in fashionable circles," said Sir Digby, with a patronizing look about the room. "But I would have thought Lord Bromhurst and Sir Jeremy might have known."

"I am not conversant with the latest on-dits, but I cannot believe that Lord Bromhurst would allow an improper person to take charge of any of our children," Jeremy said, and turned his gaze back to his friend.

"Of course not!" Bromhurst scowled. "There *was* some damaging gossip published about the lady some years ago, but I am certain the children are perfectly well in her care."

"The children?" Jeremy lifted an eyebrow. "How many of our children are at Rosemead Park?"

"Four in total. After the first case, I decided to exercise my discretion as President and allow her to take in three more."

Some of the other Governors looked surprised.

"I for one am not easy with the situation," said the Archbishop querulously. "I cannot help wondering if she is merely amusing herself by overindulging them. This might be a good opportunity for Sir Jeremy to conduct an investigation."

"But only think of the gossip that might ensue if one of our Governors were known to consort with her," said Sir Digby.

"Why *is* she so notorious?" asked Jeremy, stifling an impulse to shake Sir Digby.

"Why, she is known to have had a legion of lovers since her husband's death. She flaunts herself at the theatre and the opera, wearing the most scandalous of gowns, entertains scores of lovers in her favorite suite at Pulteney's Hotel, and they say"—here Sir Digby lowered his voice and looked apologetically at the Archbishop—"they say she holds orgies at Rosemead, with wine flowing and—I blush to say it—nude bathing in the fountains."

"Rubbish!" said Bromhurst, with a disgusted look.

The other Governors joined in a general rumble of disbelief. Jeremy knew they shared his annoyance with the middle-aged fop, who only attended meetings in an attempt to impress his wealthy father-in-law, Tobias Cranshaw the banker, one of the Hospital's most generous benefactors.

"And then there is the matter of her husband's death," continued Sir Digby.

Jeremy stared at him. Was the fool suggesting Lady Dearing had had something to do with it? Bromhurst would never have put children of the Hospital in the care of such a woman.

"What of it?" Jeremy asked.

"It happened over four years ago. Lord Dearing broke his neck taking a stone wall in the Cotswolds. They say he'd been drinking heavily and taking mad risks, all because his wife had been playing him false. They say she must have been using some damned French tricks to keep from conceiving an heir for him."

"I for one set no store by such gossip," Bromhurst snapped.

Jeremy looked at Bromhurst. "Have any other charges been laid at this woman's door?"

Bromhurst shook his head.

"But there is more!" insisted Sir Digby. He drew himself up straighter, and a creaking noise made Jeremy wonder if he wore a corset, like the Prince Regent. "No one can deny she is Lord Arlingdale's mistress."

Bromhurst snorted. "They have been seen together at the theatre and opera. It does not necessarily follow that there is anything illicit in their relationship. And there are many good reasons to allow this matter to lie."

Jeremy met Bromhurst's gaze and held it. "I do not say you acted improperly, sir, but I still believe an inspection visit may be in order. And I still have every intention of honoring my wife's final request."

"I tell you it is best to let the matter lie."

"Why?"

"For one thing, Lady Dearing has been most generous in her donations. For another, her friends the Debenhams are among our most important and influential benefactors. If we offend her, we offend them as well."

Bromhurst glared along the length of the table, daring anyone to dispute his words. Jeremy had not met the Debenhams in person, but they had responded to his letter soliciting donations for the branch hospital with a substantial pledge.

"Also," continued Bromhurst, rapping his hand on the table for emphasis, "the four children who are at Rosemead are no longer a charge on the Hospital, enabling us to take in four new children. Does anyone here need reminding of the usual fate of unwanted infants in London?"

He subjected the group to another fierce look. No one replied. "Moreover, Lady Dearing appears to have quite the way with troublesome cases, even those deemed incorrigible, like Ben Taylor."

Jeremy lifted an eyebrow. "I've not heard that name."

"Ah, that was several years ago, before you joined the General Committee. Ben started a fire at the Hospital."

A firebrand . . . Jeremy sat back and stared vacantly into Hogarth's painting. A notorious widow, entrusted with a possibly dangerous child. And Bromhurst had sanctioned it?

"But Mary Simms . . ." mused the Archbishop. "She

is the little girl who sang so sweetly in the choir, is she not? You cannot tell me *she* was incorrigible."

Bromhurst shook his head. "Of course not. However, several months ago, she insisted she could no longer sing, though the apothecary could find nothing wrong. At the same time, Mrs. Hill reported a sad change in the girl's manner. It is my hope that Lady Dearing's care will have a beneficial effect."

The Archbishop's kind eyes looked troubled. "You should have discussed this with the Committee. How can we be certain it is right to palm our difficult cases off onto this widow? I do believe Sir Jeremy should investigate."

Heads nodded around the table.

"Perhaps *I* could perform this delicate task," suggested Sir Digby. "After all, Sir Jeremy is so busy with the branch hospital project, I should not wish to divert his energies."

"A bit too eager, aren't you, Sir Digby?" one of them drawled.

Others stifled disgusted expressions. Sir Digby reddened and shifted downward in his seat, his corset creaking, the gaudy diamond in his cravat winking. Jeremy grimaced, recalling how the fop had boasted of recently found—what did they call themselves? The Select Company of Exquisites, or some such nonsense; a club of idle dandies with nothing better to do than gossip and invent ever more expensive modes of personal adornment.

From Bromhurst's deepening scowl, Jeremy deduced the Hospital's President did not trust Sir Digby to conduct the inspection. But he was not prepared for his next pronouncement.

"I believe everyone here can trust Sir Jeremy to discharge the task with the proper discretion," said Bromhurst when the room had quieted. "If anyone questions it, he is at Rosemead on Hospital business, nothing more."

Jeremy shot a grateful look toward his friend.

"I expect you will find everything in order at Rosemead," continued Bromhurst, "and that Mary Simms is best off where she is."

"Then the matter is settled," said Jeremy, deciding not to contradict his friend's final statement. "I shall speak again to Mrs. Hill and arrange to go to Rosemead tomorrow."

The meeting adjourned, but as the men filed out of the room, Bromhurst laid a hand on Jeremy's arm.

"Let's take a walk around the grounds, shall we?"

Jeremy nodded, unsurprised.

Bromhurst remained silent until they left the building. As the other Governors returned to their carriages, Jeremy and his friend strolled on the fields surrounding the Hospital.

"Does one's heart good to see, doesn't it?" said Bromhurst, waving an arm toward a group of boys playing nearby.

Jeremy drank in the sight. Bright eyes, rosy cheeks, sturdy legs: all spoke of health. Of a future.

"Indeed it does."

"Reminds us of why we do what we do."

He nodded, knowing Bromhurst was building up to something.

"One hates to think that for each child we take in, five must be turned away."

Jeremy clenched his jaw. He knew the numbers; he did not need reminding. One in five infants turned away. Nine out of ten infants left at parish workhouses, dead of starvation or neglect. Small corpses left overnight in London's parks, cleared away before genteel folk could be offended by the sight. Small corpses bobbing in the Thames.

"This place was founded over fifty years ago," continued Bromhurst, "and still the infants keep coming. People grow cynical; many say first causes must be addressed. Funds that might have come to us now go to societies for the reformation of prostitutes."

"The majority of women who bring their children here are not prostitutes," Jeremy protested. More often, they were lowly servant-girls, imposed on by fellow servants or employers, wretched creatures who liked to think of themselves as rakes. Jeremy knew better words for men who abandoned the young women they'd gotten into trouble.

"Of course," Bromhurst replied. "But until society is in a better state, what can we do but provide for the poor innocents?" He turned an intent gaze on Jeremy. "The branch hospital scheme depends on *you*. You have the reputation, the eloquence, the looks, the voice—"

"That is ridic—" Jeremy interrupted.

"Yes," Bromhurst went on, "the looks and the voice to coax the ladies into loosening their purse strings on behalf of the foundlings. And gentlemen respect and trust you. With such talents, you should be in Parliament!"

"The Whigs have approached me on several occasions," he replied in what he knew was a vain attempt to divert Bromhurst.

"What I'm trying to say is that you of all people must know what it takes to persuade people that caring for these children does not encourage immorality. If you wish this project to succeed, you must keep your own reputation spotless."

Jeremy frowned. "Are you withdrawing your approval to my plan to visit Rosemead?"

Bromhurst's mouth tightened. "I don't know why you are so set on it. Cecilia has been dead for over four years. It grieves me to see you still mourning her."

"I do not suffer."

His friend raised bristling eyebrows. "If you wish for children, why not just marry again and set up your own nursery?"

"I have an heir."

"Yes, I know, your cousin Thomas. But he is well provided for, and I'm sure he would be more than happy to be cut out."

Jeremy could not deny it.

"Lady Bromhurst and I would be delighted to see you with children of your own. You know no one was more saddened during your . . . disappointments."

Disappointments. A damned empty, weak word for the ordeals Cecilia had endured, while he suffered alongside, powerless to help her. He thrust back a spurt of unholy anger along with the memories.

"Your sympathies meant a great deal to us," he replied.

"It is time to move on, lad," said Bromhurst gruffly. "You are still a young man and—"

"I am five-and-thirty."

"A mere lad! I'm sure half the young misses at Almack's would jump at the chance to be the next Lady Fairhill. You need to go about in society more."

"I have done so, and met no one I wished to marry."

"For just one paltry Season, it must be two years ago now! Since then many pretty and amiable girls have come upon the Marriage Mart."

Jeremy remained silent. Useless to admit that he wanted none of the amiable misses thrown his way by Lady Bromhurst or Aunt Louisa. That since Cecilia's death there was only one lady for whom he'd felt more than a fleeting attraction.

And he'd frightened her off.

"You are too particular," continued Bromhurst. "You cannot expect to find another such wife as Cecilia. You set too high a standard."

I do not wish for another like Cecilia. Jeremy bit the words back. Everyone thought Cecilia a saint. They were right, and it would be disloyal to her memory to reveal that he did not wish to marry another saint.

Nor could he confide to anyone that the lady he'd sought during that one Season was a spirited but fool-hardy innocent with a ravishing figure and enchanting dimples. One who bore an oddly shaped birthmark on her left breast and made sweet, whimpering noises when kissed.

Who had run away from him.

"No," he said at length. "I have no such standards, sir. The fact is that I have no desire to remarry."

He'd inquired at costume warehouses, searched for her at balls and routs, even investigated the gossip in the aftermath of the masquerade. But all he'd discovered were the usual veiled references to the tawdry intrigues of Lord This and Lady That. Nothing about anyone who sounded like him or the ingénue he'd frightened with his ardor.

He'd never found her, never been able to apologize or make matters right.

"If you married, you could more easily pursue your plan regarding Mary Simms. You heard what Sir Digby said."

"Sir Digby Pettleworth is an ass."

"No doubt about it. He would not be on the Committee if he were not Tobias Cranshaw's son-in-law. But still I do not wish gossip to link your name with Lady Dearing's."

"Do you think I would risk it? I'm sure Sir Digby vastly overrates her charms."

"She *is* quite lovely," said Bromhurst, rubbing his nose again. "But after a marriage such as yours I can-not imagine you would succumb to temptation."

"I shall not succumb. Least of all to the overripe charms of a notorious widow."

"What worries me, lad, is what you are risking by this."

"Do you think I am being selfish to want to fulfill Cecilia's dying wish?"

Bromhurst averted his face for a moment. "No, but

it's taken all of four years for you to sort it out. You told me yourself that she had been given a great deal of laudanum at the end. How can you be certain what she meant?"

Jeremy stared back across the lawn toward the sight of playing children. Healthy limbs. Strong lungs. Smiling faces. A wrong made right. Hope.

"I am certain."

"Well then, I wish you good luck. But I beg you, be discreet. And be careful!"

"Have you ever known me to be otherwise?"

The furrows remained in Bromhurst's forehead.

Jeremy shrugged. In time Bromhurst would realize what Jeremy already knew: that he was beyond the age of foolish indiscretions, if not—God help him!—beyond feeling desire. But he'd spent most of his life mastering his passions; his disastrous lapse three years ago would be his last.

Chapter Two

"Ten thousand pounds? Adolphus, I am so disappointed. I did not think you would jest with me in this manner!"

Livvy smiled sweetly across her tea at her husband's nephew and heir. Adolphus, seventh Baron Dearing, had never impressed her with his intelligence. In this, as well as his light brown hair and the regular contours of his face, he resembled her deceased husband, though Adolphus lacked Walter's athletic physique. And unlike Walter, he was no worse than an annoyance.

"It is not a jest. I am entirely serious, dear aunt." He leaned forward, the diamond pin in his cravat catching the light. "I realize it must seem quite a vast sum to you. Just imagine the style of living it would afford you, perhaps in Greece or Italy."

The fool smiled. As if she could be so gullible!

"Ten thousand pounds, to give up my jointure and leave England? Paltry, my dear nephew."

His jaw dropped. "Paltry?"

"Paltry. You are well aware that my jointure provides me two thousand a year. I trust you are not expecting that I will die within the next five years?"

"No, of—of course not," Adolphus blustered.

"Allow me to reassure you that I intend to live a very long and very happy life," she said consolingly.

Adolphus gulped. "But Sophronia and I cannot help but wonder if you might be happier in Rome or Greece. You cannot enjoy your present position in English society."

"I am quite resigned to my lot."

"You cannot mean that. You are not received anywhere!"

Livvy nearly giggled at her nephew's thunderstruck expression. He and Sophronia could imagine no worse fate than social ostracism. But painful as the scandal following the masquerade had been, she had come to learn that a reputation ruined beyond repair—along with a fine estate and a generous jointure—meant unprecedented freedom for a widow.

"I am content with the friends I have," she replied.

"Yes, I know, Viscount Debenham and his wife. I cannot imagine how they can bear to visit with you, when you live as you do. Are you not aware of how your behavior reflects on me and Sophronia? On little Walter?"

"I do not know why it should."

"How can it not? Are you unaware of what is said about you?"

"My dear nephew, I am afraid common report has slightly exaggerated the number of my amours."

Adolphus reddened like a girl. The self-conscious prig!

"But I am content," she continued. "I have my music, my garden and the children to keep me very well entertained."

"Yes, the children . . ."

One of his eyelids began to twitch; a sure indication that she'd reached the crux of his problem.

"What about the children?" she asked with deceptive calm.

"Well, there's a new rumor."

"Yes?"

"It's being said that the little one—er—"

"Robbie. His name is Robbie. They all have names, you know," she said, picturing four dear faces in her mind. Philippa, Ben, Mary and Robbie. Her children, and Adolphus was worse than an idiot to think he could part her from them.

"It's being said that he must be yours. Of course I realize the complete impossibility of such a thing!" he said with false sympathy dripping from his tone.

Livvy bit her lip. What a cruel, small-minded *thing* he was to remind her of her failure to produce an heir for Walter.

"But think how sad if a son of mine had cut you and little Walter out of the title and estate," she murmured.

Adolphus reddened again, but his small eyes flashed. "I bore too much affection for my uncle to feel anything but regret that he never had the joy of fathering a son," he replied loftily. "It grieves me that you have so little respect for his memory, living as you do, taking in those little bast—"

He broke off as Livvy leapt from her chair.

"Do not call the children that again," she said, staring down at him contemptuously.

He cringed, plucking at his diamond pin. "B-but that's what they are, after all."

"They are innocent children," she replied, resuming her seat. "Foundlings. Yes, some or all of them may be illegitimate, but I for one cannot hold their parents' transgressions against them."

"Such charitable sentiments may be admirable, but I don't know why you cannot content yourself with making a modest donation to the Foundling Hospital," he said peevishly. "Why must you take such children into your care? Whatever you say, they are not the innocents you make them out to be. I am sure the staff at the Hospital were more than happy to see them go!"

"They knew these children required more attentive care than they could provide."

"What of the damage they may cause the house and grounds? Have you thought of that? Your father could not possibly have intended this when he settled Rosemead on you."

"Papa only wished to make provision for me and any children I might have. You must content yourself with the knowledge that when I am gone, Rosemead will go to you and your heirs."

If only her marriage settlements did not preclude her from bequeathing the property to the Foundling Hospital! It was the one thing she would change if she could. Papa had never dreamed she would not have children of her own to provide for. Having no other family, Papa had set up the default clause leaving the estate to Walter and his heirs, but he had not truly expected it would be invoked.

Only her remarriage could prevent it, but that was out of the question.

She rose from her chair and once more smiled sweetly at Adolphus, who was obliged out of politeness to rise as well.

"In the meantime," she said, "I am mistress at Rosemead. You will have to trust that I shall keep it in good repair for you. Now I have a number of matters to attend to. I am sure you will excuse me."

He got up, his face reddening, but his eyelid continued to twitch. No doubt his failure to win her cooperation would result in a dreadful scold from his darling Sophronia.

"You will not reconsider what we have discussed?" he asked, his voice rising to a squeak.

"Very well," she replied. For a few seconds, she assumed a thoughtful expression, then shook her head. "No, I am extremely sorry but I still must decline your kind offer."

"You cannot have given it any thought!" he sputtered, dragging his heels as he followed her out of the drawing room and into the entrance hall where her butler awaited with his overcoat, hat and cane. Dear old Thurlow! Always ready to rid her of unwelcome visitors.

"Perhaps—perhaps if the amount is insufficient— shall we consider increasing it to fifteen thousand—" Adolphus said quickly in a low voice, embarrassed by Thurlow's presence.

"Do not distress yourself! There is no sum large enough to persuade me to leave Rosemead."

Livvy bit her lip to keep from laughing at her nephew's appalled expression. He muttered something indistinguishable as Thurlow helped him into his greatcoat, then made an ungraceful bow and turned to leave.

"Please send my love to Sophronia! And little Walter!" she called after him.

She smiled wickedly, seeing his back stiffen at her words.

At least it was his back she was seeing.

Glancing at the clock on the hall mantel, she saw it was over an hour before the children and their governess departed for their daily ramble in the Park. Excellent! An hour of painting would restore her mood before she rejoined them.

"Thank you, Thurlow," she said, smiling at the elderly butler. "Now please see that I am not disturbed for the next hour."

"Yes, ma'am."

She hurried to the salon at the northeast corner of the house that she used as a studio, eager to work out the poison of Adolphus's visit. Despite her relish at having won this latest encounter, she was conscious of a faint sick feeling to her stomach. Adolphus would hurt her if he could. But he could not. Bless Papa for having ensured her financial independence with the most scrupulously worded of marriage settlements! Adolphus could scheme, but he had no power to coerce her.

As for his mean-spirited remarks, well, such things no longer distressed her. Much.

She put a smock over her green muslin morning gown, thinking over what he'd said about her fall from grace. The truth was there were times she missed the pleasures of society, though not enough to take up the Debenhams' offer to try to reestablish her character. Harriet and Julian were dears, but she had gratefully declined putting them in the awkward position of defending her. They had a new baby to occupy them, too.

It would have been different had she had children of her own, of course. But the children she cared for now would never enter that polite world, and she herself had learned that there was a wealth of meaningful activities to be enjoyed outside the *Beau Monde*. She'd recreated her life as she willed, and it was nearly perfect as it was.

Nearly.

She turned her attention to the canvas. The muddled image on it bore little resemblance to the earthenware jug of daffodils and hyacinths resting on a table by the wall, backed by a scrap of blue velvet. Surely it would improve with some work. She set to painting with a will, relishing the squishy feel of the oil paints, the tactile pleasure of pushing them recklessly around the canvas. Even the sharp smell of the paint was delightful.

She dabbed her brush into the yellow ochre, then realized she'd overloaded it when a splotch flew to a section of the canvas where there should have been only blue velvet. She smiled at her clumsiness, rather liking the way the golden color contrasted against the deep blue. She flicked another drop of paint against the blue background, then another. Perhaps she would start a new fashion.

Perhaps not, she decided a minute later, ruefully surveying the canvas. Since her schoolgirl days she'd been able to execute a creditable watercolor, but oil painting was a new departure. Perhaps lessons would help. In the meantime, she would scrape the mess off the canvas and try again.

She cocked her head at the picture once more, and laughed. Perhaps she should just frame it and send it to Adolphus and Sophronia as a present! But no, it really was no fun unless they actually felt obliged to display the awful thing. At least imagining them doing so put her in a better frame of mind. Adolphus was just a nuisance; a useful reminder of Walter and the life she'd left behind three years ago, which made her present bliss all the sweeter.

She glanced at the clock. Nearly time for her ramble with the children. Quickly, she began to set her brushes to soak, but dropped the last one as a voice rang out from the direction of the entrance hall.

"I must see Lady Dearing," the masculine voice said, in tones that were rich and urgent.

An unforgettable voice: a low, mellow baritone that resonated within her somehow.

Dizziness overcame her. How she'd longed to hear that voice, after that malicious article had mistakenly coupled her name with that of Lord Arlingdale, as doors had closed to her, as renewed friendships had faded and gentlemen of every description had tested their chances with the debauched widow who'd come to London seeking a lover. And he'd stayed away, whether from indifference or cowardice, she never knew.

He'd seemed so . . . *kind.*

Now he was here, rolling back months of pain and years of adjustment, tipping her world edgeways.

Why now?

She stole out of the room, quietly heading toward the entrance. Thurlow's voice sounded, too low for her to quite make out the words though she guessed he was trying to repel her visitor.

"No, I am *not* here to impose on her!" the stranger insisted.

The vehemence in his voice caused her to stumble. She missed his next words. Did it matter? Perhaps he'd been confused by the rumors about her and Lord Arlingdale. Perhaps he'd just discovered what had truly happened. Perhaps . . .

She reached the hall at a run, then stopped, breathless, to lock eyes with the man standing beside her butler.

Dear God, it was he! As tall as she remembered, his shoulders as broad. The folds of his greatcoat were flung back, revealing a sober black coat, a gray waistcoat buttoned over a flat stomach, dove-colored riding breeches molded over muscular legs. His hair was dark, a bit long, curling over a broad forehead. His chin firm, with the hint of a cleft, his lips as firm, as beautifully curved as she remembered. And his eyes— oh, those eyes! Framed by thick lashes, they were huge and dark. Focused, melting her with their intensity.

And completely lacking even the slightest glimmer of recognition.

Chapter Three

$\mathcal{L}$ ivvy's cheeks burned. Heavens, she'd all but flung herself into the arms of a man who was now regarding her as a complete stranger!

"My apologies, Lady Dearing," he said. "It seems I have come at an inconvenient time, but my business is important."

His face had darkened, as if he too was conscious of having locked gazes for a shockingly long interval. Still there was no hint that he recognized her. On the other hand, she was more certain than ever. There was no mistaking those eyes, that chin, those lips. Or that deep, rippling voice that instantly transported her back three years.

Apprehension pierced her reawakened yearning for him. If he did not remember her, why was he here?

Before she could say anything, Thurlow coughed.

"I did tell him you were not at home to visitors, my lady," he said apologetically.

"It is no matter. I had finished painting for the day," she replied, trying not to stare at her visitor.

"I am Sir Jeremy Fairhill," he said, handing her the card he'd been holding in his hand. "I am one of the Governors of the Foundling Hospital."

She stared at the card, marshaling her thoughts. "Has—has one of the children's parents come forward, perhaps?" she asked, unable to keep a quiver from her voice.

"Not exactly," he replied, eyeing her intently. "May I suggest we sit down to discuss the matter?"

A sense of foreboding came over Livvy at his unre-vealing tone, and his critical scrutiny. She did not think he recognized her, but was instead summing her up for some other reason. Had some new bit of gossip caused the Governors to reconsider her fitness to care for the children?

She reached a hand down to smooth her gown, in-stead finding the flannel of her painting smock. Good God! She must look a complete lunatic, and yes, there was a dab of yellow paint on her cheek! She saw it reflected in the mirror across the room.

"I—I shall be delighted to speak to you, Sir Jeremy. Thurlow, please show Sir Jeremy to the drawing room. Do you wish for some refreshment? Tea, perhaps?"

"I require nothing."

Sir Jeremy's tone was curt. She risked a peek at his face and saw to her dismay that his jaw was set in a disapproving line.

He *did* know her reputation, clearly.

"Then please excuse me," she said in a low voice. "I shall return in just a few minutes."

As Sir Jeremy followed Thurlow to the drawing room, Livvy fled up the stairs.

Sir Jeremy Fairhill . . . The name was familiar. Yes, Lord Bromhurst had spoken of Sir Jeremy's efforts to raise funds for the construction of a branch hospital. An eminently worthy man, then. A man of charity, who had kissed her into delirium against a pillar at the Pantheon Theatre. A member of the Foundling Hospital's Board of Governors, who could take away her children at will.

And he regarded her as if she were the Whore of Babylon.

She reached the end of the corridor and entered her bedchamber, relieved to see her maidservant, Alice, there mending a gown Livvy had torn during yesterday's walk with the children.

"Alice, one of the Governors from the Foundling Hospital is here to see me. I must look respectable. There is no time to be lost!"

The older woman looked startled but quickly set aside her work. She helped Livvy remove the painting smock and clean the paint off her face and hands. Once Alice had deftly rearranged her curls in her usual simple fashion, Livvy eyed her reflection in the glass.

One thing was certain. Until she knew his business, she could not allow Sir Jeremy to guess how they'd met. The fact that she'd kissed a stranger at a public masquerade would weigh heavily against her. The fact that she had kissed *him,* of all men, would make no difference. Gentlemen might be forgiven the occasional lapse, but ladies were expected to behave with greater restraint.

She frowned. Her sleeves were long, covering arms that had been bared the night of the masquerade. However, the gown was a frivolous pale green and cut fashionably low across her bosom, revealing the birthmark she'd struggled to hide under her costume that night. Bother! She'd long since given away all her mourning attire. There was not a single sober-hued or high-necked gown left in her wardrobe.

"A tucker! I need your tucker!"

"Yes, of course, m'lady," said Alice. "If you'll help me—"

Livvy helped Alice remove the scrap of muslin and then sat quietly as Alice pinned it into her own bodice. Surveying the result, she nodded.

"Would you like a cap, ma'am? Caps look ever so sober," offered Alice helpfully.

Livvy pondered the suggestion for a moment. Her blond curls might help confuse the matter. The black wig had hidden them completely. Or so she hoped.

"No, thank you," she replied. "It might appear that I am trying too hard to make a good impression."

"Don't worry, ma'am. You've nothing to hide. I'm sure you'll handle this Governor, whoever he is."

Livvy hurried out, wishing she did indeed have nothing to hide.

Jeremy paced the drawing room, looking about for more clues to the nature of his hostess. An interesting assortment of art decked walls of a cheery yellow color, surmounted by plasterwork in rococo swags of fruit and roses. Gracefully curved chairs with embroidered seats, a striped sofa and a pianoforte were arranged casually atop a richly patterned Aubusson carpet.

His gaze flashed back to the pianoforte. A beautiful instrument, gleaming with polish, nevertheless one of its carved, turned legs showed signs of having been broken and carefully repaired.

Surely none of the children could have wreaked such damage.

He looked toward the French doors leading to a terrace outside. In a corner, a harp stood, and a bowl of hyacinths and narcissi added color and fragrance to the feminine setting.

He'd half expected something vulgar, not a place so thoroughly ladylike. And beguiling. Lady Dearing was clearly a connoisseur of beauty. An eccentric, Bromhurst had called her.

He stared again at the paintings, but he could not guess if any of the landscapes, portraits or floral pieces were her work. That she was an amateur artist was clear from her smock and the dab of yellow paint that had blossomed on her cheek like a daffodil petal. He'd felt the most insane urge to wipe it away. To see if the peachlike skin beneath was as soft as it looked. It was hard to believe she was in her thirties.

He wished he hadn't been so curt with her in the entrance hall, but the way she had smiled up at him out of those larkspur-blue eyes had completely bowled him over. At first he'd thought she smiled for him. But how could that be? Was it her nature to try to captivate every man she met?

Now he was sounding like Sir Digby Pettleworth.

Muslin swished. Jeremy turned and promptly found himself staring again. Scrubbed clean of paint, Lady Dearing's cheeks glowed a healthy pink. Golden ringlets spilled carelessly from a ribbon the color of budding leaves. As she walked toward him, the folds of her matching gown hinted at lush curves and a trim waist. The lace high at her throat was somehow more provocative than the low necklines currently in vogue. Had she chosen this demure ensemble for just this effect?

He wrenched his gaze away.

"Please sit down, Sir Jeremy," she said.

Her voice was delightful, soft as rain. Her tone was friendly, neither coy nor cold.

He sat on the sofa while she took a seat in one of the chairs. For a moment, he struggled to remember the words he'd planned to say.

"You said you wished to speak to me about the children."

There was a tremor in her voice, echoed in the flutter of lace at her throat, the swinging of her long pearl earrings.

Annoyingly, his mind conjured the image of her naked in a fountain.

He cleared his throat.

"Yes," he replied, more gruffly than he'd intended. "I am here for several reasons. First, the General Committee has sent me to inspect how you are caring for the children."

She inclined her head, but the color ebbed from her cheeks. Was it guilt, or natural nervousness?

"Of course I shall cooperate in any way I can. And your other purpose?" she asked, her eyes meeting his anxiously.

"I also have a particular interest in one of the children. Mary Simms."

"Mary?" She scrutinized him warily.

Lord, did she think *he* had anything to do with the child's troubles?

"Yes. I have talked to Lord Bromhurst and Mrs. Hill. I am aware of Mary's situation and I assure you I have only the kindest interest in her."

"I did not mean to imply otherwise. But what *is* your interest in Mary?"

"I should like to take her into my own household, and raise her as my daughter. I have arranged the hire of a chaise to take her to London. Could she be ready to leave tomorrow?"

Livvy stared at Sir Jeremy, unable to comprehend his words for a moment. An inspection . . . and now he wanted to take Mary away. Of all her children, the most vulnerable, the one she was just beginning to reach.

"Mary? Why?" she croaked.

"I can see you are surprised. Perhaps it is rather sudden. Let me explain."

"Yes, it is sudden," she said sharply. "And I think it very unwise to remove her from Rosemead now."

"I have a very important reason for doing so."

Despite herself she was curious.

"My wife used to enjoy visiting the children at the Hospital, and—"

"Your *wife*?" Livvy interrupted, suddenly feeling ill. Had Sir Jeremy been married when he kissed her at the masquerade?

"My wife," he repeated stiffly. "She enjoyed visiting the children, and took an especial interest in

Mary. On her deathbed she begged me to care for the child."

"Your wife died?"

He stared at her and Livvy blushed. She must seem an imbecile to ask such questions. Pray he did not guess why!

His eyelids lowered. "Over four years ago."

A sigh escaped her. He had *not* been married, then.

"I am sorry," she said. "I should not have interrupted."

He looked up, dark eyebrows drawing together over those intent mahogany eyes. No doubt her reaction to his answer puzzled him. "It was only yesterday that I learned from the matron at the Hospital that it was Mary Simms my wife must have spoken of. Now I am determined to fulfill her wish, and I assure you that I intend to treat Mary with every kindness and consideration."

She clasped her hands in her lap. It was a strange tale. She looked up, reading determination in his eyes, in the set of his jaw. A more likely explanation occurred to her. As a baby, Mary had been left at the Hospital with the hundred pound fee that guaranteed admission. At least one of her parents was a person of means. Could it be Sir Jeremy?

But to ask might be an unpardonable offense.

"I am most sorry to hear of your bereavement," she said, choosing her words carefully. "A last request must of course be honored. But I beg you to consider how you might best fulfill that request. You must realize Mary is a special case."

"I am aware of that. I hope to act as a good father to her."

"But she has become very fond of me and of the other children here. What do you think it would mean to her to be uprooted?"

He frowned. "It is her welfare I am interested in. Do you not realize the advantages I can offer her?"

She clasped her hands more tightly. "What you

mean is, that growing up in the home of a wealthy and respectable gentleman, Mary will have better opportunities than with a scandalous widow."

"I did not mean to offend you."

An unexpected softness in his voice shook her. She squared her shoulders. "Let us not beat about the bush. You cannot be unaware of my reputation. All I can say is that I fell out of grace through an indiscretion, but not through actual vice. I promise you I would never do anything to lead Mary—or any of the other children—astray."

"As my ward, Mary would be well educated and carefully brought up. She might eventually make a respectable marriage."

Livvy bit her lip. Through his charitable work, Sir Jeremy undoubtedly had many connections with tradesmen, bankers, gentlemen farmers, clergymen and the like. Under his guardianship, Mary would have an opportunity to meet potential suitors, at least some of whom might not despise her for her unknown parentage.

"I do understand that you can offer Mary more than I can," she conceded, "but that is for the future. What I am trying to say is that I believe she may be on the verge of confiding in me. It would be most harmful for her to be removed at present."

He frowned at her for a moment. "Perhaps I should meet her and the other children, and judge for myself."

She sighed. It was reasonable. "Of course you may."

"I must also prepare a report for the General Committee on how the children are faring here," he added dispassionately.

She gripped her hands so hard it hurt, rather than reply on impulse. She'd almost forgotten the cursed inspection. Would Sir Jeremy understand some of the ways she'd deviated from Hospital practices, or would he judge her harshly for them?

"The children are out on a ramble with their governess," she replied, draining all emotion from her voice. "They will not return for another hour, I think."

"I can wait."

"But it will be almost time for their dinner, and it would be most improper of you to join us. Daytime visits may be excused on account of Foundling Hospital business, but if you are known to dine here, there would be gossip. I would not wish the good work you are doing on behalf of the Foundling Hospital to be jeopardized by it."

He directed a suspicious look her way, then finally nodded.

"When should I come?"

"Let us say ten o'clock. That is not too early, is it?"

"Not at all. I am an early riser. But are the children permitted to sleep so late?"

"Of course not. They rise at seven and have lessons after their breakfast. At ten they go outside to play. It would be a good opportunity for me to show you about the schoolroom while it is quiet. You may meet them when they return."

Having played out any fidgets and on their best behavior, she prayed.

"Very well. Ten o'clock it is."

She rose from her seat to leave and he followed.

"I meant to arrive earlier," he said as they walked down the hall. "But my horse threw a shoe."

His tone was friendlier, as if he wished to lull her fear of the inspection. She knew better than to be caught off guard.

"You rode from London?" she asked.

"I prefer to ride or walk whenever I can."

So he did not care to be driven. Exercise would account for those muscular limbs, the powerful way he moved. Despite her intentions, just walking beside him brought back memories of the masquerade.

A rush of desire.

Idiot, to allow a man's good looks and athletic physique to affect her so! Once in a lifetime was surely
enough for such folly. And this man no longer admired her, if his stiff manner was any indication. What
would he think if she told him the part he himself had
played in her fall from grace?

He could easily blame her for having encouraged
him.

She forced an impersonal smile to her face and bade
him goodbye on the steps as a groom brought his
horse around. She watched as Sir Jeremy mounted the
gleaming, superbly conditioned black beast and rode
off. He had quiet hands and an easy, upright seat that
spoke of long hours spent in the saddle. If he donned
some armor, and some colorful trappings, he could be
taken for a knight errant from some old legend.

She dismissed the silly fancy. In truth, the man was
a puzzle. At the masquerade he'd seemed so protective, so gentle, so tenderly passionate. Now he regarded her with hard, critical eyes and she didn't dare
tell him the truth, for fear of upsetting the life she
had carved out for herself and the children.

And yet, a mad, reckless part of her rejoiced that
she would be seeing him again tomorrow.

Chapter Four

Livvy returned to the house. Thurlow still stood in the hall, holding the door for her, a thoughtful expression on his face. It reminded her of something she must do.

"Please tell Charles he is to have two weeks' holiday," she said.

The butler blinked, then nodded. "Very well, ma'am. I will tell him."

"I have a very good reason for what I am doing, Thurlow," she assured him.

"I imagine you do, my lady," he said respectfully, but with a twinkle in his eye.

Dear Thurlow! Bless him and dear Mrs. Thurlow, the housekeeper. They'd kindly born with her tantrums throughout childhood and helped her rebuild her life through widowhood and disgrace. They'd not uttered a word of complaint when she began to bring her foundlings home from London, instead treating the children with the utmost kindness and insisting the rest of the staff follow their lead. She could count on their support in helping to make a good impression on Sir Jeremy Fairhill.

An hour later, Livvy joined the children and Jane Burton, their governess, for dinner in the schoolroom. The children, hungry from their long walk, devoured their lamb and rice pudding in silence. Meanwhile she gazed at the faces surrounding the worn oak table.

Philippa, the first child she'd brought home from the Foundling Hospital. Clever, opinionated and fiercely affectionate, she'd exhausted the patience of the teachers there. Tall for her eleven years, with piercing green eyes in a thin face framed by an unruly mass of dark hair, Philippa was at an awkward stage, but someday she would be a striking, intelligent woman, one who might find her way even in a society dominated by men who thought they knew best.

Ben, dark-haired, brown-eyed, big for his age, whose face had worn a sullen expression for weeks after his arrival, who had come so far in overcoming his tendency to stutter. Who'd once set a fire at the Foundling Hospital but now could coax the most tender of plants to grow. He was nine now . . . goodness, it was two years since she'd brought him home!

Four-year-old Robbie, with sparkling hazel eyes, ears that stuck slightly out from his head, tousled red-brown hair that stubbornly resisted all attempts at taming it. The scamp whose adventurous spirit could lead him into trouble—and did at times—but who made her laugh every day.

Her gaze fell on the most recent addition to her family: ten-year-old Mary, angelic in appearance with her pale blond hair and blue eyes. Angelic in behavior as well. *Too* subdued, Livvy thought, contrasting her with the others. But Mary was beginning to unfurl a few petals; Livvy had great hopes that they would soon reach a better understanding.

If only they would be given that time.

When they had reached the jam tarts that ended the meal, Livvy decided to prepare them for Sir Jeremy's upcoming visit.

"Children, Miss Burton," she said, addressing Jane

formally as she always did in the presence of the children. "We had a visitor today."

"We saw him riding in as we were leaving," said Robbie excitedly. "Coo! What a prime horse he rides!"

"Who was it?" asked Philippa.

"Sir Jeremy Fairhill, one of the Governors of the Foundling Hospital."

All of the children sobered, except for Robbie, who continued to shovel jam tart into his mouth.

"Why did he come?" asked Philippa, her voice echoing the strain in the faces of all the older children.

Livvy took a breath. She'd already decided not to tell them about his plans regarding Mary; hopefully Sir Jeremy would see wisdom and not force the issue. The upcoming inspection was another matter. She had to prepare them somehow.

"As a representative of the Hospital, Sir Jeremy wishes to know that all of you are thriving here," she explained.

"B-but we *are*," said Ben, his stutter giving evidence of his anxiety.

"Sir Jeremy has all your interests very much at heart," she said gently. "I have invited him to visit again tomorrow so he may become better acquainted with us. I expect you all to show him how well we get on here."

"Will he take us away if he's not pleased with what he sees?" asked Philippa.

Livvy gazed around at the children for a moment. All looked grave; Mary's face had paled. It was no use dissembling to them. "He might. But you must not be worrying that that will happen. It is quite a routine thing, you know. The Governors make periodic inspections of the wet nurses who keep baby foundlings in the country, and they sometimes visit older children who are serving apprenticeships to make sure they are being treated properly. This is not much different."

Philippa nodded solemnly. Livvy could count on her help now. Glancing around the table, she saw the same resolution echoed in the other children's faces.

"I know you will all make me proud of you," she said with forced cheerfulness. "Everything will be well."

Jane echoed Livvy's hope later that evening, when they sat together in the library sharing tea.

Livvy agreed, then took a bite of a macaroon. The children had washed, said their prayers and were safely tucked into bed for the night. Usually this was a quiet, relaxing time for her and Jane, but tonight anxiety preyed on both of them.

"I do not know what Sir Jeremy will think," Jane continued, faint worry lines creasing her smooth forehead. "We have deviated so much from the course of study the children used to follow at the Foundling Hospital."

"I can only hope that once he meets the children he will understand. But that is not our only problem."

Jane tipped her head slightly to the side.

"He wants to take Mary as his ward."

"Mary? But why?" Jane pushed a light brown strand of hair back into place.

"He says it is because it was his wife's dying wish. I do not know . . . It is a strange tale."

"You do not think? . . ." Jane's eyes widened.

"That he is her father? I don't know. Perhaps what he said *is* true. There was something about how he spoke of his wife . . . as if he bears a wound he would rather not have touched," she mused, half to herself. "Moreover, if he is the one who sent Mary to the Foundling Hospital with the hundred pounds, why would he claim her now?"

"Perhaps he and Mary's mother were cruelly parted. Perhaps she died, and it has taken him all this time to find Mary."

"You *are* a romantic, Jane!"

"Well, it might be true," said Jane with a stubborn tilt to her chin.

"It is no stranger than his own story," Livvy conceded.

"Perhaps he plans to take a new wife and thinks she will be a mother to Mary."

Was he thinking of remarrying? A chill crept over her heart. Sir Jeremy had not the demeanor of a man in love, but he might be contemplating some very proper alliance. Livvy reflected that it would be a rare gentlewoman who would tolerate a foundling— possibly her husband's illegitimate daughter—in her household.

She shook her head, baffled. "Regardless of his reasons, I hope we can persuade him to allow us to keep Mary, at least a while longer. That is, if he decides I am a suitable person to have charge of *any* of them."

"You don't think he truly would take them all away?"

"It is possible. If you had seen the way he looked at me—well, I can tell he would not hesitate to remove the children if he thought I was doing them any harm."

"Surely that won't happen!"

"In any case, you will have a home with me, dear," Livvy replied, seeing the alarm in her friend's eyes. "But it won't happen. We *will* find a way to deal with Sir Jeremy."

"Livvy, you must tell me if there is any way I can help you tomorrow," said Jane, after a little pause.

"We must go on as we always do, Jane. There is no sense in trying to deceive Sir Jeremy about what we have done for the children. We can only try to convince him that we have acted rightly."

And, she added silently, one deception was quite enough for her to manage.

Jeremy turned in to the gates in the brick wall that encircled Rosemead Park, his horse's hooves squelching through the damp earth and gravel of the drive. He'd arisen early to find that the night's rains had given way to a perfect spring day.

"Steady lad, one would think you were two years old again," he admonished Samson, as his mount playfully shied away from a swaying, bud-laden rhododendron bush.

But he himself was far too eager to be riding up that winding drive, watching the elegant, symmetrical building of rosy brick emerge from its secluded position in the wooded vale.

He thought he had talked himself into a more proper frame of mind. Yesterday he had allowed Lady Dearing to surprise him into rudeness. He'd not expected her to be so lovely and youthful. And her odd manner, bursting into the entrance hall to greet him, and responding so strangely to the things he'd told her about Cecilia—perhaps she *was* rather eccentric.

He reined in at the stables, going back over the questions he'd mentally rehearsed. They would help him concentrate on what was most important. Having left Samson with a groom, he returned to the entrance, where he was once again admitted by the grandfatherly-looking butler, Thurlow. The clock on the mantel showed he was a quarter of an hour early.

"Her ladyship is in the library, sir, doing her accounts," said Thurlow, taking Jeremy's overcoat and hat. "However, I am certain she would wish me to take you to her."

Jeremy followed the man down the hallway and into a cozy, book-lined room carpeted in a practical drugget. The furniture was scrupulously polished and dusted, but like the carpet, showed small signs of wear.

He wondered if the children played here sometimes. Twittering sounds emanated from one corner, where he saw several goldfinches housed in an enormous birdcage carved to resemble a Chinese pagoda. The French doors, matching the ones in the drawing room, were partially open, admitting spring-scented air into the room.

Lady Dearing sat at a desk leaning over an open ledger, a pair of spectacles sliding down her nose. As Jeremy entered, she looked up and pushed them back with a beautifully manicured hand. He wondered if she had donned the spectacles in order to look older. It was not working.

"What a pleasure to see you so early, Sir Jeremy," she said, rising as the butler left them.

"My apologies. I rode out early to exercise my horse and was not certain of the time."

He tried not to stare at her as he had yesterday. But she looked thoroughly fresh and appealing in a blue-striped gown, lace high to her throat, her blue eyes glowing through the spectacles.

"Did you expect to find me with a lover, perhaps?" she asked, chin tilted slightly.

It was phrased as a joke, but he knew it was a challenge. He had offended her yesterday. Or she wished him to think so.

"Of course not. I must apologize again. I realize my manner may have been a bit abrupt yesterday, but I intended no offense. It is just that you are . . . younger than I expected."

"I am two-and-thirty," she replied crisply. "Many women have borne four children, or even more, by my age."

He suppressed frustration. He'd offended her again, with a statement that would have pleased most women.

"I did not say you are too young to care for the

children. I was trying to apologize for my rude
manner."

A flush stole over her cheeks. "Do not trouble yourself about it. I suppose it is natural for you to be
suspicious."

"I am here to learn the truth."

"Very well then. There are a few things I should
like to discuss before we go up to the schoolroom.
Will you be seated, please?"

Though her words were decisive, there was something in her demeanor . . . a taut wariness. Did she
have something to hide, or was it just the natural nervousness of anyone under inspection?

Regardless, a polite and friendly manner would help
him to discover the truth.

He relaxed his expression and took a seat. "What
is it you wish to tell me, then?"

She clasped her hands in her lap, as she had yesterday. They were beautiful hands, bare of rings, he
noticed.

"First I must tell you that I have the deepest respect
for the Governors of the Foundling Hospital," she
said. "I believe that the standard of education at the
Hospital is undoubtedly well suited to the needs of
the vast majority of the children."

"There is no need for flattery. What is it you wish
to tell me?"

"I was trying to make clear that I intend no criticism
of the Hospital or the Governors, and explain that in
the case of the foundlings here at Rosemead, I have
found that somewhat . . . different . . . methods have
proven efficacious."

"Such as?"

"Their education here has been broader. I believe
that allowing them to pursue individual interests has
helped them improve in other things, especially in
their behavior."

She'd given him the lead to ask one of his questions.

"Yes, their behavior. May I ask how Ben Taylor is doing?"

"Very well," she replied. "He has taken a particular interest in gardening. Every day he helps Furzeley, my head gardener, and he has come along very well."

"Excellent. Many of the Hospital's boys become gardeners."

He turned his head, hearing a rustling outside the French doors. Ah. It was a potted shrub, its branches moving slightly in the breeze. He returned his gaze to Lady Dearing, to find her turning back from looking the same way.

"What I should really like to know is if there has been a recurrence of the fire-starting."

"Not at all," she said reassuringly. "Have you spoken to Mrs. Hill about it?"

"A little. She confided to me that he'd set it in a tin pail in a spot where there was little likelihood of its spreading. She seemed inclined to be lenient to the boy, but it is not a matter to be taken lightly."

"Not at all. Did Mrs. Hill mention that Ben suffers from a rather severe stutter?"

"Yes, she did, and that the teachers at the Hospital quite failed to cure him of it. Are you telling me there is a connection between the stuttering and the fire?"

"One of the other boys liked to tease him. He would try to goad Ben into fighting and then lay the blame on Ben. Even though Ben is big for his age, he hates fighting. I think that since he had trouble explaining what was happening to anyone, frustration led him to set the fire."

He frowned. "I trust the matter was dealt with properly."

"It was. And since Ben has come here, his behavior has improved markedly, along with his stuttering."

"You have found a way to cure him of it?" Despite himself he was impressed.

"Not entirely. We have found it helps to *not* try to correct the stuttering, but to just encourage him to speak regardless. But I am afraid you may not see the improvement. Ben still stutters when with strangers, or if he is upset."

"I must hope then that he trusts me enough to demonstrate an improvement."

"Perhaps he will," she said, her hands twisting in her lap.

"Is there something else you wished to speak of?"

She nodded. "Are you still hoping to take Mary away today?"

"Yes, I am."

She paused. For a moment all that could be heard was the finches' song and the sound of the shrubs on the terrace rustling in the breeze. He looked away, striving vainly to ignore the appeal in her eyes.

"I hope you will not persist in that plan," she said at length. "I do not think she is ready. When she first came here, she was so . . . subdued. She seemed shy of accepting a simple embrace, and cringed at the mildest rebuke. But she has become more comfortable, more affectionate. She likes to work in the kitchen with Cook, and she likes to mother Robbie, my littlest one, and help him with things like tying his shoestrings."

"I was told she used to enjoy singing."

"She will sit and do needlework while I practice on the harp or pianoforte, but when we sing in the evenings she will not join us. I think she could if she wished but fears we will think she was lying when she said she could not sing in the choir. For some reason, she dreads being sent back to the Hospital."

He frowned. "I should hate to think she was mistreated there."

"It perplexes me, too," she replied. "Mrs. Hill and the rest of the staff have always impressed me with their kindness. But I truly believe Mary will in time give me her confidence."

"I *am* grateful for your efforts on her behalf."

She paused, removing her spectacles and holding them in her lap. "Sir Jeremy, if you take Mary, who is to care for her? You are not planning to take on her education yourself, are you?"

Now she met his gaze squarely. Her questions were fair.

"I shall engage a governess, but for now my plan is to take Mary to my aunt, who lives in Russell Square with my cousin and his wife. My aunt has raised a son and daughter of her own and she has always been more than kind to me. She and my uncle became my guardians upon my parents' death. She has had some experience dealing with . . . difficult children."

Her gaze softened, as if she realized he spoke of himself.

"I see you have given this much thought," she replied. "Perhaps your aunt may succeed with Mary. Still, I wish you would allow me to continue trying."

Whether it was the sympathy in her voice or some other enchantment, he did not know. But her pleading struck him with something like an inward pang. She *did* love Mary.

"I will consider it."

She lowered her gaze, coloring a little, then looked up again. "Thank you."

For a moment he returned her gaze, pierced by the depth of feeling in her voice. Her eyes were bright with the hint of tears. Such eyes . . . Beautiful as they were, they seemed older than her fresh, glowing complexion implied. They were eyes that had seen pain. The eyes of a mother.

He cleared his throat. "May I see the schoolroom now?"

As they got up to leave, he reminded himself that even if she doted on the children, that did not mean she was a fit person to care for them.

No one knew better than he that love was not always enough.

But as he followed her out of the room, her scent—of roses, narcissus and sheer femininity—tugged at his senses, along with the rustle of her skirt, the natural undulations of her hips as she climbed the stairs ahead of him . . .

What had gotten into him? He was here on Hospital business. He was here for Cecilia.

But he'd not felt so powerfully affected by a woman's charms in years.

At the top, Lady Dearing turned and led him down a hall into a large room painted the same cheerful yellow as the drawing room. Jeremy turned his attention to the colorful artwork adorning its walls: framed samplers, pastels and watercolors.

"You are seeing some of the children's work," Lady Dearing explained, in something of a rush. "I realize the foundlings are not taught drawing at the Hospital, but Miss Burton and I have discovered that allowing them to exercise such talents has proven beneficial."

"It is unusual. But so are these children," he concurred, wishing she would be more at ease. Was this the sort of thing she was nervous about?

"I am so glad you see it so," she said, with a slight smile.

The breathless quality in her voice drew him to look at her again. She seemed so nervous, standing there with her long filigree earrings swinging slightly, her hands clasped together. He felt an absurd longing to reassure her.

Instead he looked about some more. Long shelves lay against one wall, for the most part filled with books, although one bore toys ranging from a hoop to a carved and painted Noah's ark set. A side table held a globe, a microscope and several small boxes whose contents he could only guess at.

"I see the children enjoy a rather broader education than those at the Hospital," he observed.

"But you do not think it wrong?" The strain in her voice was almost painful to hear.

"I wish such subjects were in the reach of every child in England."

"You do?" She watched him wide-eyed, not the first to be surprised by his highly progressive views on the matter.

"Most of the Governors do not agree. In any case, we cannot afford to pay masters to teach geography or natural philosophy," he continued. "The most we can do is to provide an education to prepare the children for a trade or domestic service."

"I know. They are taught their letters and how to do sums, which is far better education than they would have received otherwise. Had they lived at all," she added earnestly. "I am sure the Committee must weigh every expense against the possibility of saving more children's lives."

She *did* understand. Not even Cecilia could have expressed herself with greater sensitivity.

And Bromhurst said she had done well by these children, which now seemed likely. It would explain why, as President, he was so reluctant to allow anyone to interfere with Lady Dearing. Perhaps that was why he had avoided any discussion of her and her controversial methods at meetings.

It made Jeremy's current dilemma all the more difficult.

"We do," he agreed, then cleared his throat again. "Do the children attend Church?"

"Yes, of course."

"And—forgive me for asking—how are the children regarded by your neighbors? Sometimes there is a prejudice against foundlings."

"Not everyone approves, of course, but most follow the lead of our good vicar and his wife, who have been most kind to the children," she said with a smile. A real one this time, no polite facade. It lit up her eyes.

"I am glad to hear it."

Her smile deepened. A breeze from the window lifted her hair, brought a hint of her perfume his way.

He turned his head aside. "May I meet the children now?" he asked quietly.

"Of course."

She preceded him out of the room and he followed, focusing on everything but her. But the image remained to taunt him: her smile, the ruffled golden curls. Luscious breasts, trim waist, feminine hips, all discreetly, elegantly swathed in lace and fabric but mutely beckoning him. A woman made for loving: for touching and kissing and caressing and . . .

And she might be Arlingdale's mistress.

Even if she was not, her tarnished reputation and his role as an inspector made such thoughts grossly improper, even dangerous.

But he continued to wrestle with them as they entered the library and headed for the open French doors. Before they reached them, a young woman with light brown hair dressed in a sober brown dress burst in from outside. The governess?

She looked distraught.

"What is it, Miss Burton?" Lady Dearing asked.

"I am so sorry," said the governess, wringing her hands. "I would not have let it happen for the world. I needed to visit the—the—and I thought they would be safe—and—"

"What is it? Is something wrong?" asked Lady Dearing, her voice still calm but a fraction higher in pitch.

Miss Burton swallowed, her face pale, her eyes imploring her mistress's forgiveness.

"Please forgive me, L—my lady! The children have disappeared!"

Chapter Five

*L*ivvy could have screamed.

Out of the corner of her eye she saw the grim disapproval in Sir Jeremy's expression. How could the children do such a thing, just when it looked as if she'd won him over?

"Please calm yourself," she told Jane, keeping her voice tranquil. "Where were the children last seen?"

"On the south lawn, but that was almost a half hour ago. We have been searching ever since. I did not wish to disturb you while you were speaking to Sir Jeremy."

"It is not the time to worry about what is done. We have to decide how to proceed now."

"There's one more thing, ma'am. Cook says the sandwiches prepared for the children's nuncheon are missing, along with some of the bread and cheese that were in the larder."

Livvy recalled the noises she'd heard outside the library doors. She'd set them down to the wind, but . . .

She turned to Sir Jeremy, squaring her shoulders. "Do you recall when the shrub rustled on the terrace? I fear one of the children was hiding behind it and overheard our conversation."

"Are you saying they ran off rather than allow Mary to come with me?" he asked grimly.

"They do not know you. Perhaps they fear you. I realize it does not excuse their naughtiness, but—" She swallowed, bracing herself for his anger.

"The important thing is to find them now."

She nodded.

"Shall I have someone make inquiries in the village?" asked Jane.

"Not yet."

She took a deep breath, half-closing her eyes. Panicking about Sir Jeremy would do the children no good; for their sakes, she had to deal with the situation as if he were not present. To imagine where a child might go to hide.

She opened her eyes again. "I think I know where they have gone. There is no need to raise a stir just yet. Sir Jeremy, if you allow me some time I shall bring them back to you."

"I am coming along."

She nodded, unsurprised. Now everything depended on how she managed things; any mistake would no doubt result in *all* the children being removed from her care.

A few minutes later, she'd exchanged her slippers for half boots, pulled on a shawl and bonnet, and rejoined Sir Jeremy. They hurried out the French doors, sped across the terrace, then descended the steps to the garden level.

One look at his face and her stomach twisted.

"I hope—I hope you are not too angry with the children," she said, skirting the garden wall and heading toward the lawn and the woods beyond it.

"I'm not an ogre. Why would they regard me as one?"

"I told them only that you were here for an inspection."

She set a fast pace across the lawn; he kept up easily, his expression still stony. Her stomach clenched even as the fast pace stole her breath.

"You will not—you will not make any hasty decisions about the children, will you?" she blurted out, unable to bear the silence any longer.

She suffered a long, unblinking look.

"I never make hasty decisions."

She bit her lip and hurried on.

"Where do you think they have gone?" he asked as they passed the Grecian folly on the edge of the woodland.

"There's a cave," she said, struggling for breath. "Near the eastern border of the park. About . . . ten minutes' walk from here."

"A *cave*?"

"My grandfather had it . . . excavated. He built that folly. Later he developed a taste for . . . Gothic features. My father thought the cave . . . unsafe, and had it blocked up. As a child I found a way in."

"Is there any danger?"

"I hope not. If it has not . . . collapsed in all these years . . . perhaps the roof is solid."

She redoubled her pace and skidded over a particularly slippery patch, and would have pitched face-forward into the mud had Sir Jeremy not reached out to catch her. For a moment, he held her tightly, one arm around her shoulders, another just under her breasts. Her heart all but stopped as his large hands steadied her, their firm grasp bringing back memories of his protective embrace at the masquerade. Of their kiss. Knees shaking, she summoned up all her strength to regain her balance and pull away.

"Thank you," she breathed, risking a look at his face.

His face was even stormier than before, but she saw no signs that he'd recognized her. A moment later he looked calmer, as if he'd forced back his anger.

"What do you intend to do when we find the children?" he asked, a hard edge to his voice.

His question brought a sick taste to her mouth. How

did he expect her to deal with them? She'd never beaten the children, and in fact the staff at the Hospital now used isolation in preference to physical punishment. But if Sir Jeremy was of the old school . . .

"I shall talk to them . . . of course," she said, a sharp running pain across her chest adding to her sense of nausea. "To try . . . if I can discover why they did this. Then I must devise a suitable punishment."

An anxious moment passed before he answered.

"I trust you do not intend anything too harsh," he said at length.

Stunned, she turned to look at him, and her legs nearly buckled under her. He'd reddened, looking distinctly uncomfortable. He did *not* wish her to beat the children.

Relief brought her renewed strength. She ran up a slight rise and down into the next hollow, a lovely quiet spot in the center of the ancient woods, where drifts of bluebells released their wild-sweet scent.

Now she could see the entrance to the cave, a narrow, almost invisible gash among the tree roots, overgrown with ivy. "Philippa! Ben! Mary! Robbie!" she called.

Nothing could be heard but birdsong and the rushing of the nearby stream.

As she approached the entrance to the cave, Sir Jeremy beside her, Livvy prayed once more that she was right.

"Come out. You are discovered," she shouted.

There was no answer.

She moved a tangle of ivy aside to reveal the opening. It was smaller than she remembered, and too dark to see the interior. She heard a scuffle and a muted whisper. Her shoulders sagged with relief.

"I know you are in there. Come out this instant, all of you," she said in a fierce tone she rarely used.

Please don't disobey me now.

A moment later Philippa poked her head out of the

hole. Pale despite smudges of dirt on her cheeks, the girl had clearly screwed up her courage to be the first out. Livvy stretched out her hand and helped her climb out of the gap to emerge, staring wide-eyed at Sir Jeremy.

"Sir Jeremy, this is Philippa," said Livvy.

She gave the girl a pointed look until Philippa dropped Sir Jeremy a polite curtsey, which he returned with a grave nod.

Livvy turned back to the gap. The next face to appear was Robbie's; his eyes seemed enormous in his puckish little face, beseeching her understanding. She lifted him out bodily, taking the opportunity to give him a quick squeeze before setting him down and introducing him.

Ben emerged, his face sullen. Though he dared not try to speak, he made a little bow when introduced to Sir Jeremy.

Finally, Livvy helped Mary through the gap. The girl scrambled out, bearing a basket containing the food they'd stolen. Paler than the rest, she kept her eyes downcast.

"Sir Jeremy, this is Mary," Livvy said, watching Sir Jeremy closely to see his reaction as Mary curtseyed to him.

The moment stretched awkwardly as he stood staring down at Mary with an odd yearning in his eyes. Livvy's heart, which had started to slow, resumed its gallop. Then as if suddenly released from a spell, Sir Jeremy bowed.

Livvy drew a ragged breath. "Perhaps one of you will explain what you were doing in the cave. Philippa?" she said, turning her gaze toward the eldest.

Her heart bled to see Philippa's look, defiant and pleading at the same time.

"I—we could not allow Sir Jeremy to take Mary back to the Foundling Hospital," the girl returned at length.

"So you were listening to us in the library? You know how I regard eavesdropping."

Ben stepped forward, dark eyes large in his face. "It was m-m-m-m-me," he said, with a painful effort.

"Thank you for being honest," said Livvy more softly, then looked around the small group. "But what an ungrateful thing to do! Do you not realize that you very likely owe your lives to the kindness of gentlemen like Sir Jeremy, who manage and fund the Hospital?"

Robbie began to sob.

She longed to cuddle him, but resisted. "How do you think Sir Jeremy must feel now?" she said, raking the group with her eyes.

Philippa and Mary both burst into tears; Ben was scowling with the effort of holding his own back. Sir Jeremy shifted his stance uncomfortably.

She'd done enough.

"You must all apologize to Sir Jeremy now."

The children broke out into a chorus of frightened apologies, which Sir Jeremy accepted gravely but politely. Then Livvy went to hug each one in turn.

"But we still don't want Mary to go!" blurted out Robbie, as she embraced him.

Livvy moved on to Mary, whose face was still streaked with tears.

"Don't make me go, my lady!" whispered Mary, clinging to her. "Please don't ask me to tell you why!"

Livvy glanced over Mary's head toward Sir Jeremy. His expression smote her: stark misery. He'd heard.

"Listen, all of you," she said, still holding Mary. "You must not have heard all of our conversation. Sir Jeremy was not talking of returning Mary to the Hospital."

"No?" Mary lifted her head to stare up at her.

Livvy gave Sir Jeremy a questioning glance. He nodded.

"Sir Jeremy was thinking of taking you to his aunt's

house, which is in London. His wife used to enjoy playing with you, years ago, and she commended you to his care."

Mary looked puzzled.

"Do you remember Lady Fairhill?" Livvy asked. "You would have been about six when she visited the Hospital."

Mary nodded. "Yes. She brought us gingerbread, and taught me some embroidery stitches."

"Sir Jeremy is her husband. He wants to take you into his own family and care for you."

Mary eyed Sir Jeremy but continued to cling to Livvy.

"Mary," said Sir Jeremy in the gentlest of voices. "I do indeed have a particular interest in your welfare, but I don't wish to cause you pain. I shall not insist that you leave Lady Dearing at present."

Mary wilted in Livvy's arms.

Sighing, Livvy looked around and saw the color returning to the other children's faces. She turned her gaze back to Sir Jeremy and gave him a grateful look.

"Children," she said briskly. "It is time all of you returned to the house and got yourselves cleaned up."

She loosened her hold on Mary, who slowly withdrew from her embrace and went to stand near Philippa.

"Go on, all of you. Hurry so you may be clean in time for our meal. And there will be no sweets for any of you for a week!"

Philippa led the rest of the children as they ran off in the direction of the house. Livvy suspected they were all relieved to have gotten off so lightly.

Then she turned back to Sir Jeremy. Furrows had formed above his brows; his jaw was set at a harsh angle. But the bereft look in his eyes belied everything else, softening her fear into pity.

"If you continue to be so gentle, Mary will learn not to recoil from you," she reassured him.

He stared after the retreating children.

"Allow her some time. I am sure it will be well."

He turned back to her, a muscle flexing in his cheek. "I believe you are laboring under a misapprehension, Lady Dearing. Do you think I am Mary's father?"

"I meant no offense," she said, coloring. "If you say you are not Mary's father of course I believe you. It is just that . . . you looked at her with such yearning. You have no children of your own?"

"It was not . . . not possible."

"I am sorry," she said quietly. "I must thank you again for being so patient with Mary."

His jaw tightened again. "I'm not such a brute as to drag her away forcibly. But neither can I leave matters as they stand. I cannot give a good report to the General Committee after such an incident."

She shivered. Things had been going so well . . . but he had all the power. It was time to abandon pride and plead, cajole, whatever was necessary.

"I know how badly this looks," she said. "But the children usually mind me very well, I assure you!"

"Some of the Governors speculate that you overindulge the children. I have seen nothing to refute that claim."

"But you will. At present the children are too upset to make a proper demonstration of their progress, but perhaps, if you return tomorrow . . ."

"Do you think they will not run away again?"

"They will not," she said, clasping her hands tightly in front of her. "Perhaps, if they become better acquainted with you . . ."

"Do you know how that might be accomplished?"

"You are of course welcome to make more visits. Perhaps spend a few days with each child, over a period of a month," she said recklessly.

He turned from her, broad shoulders tense. He seemed lost in thought; she could not see his face or guess if he liked the idea. It was beginning to terrify her.

"I realize you are busy with the branch hospital

project, and of course you have an estate to manage," she said, unnerved by his stillness.

"This is important," he replied, turning back to her, his gaze darkly intense. "Very well. I shall come for a few days during each of the next four weeks."

"As long as you do not think it would give rise to gossip."

"I can care for my own reputation. Anyone who knows me would realize I am here on Hospital business, nothing else."

A blush rose to her cheeks. "Very well," she said. "I must thank you for giving us a second chance. I hope we shall be able to satisfy you."

"I hope so too," he said unexpectedly.

His deep voice soothed her like a caress. She smiled. The children's escapade had *not* ruined everything.

Stillness surrounded them, scented by damp earth, ancient trees and bluebells. His eyes were soft, full of unfathomable longings. Here, again, was the man who had kissed her back to life when she'd thought such a thing was no longer possible. Desire seeped into her, heightened by the lingering memory of his arms around her on the path.

She shivered and looked away. She must have been mad to suggest a plan so fraught with opportunities for her to betray herself. If he guessed how scandalously she had behaved, how he'd been deceived, or how powerfully his presence, even his voice, still affected her . . .

"Shall we return to the house, then?" Without awaiting a reply she headed down the path.

Painfully aware of him beside her, she set a pace too quick for conversation and watched her every step, not daring to risk another touch. Desire was a cheat. She would not succumb to it again; she would not allow it to rob her of everything that mattered.

Never again.

*　　　*　　　*

*Livvy shifted her position on the edge of the bed
and glanced toward the doorway once more. Where
was Walter?*

*It felt as if it had been hours since Alice had brushed
out her hair, had helped her into her new nightrail and
dressing gown, both white and shimmering, the dressing
gown tied in front with knots of blue ribbon. She
caught herself toying with the knots, and stopped.*

*She wasn't afraid; she was nearly eighteen after all.
Her stuffy old aunt had to be wrong; this was not going
to be an ordeal. It would be as the poets described
it. Rapture. Abandon. A brief, glorious death in each
other's arms.*

*For weeks, she'd hungered for it, tasted it in his
greedy kisses. She loved him; loved the way he'd followed her to London, which he despised, for her Season; the loyal way he'd glowered at every other suitor
for her hand.*

*She started, hearing the door open. She turned and
drank in the sight of her husband.*

Her husband.

*Tall, with light brown hair waving over his forehead,
a dressing gown half open over his broad chest, his
face ruddy in the candlelight, his gray eyes dark and
gleaming with passion. With need.*

She loved to be needed.

"God, Livvy, you're beautiful," he said.

*She stood to greet him, trying to smile though her
mouth was dry. She licked her lips to wet them again.*

*"You're beautiful, and you're mine," he gloated. "I
must be the luckiest man in England."*

*In two quick strides he crossed the room and crushed
her to his chest. Her stomach fluttered at the contact,
at the power she had to arouse him. She tipped her
face up and he captured her mouth in a hard, posses-
sive assault, rougher than he'd ever kissed her before,
filling her mouth with the taste of brandy, bruising her
lips, scraping her chin with the stubble on his cheek.*

She flinched, then forced herself to relax. He loved her; he needed her; the fierceness of his kisses proved it. The thought sent heat rushing to her breasts, belly, places she didn't have names for, just as it had during the few stolen kisses of their courtship.

This time there would be more. She wasn't afraid. She wanted it, had longed for it for weeks.

He broke the kiss and snatched at the top ribbon of her dressing gown. She flinched again as he cursed loudly at the ties. By the time she had lifted her hands to help, he'd ripped the top one. Before she knew it, he had ripped through the remaining ties, then roughly pushed the dressing gown she'd chosen with such care off her shoulders.

He was so impatient. Passionate. Men were like that, perhaps. Perhaps it was going to be well.

He tugged at her nightrail until the draw-string gave way, and pulled it impatiently off her. She shivered and held up her hands to cover herself.

"Ah, don't be so modest. You're my wife, damn it, let me look at you!"

He grasped her hands, pulling them to her sides as easily as if she had been a doll. Then raked his eyes over her for a moment while she stood shaking, assaulted by the suspicion that it was not love that shone from his eyes, but mere pride of possession.

He released her hands suddenly. She shrieked as he picked her up, took a few strides and flung her up onto the bed. Then his weight was upon her, crushing her, thick legs shoving hers apart.

Her stomach contracted with fear. Something was not right. Was he not going to kiss her again . . . or something?

She opened her eyes. "Walter, I—"

He stabbed into her, and her words fused into a cry. The pain was so sharp, so searing, it seemed he wished to split her apart. Then he plunged in again. She knew there would be pain, but she could accustom herself to the burning, the stretching. If only he would give her some time.

"Please," she whispered.

He withdrew a second time, and she sobbed in relief. An instant later she heard a grunt, felt the pain again. Tears clouded her vision. She could not see him; she could only smell his brandy-laden breath and listen to his rhythmic grunting as he jabbed into her again and again, and she realized he was too lost in drink and lust to hear her.

He shifted suddenly, aiming for a deeper angle. She braced herself for another onslaught, more violent then before. And another, and another, and she lay beneath him, weeping and trembling, praying for it to end.

Her prayer was answered a moment later when he let out a bellow and collapsed, crushing her bleeding, shaking body beneath him.

And slept.

Chapter Six

$\mathcal{J}$eremy turned Samson into Russell Square, glad to see the elegant brick townhouse that his uncle had bought as a young barrister. Though Jeremy had moved into Fairhill Abbey, the family seat in Hampshire, upon reaching his majority, Aunt Louisa, Tom and his wife all insisted he stay in his old room whenever business took him to London.

It still felt like home.

Leaving Samson at the stables in the mews behind the house, he entered through the garden door. He found them seated in the drawing room: Aunt Louisa, her small, plump form in a cozy wing chair, his cousin Tom sitting on the sofa, his arm fondly around the shoulders of his pretty wife, Charlotte. As Jeremy expected, they all turned quickly toward the doorway, their eager expressions fading to confusion.

"Jeremy! So where is the little girl?" asked Aunt Louisa, gazing up at him, eyes bright with affectionate worry.

"She was too frightened to come with me," he said with forced calm. "I was obliged to leave her in Lady Dearing's care."

His aunt stared up at him for a moment. Then she pursed her lips and bounced up from her chair to hug him.

"You must be so disappointed, dearest," she said, trying to pat his shoulders but only reaching the middle of his back.

"I am not unhopeful of a good outcome," he said, gently disengaging from her embrace.

"Well, come sit down and tell us all about it. Dinner is not for another half hour."

He took a seat next to his aunt.

"So what happened?" asked Tom. "You mentioned there was something amiss with the poor little girl."

"Something *is* troubling her, but at present she clings to Lady Dearing. I thought it cruel to remove her."

"Oh dear," said his aunt. "One hates to think of a young girl under the influence of such a woman."

He looked down, surprised by the strength of his urge to defend Lady Dearing. "I believe her ladyship is sincerely fond of the girl. She suggested, I believe quite sensibly, that I must become better acquainted with Mary. She has invited me to make several more visits to Rosemead and I have accepted."

Tom and Charlotte shifted in their seats.

Aunt Louisa raised her eyebrows. "But is it wise for you to be seen on visiting terms with a—a vulgar widow?"

"I did not think her vulgar. She is . . ." He paused, struggling for words to describe Lady Dearing. Unconventional. Intriguing. "Unusual."

"She must have a kind heart, to have taken those foundlings into her own home," said Charlotte in her gentle way.

"Yes, as long as she takes her responsibilities seriously, and does not regard the children as puppies to be played with," said Aunt Louisa sternly. "Bringing up children is no small task, as you both will learn soon enough!"

Tom and Charlotte tried to look cowed, but both

exuded an air of suppressed excitement. Jeremy averted his eyes when he saw Tom stroke his wife's burgeoning belly.

"That is another reason I shall continue my visits," he said. "I must make sure everything *is* in order at Rosemead."

"I only wish you may not allow yourself to be taken in by that woman," his aunt warned him.

"Of course not."

Conversation passed on to news of various acquaintances and the progress of Tom's legal practice. Throughout dinner, Jeremy caught his aunt eying him with concern, so he was not surprised when she beckoned him to her side later that evening, when they'd gathered in the drawing room over tea.

"Dearest," she began as soon as he'd settled into a chair beside hers. "I did not wish to argue with you in front of Tom and Charlotte, but I really wish you would reconsider this resolution to continue your visits to Rosemead Park."

"I need to know those children are well there," he said reasonably. "You yourself said Lady Dearing might be overindulging them."

"Well then, perhaps I am wrong," she said, vigorously stirring her tea. "Lady Dearing is certainly wealthy enough to provide everything those children could need. Perhaps the child is well enough where she is."

"I must be certain of that before I make any decisions."

"But dearest, what I really wish to say is how much I should prefer to see you with a child of your *own*."

"That is *not* why I am interested in Mary."

"Hmm . . . it has been over four years since Cecilia's death. I loved her, too, but it is time enough for you to give up mourning her."

"I am not still grieving."

He looked down, guilt weighing on his chest. He

could tell no one that relief had mingled with his sorrow over Cecilia's death. But at least now he'd been offered the opportunity to assuage that guilt.

"Then why not look about you for a bride? I wish you would not set yourself against love. And desire." Aunt Louisa winked at him.

"Aunt Louisa!"

"I am old enough, I hope, to speak my mind. It would do you good to allow your passions just a little rein."

He looked down into his empty tea cup, embarrassed and appalled that his aunt might make such a suggestion.

Had she forgotten about his parents?

"I know why you made such a careful choice in Cecilia," she continued, as if guessing his thoughts. "But I am certain you will find another amiable and virtuous lady to suit you, if you would only try."

And because he did not try, Aunt Louisa and Lady Bromhurst had thrown enough amiable and virtuous young women his way to satisfy half a dozen inconsolable widowers. He was an ingrate, no doubt, but since that masquerade at the Pantheon no woman had been able to ignite more than a spark of desire.

Except now, Lady Dearing had done it.

Memories of the day tormented him. Her breathless voice, pleading with him on behalf of the children. Bluebells. Mud. Soft, bounteous breasts pressed against his arm as he'd held her to keep her from falling. His flaring reaction to her warmth, her scent.

Had he allowed it all to affect his judgment?

"Dearest Jeremy." Aunt Louisa's softened voice recalled his attention. "You must remember that when passion is allied with true affection, only happiness can result."

She gazed toward the sofa, drawing his eyes to where his cousin sat with Charlotte. Both were touching her belly and exclaiming over the lusty kicks of

their unborn child. Then Tom slid a hand up to cup
Charlotte's bosom. She started, blushed a little, then
whispered in his ear.

Jeremy averted his gaze. This was going too far,
even for an informal family gathering. Did they not
have a bedchamber? But a minute later, they both
arose and excused themselves.

As Jeremy joined his aunt in bidding them good
night, an unexpected spurt of jealousy wracked him,
as strong as he'd felt the first day he'd come to visit,
a sullen five-year-old, and given Tom a violent thrash-
ing for no reason he or Tom could fathom, at least at
the time. But Tom had forgiven him, and so had his
aunt and uncle. The happiest days of his life had been
spent in this house, and he would never forget it.

He forced himself to return Aunt Louisa's smile and
thrust the ugly, twisted, unworthy feeling deep within
himself, where it would hurt no one.

"So how did you fare with the Wicked Widow?"

A heavy rain pattered on the roof of the Foundling
Hospital as Jeremy looked across the table toward Sir
Digby Pettleworth, disgusted as always by the fop's
insinuating tone. But everyone else was curious as
well.

"We had an interesting meeting," he began cautiously.

"How are the children faring?" asked the Archbishop.

"They appear to be well."

"You saw no evidence of lewd goings-on?" Sir
Digby asked.

What an ass. Jeremy suppressed the angry retort. "I
did not," he said shortly. "All seems to be in order.
Lady Dearing has fitted up a schoolroom with everything one could desire, and engaged a governess who
appears to have the requisite character and qualifica-
tions. The children are quite fond of her ladyship."

He ignored a twinge of conscience for not revealing how the children had run away. But it was better to wait until he understood their reasons and could give a full report.

"You don't seem certain of anything," objected the Archbishop.

"I need more time there."

"We are fortunate that you are so *thorough*," Sir Digby murmured.

"I am sure there is no one here who does not trust Sir Jeremy to conduct himself with the utmost integrity," said Bromhurst, frowning at Sir Digby.

Jeremy shot his friend a grateful look. "Thank you. It is my intent to go there for several days each week over the next month. That should be sufficient time for me to make a proper assessment."

"But is this necessary? Do you really suspect anything is amiss?" asked Bromhurst.

Jeremy felt all eyes on him. "I cannot pass judgment until I am certain. I also hope that this course will help me gain the trust of Mary Simms. At present she is too much attached to Lady Dearing to be removed from her care."

"Why not just let her stay with the woman, then?" asked someone farther down the table.

"I must be certain that it is best for Mary. It is what my wife would have wished."

Heads nodded in agreement.

As before, when the meeting ended Bromhurst grasped Jeremy's arm. "Let's take a stroll to the Court Room, shall we? Too wet to go outside today."

Resigning himself to another lecture, Jeremy accompanied his friend out of the Committee Room. Once in the Court Room he gazed about, remembering, as he always would, the one admission day he'd attended. Despite its ornate decorations, including Hogarth's portrait of Thomas Coram, the Hospital's founder, the room echoed with anguished cries: those of mothers parting from their infants no more bitter than those of the desperate women whose children were turned away in accordance with the harsh justice of a lottery.

"What is it you wished to say to me?" he asked, after Bromhurst had stood frowning at Coram's portrait a few minutes.

"You know I will not undermine your efforts at the meeting, Jeremy," Bromhurst began. "But this schedule of visits to Rosemead Park is outside of enough! You are jeopardizing your reputation, all you have worked for."

Jeremy kept his countenance serene. He'd expected another lecture. Perhaps he deserved it for the risk he was taking.

"Think of *his* vision," said Bromhurst, gesturing toward the plump, benevolent figure of Coram.

Coram and his wife had been childless, too.

"Think of the branch hospital. Think of the infants we turn away now. Think of their fate."

Workhouses. Poorhouses. The parks. The Thames.

"I have not forgotten them. And I promise you I'll not allow my present course to affect the branch hospital project," he said through his teeth.

"You cannot have thought how our patrons, people like Tobias Cranshaw, would regard any rumors linking your name with Lady Dearing's. You must give up this obsession with Mary Simms."

"Cranshaw will understand my determination to fulfill Cecilia's last wishes."

Yet another wealthy patron who was convinced that his marriage to Cecilia had been perfect. Perhaps he could use that to his advantage. To find peace. To finally make things right.

"Mary is well enough in Lady Dearing's care, I'm sure," Bromhurst continued.

"How can I be sure all is well? Mary and the other children ran away the day I was supposed to meet them!"

"What of it? Children do such things. We have hundreds of foundlings to care for, Jeremy. Leave these four be. Lady Dearing dotes on them. Is that not enough for you?"

He faced his friend, Bromhurst's advice drilling into his resolution. Was it wrong to persist? Yet it felt even more wrong *not* to do so.

"No. In my experience, love is *not* always enough. I must be sure."

Bromhurst's face twisted. He knew the old rumors. "Oh, very well, go if you must."

"Thank you."

Bromhurst nodded, but his brows were still creased with worry.

Stay here and ride your rocking horse, lambkin, Nurse had said, then she'd taken the breakfast tray away. Jeremy wished Nurse would remember he was five years old and too old to be called lambkin. And he was too big for his old rocking horse. He had a pony now.

Comet awaited him in the stables. The house was finally empty of all its guests, and he was going to ride out for a picnic with Mama and Papa. How could Nurse expect him to just play by himself? Maybe he should go wake Mama. Maybe she'd overslept or forgotten.

Jeremy got up from his chair and left the nursery, feeling very bold. He strode down the hall enjoying the clomping sound of his boots, until he stopped. He could hear Mama and Papa arguing again. Why did they have to do it this morning?

He would end it, he decided, marching on. They always stopped arguing when he was there. He'd make them stop now.

But even though he stomped his feet as hard as he could when he got near, they didn't notice. Through the closed door he heard them say names he didn't know, and words he didn't understand. Bastard.

Whore. Damnation. Christ. *The last one he knew but it didn't fit with what they were saying.*

He was going to stop it.

He pounded on the door, feeling brave. He would make it right. They would be happier when they stopped arguing.

The shouting continued, so he pushed the door open and walked in. Papa was standing in the middle of the room, in riding clothes, Jeremy saw with relief. And Mama stood by the hearth, also in her riding habit.

They had not forgotten.

"Mama," he called, but she didn't notice him. His father was still shouting, using new words. Strumpet. Cuckold. *It sounded like some sort of bird.* Then his mother said something about geese and ganders he didn't understand. *But before he could puzzle out why they were talking about birds* his father suddenly dodged to one side.

Jeremy barely had time to recognize the thing spinning through the air—one of the shiny candlesticks Mama kept on the mantle—then it struck him on the forehead. He howled with pain. Mama screamed. Papa cursed again.

He kept screaming because it hurt, and it scared him when blood trickled into his eye, and his legs went wobbly. Mama caught him in her arms and they dropped to the floor together and then she shouted to Papa to go fetch a surgeon.

And Jeremy screamed some more because he was so angry. He hadn't stopped the fighting after all and maybe now they wouldn't go for their ride.

Then Mama started weeping and calling him her baby, and he wondered why. He was not a baby anymore. He wanted to tell her but couldn't stop crying. She began to rock him in her arms, and he was too old for that too. But he stopped howling. It felt so good, and he was tired.

Then he slept.

Chapter Seven

*M*ist curled around the quaint red conical roof of one of the distinctive oasthouses that dotted the Weald of Kent. Jeremy guided Samson along the narrow lane near Cherrydean, the nearest village to Rosemead Park. Despite the comfortable room he'd hired at the Hare and Hounds, he'd awoken early, restless and deplorably eager to keep his appointment with Lady Dearing and the foundlings. Now even the Kentish countryside beguiled him. Though his native Hampshire was lovely and fertile, he'd never seen such hop vines, such orchards laden with blossoms.

Samson snorted. Hoofbeats sounded around the bend, and a moment later Lady Dearing rode out of the shifting mists on a gray hack. A patch of sunlight glimmered on golden curls peeking from the hat that matched her blue riding habit.

"Good morning," he called out, more eagerly perhaps than he should have.

She looked startled for a moment, then rode forward to greet him. A smile lit her face, but all too quickly her expression faded to a polite mask.

"You are not lost, are you, Sir Jeremy? Rosemead is quite the opposite way."

"Thank you for your solicitude, but I am not lost," he said, turning his gaze between his horse's ears. "I promise you I shan't be late for our appointment."

"I am just returning," she said in a friendly tone. "I am going to take Galahad for a gallop across the Park, then join the children for breakfast. You may come along if you wish. We have much to discuss."

He nodded and turned Samson alongside her horse, steadied by her direct, businesslike manner. At the same time he couldn't help but enjoy the brightness of her eyes, the healthy color in her cheeks. The alluring curve of her hip over the cantle of her sidesaddle.

"Do you make a habit of riding out this early?" he asked on impulse.

"Yes, or I take a brisk walk around the Park. I like having a bit of quiet time before the children are up."

Early rising, breakfast with the children . . . None of it fit with the debauched life gossip credited her to lead.

"I have spoken to the children about their behavior last Thursday," she continued. "Mary is still reluctant to reveal why she fears a return to the Hospital, and the rest of them merely acted out of loyalty. I must beg you to be patient."

"It is not my intention to coerce information out of Mary."

"I did not imply you would," she said softly. "Perhaps you will allow me to tell you what I have planned."

"Of course."

"I think it would be best if each week you concentrated your efforts on just one child, spending as much time as possible with him or her alone."

"But they do not trust me."

"Exactly. As long as Miss Burton and I are present, the children will expect us to shield them from you. Only if you are alone together will they realize they have nothing to fear. They will also look to you to help them with any difficulties that arise, and may learn that they can rely on you to help."

It sounded reasonable. If daunting.

"Will you do it?"

She flashed him a challenging look.

Almost as if *he* were being inspected, or—came the sudden thought—tested to see if he was suited to the role of fatherhood. Well, he'd spoken to dukes, bankers and even the Prince Regent on behalf of the Foundling Hospital; he could not admit to misgivings about dealing with four children.

"Of course. It sounds an excellent plan."

She quirked an eyebrow at him. "I am glad you think so. I have planned for each child to spend some time showing you something in which he or she is interested. Asking questions will help draw them out."

"I will remember that."

"Good. Then you shall begin with Robbie."

"The youngest? Do you think it wise?"

A hint of amusement lurked in her eyes. "It is because he is the youngest that Robbie is the most trusting."

"Is he not the one who tried to run away to his wet nurse?"

"Do you think that signifies a timid nature?" Her smile broadened. "Robbie is the most redoubtable character. He knew what he wanted, and he did all he could to achieve his goal."

"An interesting interpretation of his actions."

"Did you know that he tried to stow away in my carriage?" she continued, a dimple appearing in her cheek.

"No, I did not."

"I was visiting the Hospital, and when he asked me from whence I came, I told him it was Kent. I'd no idea why it gave him such delight, until I found him under my carriage blanket and he admitted that his wet nurse lived in Kent. It quite broke my heart to return him to the nurse in charge of the little ones. Later I asked Lord Bromhurst if I could take him home with me."

"Was that not condoning Robbie's misdeed?"

"I see it as understanding a small child's desire to be near the only mother he ever knew. All the little ones cry when they come to the Hospital from their wet nurses. How can they help it? They are but three or four years old!"

"What else can we do? Physicians advise that wet-nursing is superior to any other form of sustenance for infants. But the simple country girls available as wet nurses are not capable of educating their charges. The children must return to the Hospital or they will be unprepared to earn a living."

"Please do not think I am criticizing. I am sure it is for the best. In a more ideal state of things, mothers would be able to nurse their own children."

He couldn't agree more, but her vehemence unsettled him.

"How is it that you have kept Robbie from escaping again?"

"I suggest you ask Robbie," she said.

The dimple reappeared briefly in her cheek. A delicious little dent in her glowing skin, it reminded him of something . . . . Some*one*. Nonsense. It meant nothing, just that he seemed to be partial to ladies with dimples.

They turned up a wider lane and the brick wall surrounding Rosemead appeared before them. Lady Dearing urged her horse into a trot, and a few hundred feet later they approached a small gate, presumably an alternate entrance to the Park. There she neatly maneuvered her horse along the gate, unlatched it and held it open so Jeremy and Samson could pass through. A velvety patch of green sward beckoned; Jeremy was not surprised to see Lady Dearing's horse prance. Samson pricked up his ears.

"Ready?" she asked, smiling over her shoulder.

He nodded, gave Samson his head and followed Lady Dearing in a mad dash across the Park. Ten minutes later, still distracted by her bright eyes and wind-reddened cheeks, he accompanied her into the schoolroom. The children had already sat down to their porridge. High-pitched chatter he'd heard from the hall gave way to a nervous hush, and he knew he was the cause. He smiled and bade them good morning and they replied in polite, well-rehearsed unison. Mary avoided his gaze.

Lady Dearing gave him an encouraging smile. "Would you care for some porridge, Sir Jeremy? Coffee or tea?"

He declined breakfast but allowed her to pour him coffee before she sat down with the children.

"Robbie, when we are finished you shall show Sir Jeremy our pets," Lady Dearing said, filling the awkward silence.

"I should like that very much," he said, smiling at Robbie.

The boy returned his look with the wide-eyed intensity of a very young and curious child. "O' course you will. We have some—some bang-up pets!"

Miss Burton blushed, clearly embarrassed by the child's use of cant, but Jeremy kept his countenance serene. He noticed Lady Dearing kept her eyes lowered as she brought a spoonful of porridge to her mouth. A bit of it remained on her lower lip; surreptitiously she licked it off. Jeremy wrenched his gaze from the sight of her rose-petal tongue and turned to watch the older children clear the table.

Robbie slipped eagerly out of his seat. "Now let's go see Mr. Wiggly-nose," he said, bouncing up and down.

Jeremy followed the boy to the other end of the schoolroom. Near the hearth sat a large, deep wooden box with several wisps of straw protruding from it.

Robbie bent over the box and to Jeremy's surprise lifted out a small, plump hedgehog.

"This is Mr. Wiggly-nose," he announced proudly. "I named him myself."

He lifted the creature up for Jeremy's inspection. The hedgehog's dark eyes glittered and its nose twitched.

"It does not hurt you to hold him?"

"No, he's only a bit prickly. Would you—would you like to hold him?"

Aware that everyone was watching him, including Mary, Jeremy nodded and carefully took the hedgehog from Robbie. The creature curled up in his arms.

"How curious. It is no worse than the bristles of a hairbrush," he commented.

Robbie reached up and stroked the creature, eliciting an odd snuffling, purring sound.

"However did you come to have him as a pet?"

"He—he was hungry," Robbie answered. "Lady Dee says he was born too late and—and wasn't fat enough to sleep all winter, like other hedgehogs do."

"Hedgehogs born of a second litter do not always survive," she explained. "So we brought him indoors, and—oh dear!"

Just as she broke off, Jeremy felt a warm, wet trickle down his leg. The hedgehog had relieved himself on his breeches.

"I'm so sorry!" said Lady Dearing, white-faced. "Miss Burton, fetch a wet cloth. Quickly, please!"

Miss Burton bolted from the room. Silence fell; all eyes fixed on him as if he might explode at any moment.

It was another test.

He lifted the hedgehog to face him and looked sternly at the creature.

"Mr. Wiggly-nose, where are your manners?" he demanded.

The children's eyes widened.

"I am sure your master taught you better," he continued in the same mock-lecturing voice.

Robbie's shoulders began to shake. "You're silly, Sir Jeremy!" he exclaimed, and burst into giggles.

"Mr. Wiggly-nose, I must demand an apology," he said, noting that Ben and Philippa were covering their mouths with their hands. Even Mary was watching, wide-eyed.

The creature obligingly warbled and grunted back at him.

"Ah, very well, I accept your apologies. I trust you will not behave so, disgracefully again."

The older children began to laugh. Even Lady Dearing began to chuckle softly. He drank in the delicious sound; suddenly, it occurred to him how rarely Cecilia had laughed. He looked up to see dimples puckering Lady Dearing's cheeks. Those luscious dimples . . . Making a fool of himself was worth it, just to see them.

And to please the children, of course.

As their eyes met over the heads of the children, Lady Dearing's smile faded.

Miss Burton rushed back into the room with a damp cloth and held it out to him, her cheeks red. He took it and scrubbed at his breeches, finding them only lightly stained.

"Well then, Robbie," Lady Dearing said. "Once Sir Jeremy has cleaned his—himself, you may take Mr. Wiggly-nose out to the garden for his breakfast. Then you may show Sir Jeremy the kittens. I'll meet you again in the library. You can feed Freddy and Ferdy last."

Jeremy followed the boy out of the room, still wondering what he had done to wipe the smile from Lady Dearing's face.

Livvy stared out through the window of her bedchamber. She'd come upstairs to change out of her riding habit, but instead of summoning Alice, she found herself watching Sir Jeremy and Robbie in the garden.

The sight of Sir Jeremy's tall form beside Robbie's small, bouncing one warmed her. A moment later, the hedgehog rolled down the slope to the lawn, his usual mode of traversing inclines. A captivating sound rang out: baritone laughter, mingled with Robbie's piping giggles.

Livvy withdrew from the window, deciding not to risk being seen spying on them.

But what a surprise it had been, to see such a grave, rigidly proper gentleman abandon all dignity to reassure the children. He seemed once more like the gentle, passionate man who'd kissed her at the masquerade.

Half-consciously she touched a hand to her lips, then lowered it. No, she didn't want to think about it; it only made her feel guilty. But having begun this deception, she could not risk everything by confessing now.

Besides, there was no point. There never would be.

Jeremy followed the chattering boy into the library. As they entered, Lady Dearing got up from her desk, now wearing the pale green gown he'd first seen her in. Jeremy watched Robbie run to her for a quick hug, saw the fond look she gave the child fade into a more guarded expression as she turned toward him.

He turned toward the birdcage, stifling a vague sense of disappointment. "So these are Freddy and Ferdy?"

"Yessir. Their real names are Frederica and Ferdinand," said Robbie, carefully enunciating each name as he poured water he'd brought from the kitchen into one dish, then poured seeds into another.

The birds fluttered around, twittering excitedly.

"They sing very nicely," Jeremy commented.

"If you whistle to Ferdy, he'll whistle back," said Robbie proudly as he closed and latched the cage door. "See?"

The boy whistled and one of the finches trilled back.

"A most intelligent bird. Thank you for introducing me."

"I'm glad you like them. But Sir—Sir—Sir Jeremy?"

"Yes, Robbie?"

"Could you—would you—would you—"

He waited patiently for Robbie to finish his sentence.

"—would you take me up for a ride on your horse?" finished Robbie, bouncing a little in anticipation.

"Yes, of course. That is, if Lady Dearing permits," he added, looking toward her.

She nodded.

"Thank you! Thank you!" shouted Robbie, bounding higher in that tireless way he had.

"Now you must go back to the schoolroom, dear," said Lady Dearing. "We will talk a bit, then we will come upstairs and Sir Jeremy will help you with your letters."

Once Robbie had gone, Lady Dearing seated herself in one of the wing chairs flanking the hearth and invited Jeremy to take the other.

"I hope you will tell me how you fared with Robbie. It went well, did it not?" Though her voice was calm, a slight tension in her posture betrayed her.

He nodded reassuringly. "He is a charming child. I hope you do not mind my agreeing to take him up on my horse. I assure you Samson is very well-mannered."

"No, I have no objection. It is kind of you to give Robbie such a treat. And I must also thank you for not making a fuss over the incident with Mr. Wiggly-nose."

"I am sure my breeches will come clean."

As he said it, she glanced toward his leg for a moment, then averted her face, blushing a little. Too late, he realized the gaffe he'd made: one never mentioned breeches in a lady's presence. But it was the first time she'd seemed to notice him as a *man*, not merely a Governor of the Foundling Hospital. Perhaps she was merely disgusted.

Time to move on to safer topics.

"Now perhaps you will tell me some more about Robbie," he said quickly. "I must admit I'm quite ignorant of children his age. Do they all have such difficulty completing a sentence?"

"Most of them do." She gave a slight smile. "You must realize speech is a skill they have only practiced for a few years. One learns to be patient."

"Robbie told me you take him now and then to see Nan Brooks."

She nodded. "It has helped him to adjust to life here."

"He told me she has a baby girl with her now, but I saw no sign of jealousy."

"No. Robbie regards the little girl with tolerance. You see, he is a *big* boy now." Her smile broadened.

"And now I have a more serious question," he said, lowering his voice.

"Yes, what is it?" she asked breathlessly.

"What are light-fairies?"

The dimples puckered her cheeks again, a sweet reward. "Ah, light-fairies," she said. "One morning the locket I was wearing caught a sunbeam and reflected it about the drawing room. Now we make a game of dancing the light around and pretending it is a fairy."

Finches, hedgehogs, light-fairies.

What a life for a child. What a beautiful life.

But as he gazed at Lady Dearing, her smile faded

again. The feeling stole over him that he was wasting his time. All was well here. Perhaps he should just let it be, as Bromhurst and Aunt Louisa counseled. He was not needed; he just made them all nervous.

But he'd promised to spend the rest of this day and tomorrow with Robbie, teaching him his letters, playing with him, earning his trust and that of the other children. He had promises to fulfill, and so many unanswered questions.

And perhaps he could make Lady Dearing smile again.

"I wish I'd been there to see it!" Bromhurst laughed heartily after Jeremy had related the tale of Mr. Wiggly-nose and his breeches.

Jeremy hoped it would ease his friend's anxiety; he knew why Bromhurst had taken to inviting him for a stroll on the Hospital grounds after each weekly meeting.

"But seriously, I am pleased to hear your good account of how matters stand at Rosemead. Perhaps you need not continue?"

Jeremy had braced himself for this.

"There's so much I still don't know, and the older children are still shy of me. Why do you ask? Has there been talk?"

"No, but you are running a risk by continuing this course. Lady Dearing *is* a fascinating woman, but if it is said you are succumbing to her charm—"

He forced all expression from his face. "I know the risks. So does she, I believe. She's given me no reason to think she sees me as anything but a Governor of the Foundling Hospital."

And it was just as well, he told himself fiercely. Her continued restraint, tinged with a hint of anxiety, kept him safe from succumbing to the temptation to become more closely acquainted than necessary.

He needed no reminders of the importance of maintaining a spotless reputation. Or any reminders of the consequences of undisciplined passion.

"Well, I am glad to hear that," said Bromhurst. "I just wouldn't wish you to start feeling sorry for the woman, or thinking she's the victim of false reports."

"Surely you do not believe all that nonsense Sir Digby spoke about her?"

"Most of it is rubbish," said Bromhurst bluntly. "But the rumors about her and Arlingdale might not be. I've seen her in his presence myself, at the theatre. He has been seen escorting her into the Pulteney as well."

Jeremy clenched his jaw. "Does that mean they are lovers? But earlier you said—"

"Don't look so stunned. Since she has dealt successfully with some of our most troublesome cases, I see no use in encouraging idle rumors," said Bromhurst, raking his fingers through his grizzled hair. "She's an independent and eccentric woman; Arlingdale's a charming rake, said to have many mistresses. The ladies are all agog over his golden hair and Grecian profile. Perhaps she leads a double life: mothering her children at Rosemead and meeting Arlingdale in London on occasion. It does not necessarily follow that the children will suffer for it."

"I am shocked to hear you say it. But perhaps you are right," he conceded, knowing he was on slippery ground.

It was painfully easy to imagine Lady Dearing sighing in the arms of a lover. The possibility that she was one of Arlingdale's many mistresses should have killed any attraction he felt toward her.

Yet it did not. What was the matter with him?

"Moreover," Bromhurst continued, "she's shown no wish to be brought back to respectability. If she did, she might have asked Viscount Debenham and his wife to help her. Have you thought about that?"

"No, I have not." It was only a small lie.

"And she's never shown signs of wishing to remarry. She might have done so, with her looks and that comfortable estate of hers. Undoubtedly some men would overlook the fact that she never gave Dearing an heir."

"I suppose."

"On the other hand, her barrenness as well as her looks make her the ideal mistress," continued Bromhurst.

Jeremy's jaw tightened.

"And it helps to explain why so many men have pursued her."

He looked away, so Bromhurst could not read the frustration in his expression. He didn't even know with whom he was annoyed: his friend for saying such things, Arlingdale and the others who sought Lady Dearing as a mistress, or the lady herself for behaving like such an enigma.

Or perhaps with himself, for allowing himself to be intrigued by a woman who, intentionally or not, threatened all his goals. The branch hospital. The fulfillment of Cecilia's last wish. Mary.

And yet he was intrigued.

"Whatever the case," Bromhurst lectured on, "gossip will always surround Lady Dearing. You know what is at stake. You cannot afford to behave rashly."

"Do I ever?" Jeremy muttered.

After a long look at Jeremy, Bromhurst shook his head.

Grimly, Jeremy congratulated himself on his acting. For the first time in years he wanted, very badly, to behave rashly.

Chapter Eight

R ippling notes from the pianoforte greeted Jeremy as he entered the drawing room at Rosemead. Lady Dearing gazed at her music, unconscious of him, her eyes glowing, her body swaying as she played in a manner as unconscious as it was innocently seductive.

Quietly, he inched into the room.

A soft cry erupted, and the music faltered.

Then he saw Mary seated on the sofa, staring down at a spot of blood on her thumb, her other hand still clasping some needlework.

"My dear, have you pricked yourself?" Lady Dearing's gaze swung from Mary to him.

"Let me help." He hurried to Mary and handed her his handkerchief as Lady Dearing joined him near the sofa.

"I am so sorry," he said. "I would not have interrupted, but Thurlow advised me to come in."

"I told him to bring you here as soon as you arrived, so there is no one at fault," Lady Dearing reassured him.

But Mary clutched the handkerchief to her finger, her face pale. It seemed the time he'd spent here last week had not done much good. *Yet*, he reminded himself.

"Mary, you may go up to the schoolroom now,"

said Lady Dearing. "Send Philippa down to the library, please."

The girl scurried from the room, leaving him to feel like a wretched interloper.

What *was* he doing here?

"Shall we go to the library?" asked Lady Dearing.

He nodded. "I must apologize again for having interrupted. I've rarely heard music so beautiful. What was it?"

"A sonata by Mozart," she replied, looking a bit surprised by his interest.

"You play marvelously." The words tumbled out.

Her face froze into a tight smile; not quite the reaction he wished for. "Thank you. I have had many years in which to practice. More than I wish to admit."

A decade of childless marriage.

"Does Mary enjoy listening to you play?" he asked, following her out of the room.

Her shoulders relaxed. "Yes," she said, more easily. "I have offered to teach her but one cannot force such things. It is my hope that if I allow her to listen, in time she will wish to play herself."

He nodded. "Yes, I am beginning to see that one cannot rush matters with children. I see Mary still fears me."

"She will become more accustomed, I assure you. Perhaps, even if you do decide she can remain at Rosemead, I could bring her to the Foundling Hospital so you can meet with her for a few hours now and then."

Her softened voice felt like a caress, but it was only friendly sympathy, he reminded himself. He cleared his throat. "I should like that."

As they approached the library he braced himself for his encounter with Philippa. To endear himself to Robbie had been so easy, but to earn the confidence of an older child might prove more challenging.

"I thought perhaps you could assist Philippa with

her mathematical studies," said Lady Dearing, as they entered the library. "How is your mathematics?"

"Sufficient to teach a girl of ten years, I would assume," he said, raising an eyebrow.

"Excellent."

He thought he detected the hint of a twinkle in her eyes.

A moment later, Philippa had arrived. Lady Dearing gave the girl's shoulder a pat before leaving them alone together. As he watched Philippa pick up a yellowed periodical from a pile of almanacs and lexicons on a side table, he noted that she was dressed with extreme neatness, her dark, curly hair confined by a dark green ribbon; her manner was subdued, cautious. How had the schoolmistress at the Hospital described her? Pert, inattentive, above her station.

The girl seemed none of those at present.

"Philippa, please be at your ease," he said. "I shall not continue to blame you for having led the children to run away. What's done is done, and I should sincerely like to become better acquainted with you."

She curtsied stiffly, and her hands trembled as she opened up the periodical.

"Lady Dearing has assigned me this problem for today," she said in a tight, expressionless voice.

"Read it aloud, please."

" 'Walking through Cheapside, London, on the first day of May, 1709, the sun shining brightly, I was desirous to know the height of Bow steeple. I accordingly measured its shadow just as the clock was striking twelve, and found its length to be 253 and one eighth feet; it is required from thence to find the steeple's height.' "

Jeremy stared at the girl. "This is the sort of problem Lady Dearing arranges for you?"

It made one wonder about the lady's own abilities.

"Yes, sir," Philippa replied.

Her voice was meek, but held a suggestion of smugness. Was this another test? Well, he was not going to fight shy, any more than he had with the hedgehog.

"Then let us begin."

Half an hour later, he verified Philippa's calculations against the answer provided to him by Lady Dearing, written in a graceful, flourishing hand on a slip of paper that was slightly yellowed, though not as ancient as the periodical.

"Excellent," he said, enjoying Philippa's shy smile in response to his praise. "Does Lady Dearing enjoy such puzzles as well?"

"She said her grandmother had an interest in mathematics and natural philosophy and used to work such problems with her."

"Quite admirable. I am glad she has found interesting methods to enhance your studies. You have a keen mind. Perhaps you would enjoy attending some lectures in London someday?"

"Yes, I—I would," said the girl, looking startled.

"I shall see if I can arrange something," he said. "If Lady Dearing permits, of course."

"Thank you, sir," said Philippa soulfully as she departed.

He'd gone only a few steps toward the drawing room when he heard voices emanating through the suspiciously closed door: an angry, masculine rant followed by Lady Dearing's softer accents.

Thurlow appeared from the direction of the hall, the lines in his face deeper than usual.

"Lady Dearing is . . . engaged at the moment, sir," said the butler apologetically. "Perhaps you may return to the library to await her?"

"Is something amiss? Could I be of any help?" he asked sharply.

The elderly butler gave Jeremy an appraising look.

"Thank you, sir, but I believe her ladyship is equal to dealing with this particular visitor."

Something was definitely wrong. Jeremy crossed the

hall to the door of the drawing room and pulled it open. There he saw his hostess standing with her back to him, facing a young gentleman of dandyish appearance. Neither of them noticed him.

"You have gone too far!" shouted the dandy. "How dare you dispose of those jewels in such a manner! Ungrateful creature!"

Jewels? The puppy's gift to her, perhaps? Jeremy watched from the doorway, biting back questions that would betray his presence.

"I did dispose of them, and there is nothing you can do about it," she said, her posture tense but her voice devoid of passion. "I suggest you leave now."

The young fop paced about the room. "I will not be put off so! Sophronia and I know our rights!"

"I consulted my solicitor on the matter and he assured me I was free to dispose of the diamonds as I chose. So I did."

Jeremy frowned. Who the devil was Sophronia?

"But my uncle surely intended them to be an heirloom, to be passed down to each new Dearing bride!" moaned the young man.

"How could you sell them—his wedding present to you? Have you no respect for his memory?"

"Not as much as you, my dear nephew," she retorted.

Relief flooded Jeremy. But the young man—presumably the present Lord Dearing—reddened, and one of his eyelids began to twitch.

"And all to benefit a pack of bastards!"

Jeremy coughed.

"Ah, there you are," said Lady Dearing, turning to look at him, her expression veiled. Then she turned to the other man. "Adolphus, this is Sir Jeremy. One of the Governors of the Foundling Hospital."

Dearing goggled at him.

"Sir Jeremy, this is my nephew Adolphus, Lord Dearing."

Jeremy gave a slight bow. Dearing jerkily reciprocated. A diamond pin in his cravat caught Jeremy's eye. Good God, not another one of *them*. And judging by his pallor, just as lily-livered as Pettleworth.

"I am sorry to say, Sir Jeremy, that my agitation led me to speak improperly of your fine institution," Dearing quavered.

"No offense taken," he said coldly.

Dearing seemed to shrink into himself.

"But I must say," Jeremy continued smoothly, "as one of the Governors of the Hospital, I am more than grateful for Lady Dearing's generous donations."

Dearing's eyes darted between them. "My aunt is generous to a fault sometimes. I'm afraid her warm heart leads her to overindulge the foundlings she has here."

"Has there been any trouble?" asked Jeremy.

"No, but—well, you must be conscious of the risks of allowing a lady with my aunt's lenient nature to manage children who are known to be difficult cases!"

"I am here on behalf of the Foundling Hospital to determine whether the children are being properly managed. Thus far I have seen nothing to give concern."

"But you must know one of these children set a fire at the Hospital. What's to prevent a reoccurrence? I am the heir to Rosemead. You must admit I've a right to know."

"I shall discuss your concerns with Lady Dearing and the other Governors. I believe your business here is finished now."

He set a hand on Dearing's shoulder and put a subtle pressure on it. Dearing's eyelid twitched wildly but he allowed Jeremy to steer him out of the room, toward the entrance hall and all the way to his carriage.

When Jeremy returned, he found Thurlow standing in the hall. The butler's eyes twinkled with gratitude.

Jeremy smiled to see that Thurlow's earlier wariness had given way to approval.

"He is gone, my lady," said Thurlow to her ladyship as she peered out from the drawing room.

"Thank you for your assistance, Sir Jeremy." Her voice was calm, but her hands were clasped tightly in front of her.

"I was glad to be of service."

Her lip trembled, then she stilled it. "Shall we sit down now? I should like to hear how you fared with Philippa."

He followed her back into the drawing room, wondering why his solicitude unsettled her so much. His own feelings were in a jumble. Suspicion and jealousy now gave way to guilt over having misjudged her and a fierce protectiveness.

Jealousy. Guilt. Protectiveness.

Burning curiosity as to why a widow would so readily part with her husband's wedding gift.

Dangerous feelings.

Her fragrance wafted back toward him, igniting baser passions. He tried to focus on something, and his eyes betrayed him by seeking out the small buttons on the back of her bodice. He longed to see if his big fingers could manage the tiny openings, how her skin would feel under his touch, whether she might enjoy it . . .

God help him, he was mad.

Livvy quailed inwardly as she saw Sir Jeremy's uncompromising expression.

"I am sorry you had to be subjected to such an unpleasant encounter," she said as she sat down. "My nephew's views on the foundlings are most backward and hypocritical."

His expression softened. "Do not apologize. I'm accustomed to encountering such views. Since you have

incurred his wrath on behalf of the foundlings, I must
ask if there is anything I may do to help."

He was so touchingly protective . . . it reminded her
of the masquerade. She stiffened. The gruff concern
in his voice, the determined set of those broad shoulders all coaxed her to trust him. But she could manage
without assistance; she had for years. It would be foolish to lean on Sir Jeremy, even for moral support.

"Thank you, but no. Adolphus can do little more
than bluster at me. It is of no consequence. Please tell
me how you fared with Philippa."

His eyes narrowed, first with suspicion, then with
amusement. "I should have realized you were preparing a surprise for me. I can see why the schoolmistress
at the Hospital found Philippa a daunting pupil."

"She *is* very precocious," she said, reassured by the
humor in his rich voice. "Miss Burton and I fear that
soon she will outstrip our own abilities."

"Which are not inconsiderable, from what Philippa
tells me."

"My abilities are commonplace in comparison."

He gazed thoughtfully out the window. "I realize
you have gone beyond the usual course of instruction
for girls at the Foundling Hospital, but Philippa is an
unusual case. Have you given thought to her future?"

"Of course. I promised Lord Bromhurst the children would each be prepared for useful employment.
I myself have only a small personal fortune to be-
queath to them, since as you know my nephew stands
to inherit Rosemead." She paused. "I think Philippa
might prove to be an excellent teacher. Although she
is so precocious herself, she does enjoy helping the
other children with their studies."

Livvy clasped her hands in her lap, wondering at
the slight crease in Sir Jeremy's forehead as he pondered her words. She'd given what she believed was
the most acceptable answer to the Governors of the

Foundling Hospital. She didn't dare confide her secret hopes for Philippa: that the girl might somehow, despite her birth and her sex, find a way to exert her considerable talents in mathematics, or natural philosophy, or perhaps medicine.

Finally he nodded. "I certainly cannot imagine her enjoying the life of a chambermaid, or in a dressmaker's establishment. Well, I suppose time will reveal how she could best use her abilities. In the meantime, perhaps I would be able to arrange for her to attend some lectures in London on scientific matters. With your permission of course."

"Thank you. You have been more than kind."

She gave him a glowing smile. Then his expression altered, and she quickly lowered her gaze. He'd been so stern, so rigidly correct in all their dealings, but now she could not mistake the hunger in his eyes.

Heavens, *that* was why he looked so severe at times.

She leapt from her seat. "Shall we return to the schoolroom? I think you will find Philippa excels in more than one area of study."

She hastened out of the room, not daring to look back. He was such a *good* man. Too aware of his role as the prime mover in the branch hospital project to court scandal; too gentlemanly to insult her by exploiting his position as an inspector. And perhaps whatever gleamed in his eyes was probably just a fleeting attraction.

Her own feelings might be a tumult of fear and guilt, loneliness and desire. But while his passions were firmly in check, she could keep from betraying herself.

Jeremy rode slowly up the drive, determined not to arrive too early this week, his third visit to Rosemead. Samson tossed his head, perhaps sensing his rider's unrest. Jeremy patted the horse absently, trying and failing to banish the image that had lingered with him long after he'd risen that morning: of Lady Dearing, lying back on a snowy pillow, golden curls spilled around her, her face lit by sunlight, her eyes dreamy, not wary as they usually were when she spoke to him. In his dream, she wore a simple white nightrail. He'd eagerly loosened the tie and pulled it down off her shoulders. And then his imagination had failed to conjure up the sight of her, and he'd woken up.

Samson broke into a trot. "Sorry, friend, I didn't mean that," Jeremy murmured, reining his horse in.

To steady his mind, he thought of Ben, with whom he would spend the next few days. The boy had already begun to soften to him, venturing to speak a few words now and again and even persevering past some rather painful stutters when he saw that Jeremy could be patient. Today would go further to establish the boy's trust in him, he was sure of it. Lady Dearing's plan was working. Even Mary watched him with covert curiosity and cringed less when he spoke to her.

It was all going so well; he could not risk ruining everything by allowing Lady Dearing to guess his fantasies. She was so skittish around him, as if afraid he would judge her by gossip rather than the evidence of his own experience.

Only two more visits, and he would likely not see her again.

Samson snorted and cantered up the drive to the stables; this time Jeremy saw no use in pulling up. He had just handed Samson over to a groom when he heard the sound of galloping hoofbeats. Looking up, he froze.

A fine chestnut mare thundered into the yard, bearing an extremely handsome gentleman with a Grecian profile and golden hair curling from under his hat.

Jeremy stood rooted to the ground, disbelief and jealousy raging through his body.

It couldn't be. He couldn't believe it.

But it had to be.

The man leaping down from the chestnut answered perfectly to Bromhurst's description of the Marquess of Arlingdale.

Chapter Nine

Jeremy stood burning as Arlingdale dismounted from his mare. Up close, the damned Adonis was even more handsome, sporting fresh, youthful features. Jeremy had thought the notorious marquess was older. Did the rogue enjoy eternal youth as well as the favors of numerous lovers?

Could Lady Dearing be so thoughtless as to conduct a liaison with Arlingdale at Rosemead, where the children could witness their licentious behavior?

"Good day, sir." Arlingdale strode forward to meet him. "I believe we've not met."

There was a bite in his voice, as if *Jeremy* had no right to be here.

"I am Sir Jeremy Fairhill," he returned coldly.

"Oh—ah, yes! The Foundling Hospital!" The other man's brow cleared. He flashed a despicably winsome smile and offered his hand.

Jeremy shook it, pressing hard enough to show he was unmoved by the friendly gesture.

"I'm Debenham, you know," the other said easily.

Debenham. Jeremy released his hand, hoping he hadn't crushed any bones.

"M'wife and our daughter are already with her." Debenham grinned. "I know it's early for a visit, but it's Annabel's best time of the day."

"Yes, the children have told me about little Annabel."

"They do dote on her." Debenham sobered. "Sorry I pokered up a trifle when I first saw you. Begging your pardon, but some deuced loose fish sometimes come here thinking to impose on dear Livvy. I'm glad you're not one of them."

"Indeed not."

Livvy. So that was what her friends called her. Staunch friends, apparently, who wished to protect her from those who would take advantage of her reputation. He frowned, remembering how eager Sir Digby Pettleworth had been to come to visit her in his stead. No doubt he was the sort of loose fish of whom Debenham spoke.

The viscount's ready smile returned. "Livvy's told us you are here on an inspection. I hope you're satisfied with what you've seen. A kind soul, isn't she?"

"Indeed she is."

"Well, we'd better go in." Debenham headed toward the entrance. "My wife and daughter came in the carriage, but we forgot to bring Annabel's rattle. She's cutting a tooth now and loves to bite on the coral bit, so I was sent home on an urgent mission to fetch it."

He patted his coat pocket as if to assure himself the rattle had not fallen out along the way, and breathed an audible sigh of relief. "Still there. I should have been in hot water otherwise. You know how it is." He winked.

"I can imagine," Jeremy murmured.

It took no imagination to picture the Debenhams' happiness once Jeremy had entered the library with the other man. A slim lady with short, curling brown hair and a sweet face, presumably the Viscountess Debenham, sat on the sofa beside Lady Dearing, who dandled a plump baby on her knees. The room echoed with giggles; the foundlings were all busily jumping up and down from behind chairs and tables, playing a wild version of peekaboo with the infant.

The viscount crossed the room to give his wife the rattle and a kiss, but Jeremy hovered on the threshold.

"Sir Jeremy!" Robbie cried out. As the boy bounced out from behind a chair to greet him, all heads turned his way.

"Sir Jeremy!" Lady Dearing called out, with a welcoming smile. "Come and join us. As you see we have some visitors this morning."

Jeremy allowed Robbie to drag him into the room, smiling and responding cordially to all the introductions. A few minutes later, Thurlow and another servant appeared bringing tea, coffee, and plum tarts. The children devoured their treat while the Debenhams engaged Jeremy in conversation about Foundling Hospital matters. Warmed by their friendliness, he did his best to reply suitably to all their questions while trying not to allow his eyes to be drawn to Lady Dearing.

After her initial greeting she'd become absorbed with the baby. Now Annabel grabbed the lace at her breast with a chubby hand, pulling it slightly out of her bodice. Lady Dearing started, looked up and caught Jeremy watching her. Blushing, she gently pried the baby's little fingers from her tucker and smoothed it back into place.

Firmly, he looked away. If only she did not feel it necessary to hide under those layers of muslin and lace. He felt certain it was on his account; but it would be unpardonably offensive to tell her he yearned to see her in the revealing low gowns worn by every lady of fashion. He could only hope she hadn't sensed his crass thoughts.

Against his will, his eyes were drawn back.

"And how comes the branch hospital project?" Debenham asked, recalling his attention.

Jeremy struggled to reply. Young Annabel, de-

prived of the lace, began to toy with one of Lady
Dearing's long, sparkling crystal earrings. Cooing, she
removed the earring and dangled it so the baby could
bat at it in harmless delight.

Jeremy responded absently to Debenham's questions. As Lady Dearing continued to play with the
infant, oblivious to his hungry gaze, moisture gleamed
under her lashes. Suddenly she bent down to kiss the
infant's downy head. When she straightened, her lips
trembled.

He was enthralled.

He wrenched his gaze away. When he dared to look
at her again he saw a look of strain on her face. It
sobered him, reminding him that despite his growing
conviction that she was a steadfast, loving woman,
wronged by society, there was so much he did not
know about her: why she hid behind a sordid reputation she showed no desire to repair, why she did not
seem to trust him. Ominous questions when his emotions toward her swung between jealousy and
tenderness.

And since she showed not the faintest hint of returning his interest, how could he hope to find answers?

Rosebuds surrounded him.

They hung in swags above him, trellised on the
walls, swooping and draping from arches, rising from
shrubs thickly planted within neat boxwood borders,
underplanted with lavender and violets. He could only
imagine how it would all look and smell in less than
a month.

It was not likely he'd be there to see it.

For all was going according to plan, except for his
wretched blunder earlier. Lady Dearing had caught
him looking at her like a starving man; nothing else
could explain the strained look in her eyes ever since
the Debenhams had taken their leave.

He had to make it right somehow.

He looked down at Ben, who was supposed to be giving him a tour of the gardens before commencing his assigned tasks there. The boy stared back, his fawnlike eyes wide and anxious.

Damn. He'd been frowning. He was scaring everyone now.

"I'm sorry, Ben," he said, forcing a smile. "I was looking at all these roses and wishing I could be here when they blow."

"You—you won't come back then, s-s-sir?"

He couldn't even tell which Ben wanted.

"I wish I could," he replied quietly. "But I have an estate to manage in Hampshire and much work to do on behalf of the Foundling Hospital."

"W-would you like to see the flower garden now? There's m-more there."

"I would."

At least the lad was making an effort to speak to him, Jeremy reflected, as Ben conducted him slowly through the extensive gardens, surrounded by an immense brick wall and divided into neat rectangles by hedges of yew and sweet-smelling hawthorn. From the rose garden they proceeded to a flower garden, where a fine plane tree with a circular seat beneath it provided shade from which to view informally laid out beds presently bright with tulips. The next enclosure contained strawberry beds and raspberry canes, all in bloom, and a vast array of fragrant herbs; the next devoted to vegetables and hotbeds.

The sun beat down as they wended their way to the final double-sized enclosure devoted to fruit trees. There Ben introduced Jeremy to Furzeley, the head gardener, who gave Jeremy the same appraising scrutiny he'd received from all of Lady Dearing's elderly servants.

"Has our Ben been showing ye the gardens, Sir Jeremy?" Furzeley's eyes were bright in his lined, brown face.

Jeremy nodded. "I am most impressed with his knowledge."

"Aye, he's a likely lad," replied the gardener with a fond look at the boy.

Ben looked shyly pleased.

As Furzeley gave Ben his orders for the day, Jeremy gazed around at the long rows of espaliered trees, their shapes somehow both tormented and graceful. More fruit trees were pinned against the southern wall to receive the sun and yield up their fruits. In one corner stood a long brick building, which he guessed housed tools and gardening supplies.

A few minutes later he stood by Ben near one of the wall trees. The boy carefully examined the branches and began to cut off small shoots with a small, sharp knife.

"Can you explain what you are doing, Ben?"

"You have to n-n-nip off the bits that are growing the wrong way. It keeps the strength in the b-branches that will bear this year and next."

They moved to the next tree. The sun warming his back, Jeremy watched Ben work, impressed by the boy's intent examination of the shoots, the sure skill in his hands.

"What sort of tree is this?"

"P-peach," said Ben, looking up briefly. When Jeremy nodded his encouragement, the boy continued. "It's—it's a—D-double Montagne. They're some of the best, but the French Mignonnes are good, too."

"What other fruits are grown here?" Jeremy asked, careful not to appear conscious of the increasing flow of Ben's words.

Ben waved toward the rows of espaliers. "Apples and pears. They're the hardier ones. Along the wall we have peaches, apricots and plums. They like it where it's sunny and warm."

"You've learned a lot from Furzeley. I am impressed."

The boy reddened a little but looked pleased.

"It would be foolish to remove a plant from a place where it is thriving, wouldn't it?"

"Yessir." Ben stiffened and gave him a wary sidelong glance as he moved to the next tree.

"I know you do not wish to speak of this, but we must. Setting a fire in a corridor of the Hospital was very wrong. But Lady Dearing told me why you did it, and I believe her."

"I d-d-didn't hurt anyone." Ben stopped his trimming and stared sullenly at the ground.

"I know. I've been told you set the fire in a metal pail from which it was unlikely to spread."

Ben shot him another wary glance, then fixed his gaze on the roots of the next tree.

"You were angry, weren't you?"

Ben shifted his feet uncomfortably.

"I was an angry boy once." Jeremy laid a hand on Ben's shoulder. "The first time I visited my cousin I gave him a black eye."

Ben went very still.

"Yes. My cousin Tom and I are the best of friends now. But there was a time I was so angry that I thought I hated him, because he had everything I wished for. We made up, and in time I learned better ways to release my anger."

"What ways, sir?" Ben lowered his pruning knife and stared up at Jeremy.

"Physical exertion helps. I used to run as fast as I could until the mood passed. Now I walk or ride when I'm out of temper. I imagine gardening does the same for you, doesn't it?"

Ben nodded slowly. "I like seeing things grow, too. Nothing stays the same in a garden."

The boy's eyes glowed up at him with budding admiration. Jeremy found himself wishing he could return to Rosemead for regular visits, if only to help the lad. But it was not possible, of course. All risk of scandal aside, he could not force himself where he was not wanted. He might never come to know the woman who had achieved so much with Ben and the others. *Livvy.*

He longed to call her by that name. It was not likely he'd get the chance.

"We're done here, sir," said Ben.

"On to the next task, then," he replied, hoping the boy hadn't sensed his restless mood.

Jeremy followed Ben into the toolhouse and stood by the long potting table in the center while Ben exchanged his pruning shears for a short, pronged hoe.

"What are we doing next?" he asked.

"The turnips need hoeing, sir."

"Then find me a hoe. I'm going to help you."

Jeremy could not explain it to Ben, but hard work might help to assuage other feelings besides anger.

Livvy stared down from her bedchamber, riveted by the sight of Sir Jeremy hoeing the turnip beds beside Ben. She couldn't doubt that they were dealing well together now. There was no excuse to keep watching. But she couldn't pull away either.

Sir Jeremy had removed his coat and hung it up from a nearby stake used to support beans. No dandy, Sir Jeremy! She smiled, remembering the hedgehog incident and a few others like it during the past weeks. Weeks she'd spent caught between guilt and joy, laughter and tears, watching him earn the children's trust while she continued to deceive him.

He stretched, then removed his waistcoat and hung it over his coat. Well, it *was* unseasonably warm, excusing what some would consider a moderate impropriety. Livvy fanned herself with her hand, continuing to stare, knowing she should not, as he pulled the cravat from around his neck and then unbuttoned the top buttons of his fine white shirt. Even at a distance she could plainly see a triangle of skin revealed at his throat, the breadth of his shoulders, the shape of his legs in their snug breeches.

And desire, her old enemy, had her in its grip.

She turned from the window and paced about the large, airy room, trying to banish thoughts of him. Catching sight of her reflection in the mirror, she paused and stared as she had not in a long time. Her face was still unlined, her complexion still bright. Her figure . . . it was still just as Walter had first admired and then despised. For a while she'd even seen herself as he had: all false curves, a mockery of a woman with round hips that would never support a babe, bountiful breasts that would never be suckled. Now men ogled those same charms but thought her barrenness made her the most desirable of mistresses.

But she had come to see her body for what it was. Pleasing in its own way.

For a moment she wondered what Sir Jeremy saw, then a lump came to her throat as she remembered how he had watched her playing with Annabel. But it was foolish to dwell on it. He was doing his best to hide his attraction from her; her own wisest course was to pretend not to notice.

Impatiently, she turned from the mirror. She ought to go down to the schoolroom, but like a moth to a flame she returned to the window. Sir Jeremy was still hard at work, and she drank in the sight of him flexing and bending and laboring in shirtsleeves and closely fitted breeches. How could she find the sight of a powerful man's body so arousing? It was insane.

But she did.

She hugged herself. She tried not to think of his slow kiss, his big gentle hands. She turned to study the familiar pattern of exotic birds and vines she'd painted herself on the pale turquoise moiré wallpaper, the mismatched but beloved furniture, some of it simple pieces original to the house, others bits of inlaid and carved chinoiserie she'd bought on a whim in

London. This was her bower, the sanctuary she had made for herself after Walter's death.

And there was her bed, large and comfortable, draped in silk a few shades darker than the walls, where she slept peacefully, safe from intrusion. Safe and alone.

To think of anything else was madness.

Gulls wheeled and cried. Livvy sat looking out of the window of her bedchamber, focusing on the birds' free flight in the sky, their wild cries. Breathing the salt-tanged air of Brighton that flowed through the window and fluttered her nightdress.

Her stomach gurgled and she tried to ignore it. Dr. Croft's instructions were precise, and she would have followed them religiously even had Walter not watched her like a hawk through every meal.

Plethora. Excessive fullness. That was what she suffered from, what kept them from conceiving during two years of marriage. Sea bathing, the lowering diet, and today, her first bloodletting, were the suggested remedies.

She would try anything. She wanted a baby, and Walter wanted an heir so badly. It would please him so much.

Her stomach gurgled again. Fullness! She'd rarely felt so empty. Perhaps it was the bloodletting that caused her spirits to droop.

She started as the floor across the room creaked. She knew those heavy footfalls. She got up, forcing a welcoming smile to her lips.

Walter stood watching her for a moment, still fully dressed. He'd missed dinner again; perhaps he had been walking on the seafront. His face was wind-roughened, his expression anxious. Vulnerable.

"How went the . . . bloodletting?" he asked, his eyes everywhere but the bandage on her arm.

"It was not as bad as I feared." Indeed, she'd suf-

fered worse. This was worthwhile pain, if only it was successful.

"Good," he boomed, and crossed the room to take her in his arms, more gently than usual.

He'd been so solicitous for her health lately, almost tender. Perhaps the air of Brighton agreed with him. Perhaps he was remembering the affection he'd once shown her.

"I think I'd forgotten how beautiful you are," he murmured.

She gave him a shaky smile.

He pulled down the nightdress she'd left intentionally loose and cupped one breast in his hand, then pinched the nipple. Out of long habit she turned her flinch into a gasp that might be mistaken for pleasure.

"Ah, you like that."

She nodded, lowering her face. She didn't dare bruise his pride, and it was far too easily done.

He manhandled her breast for a moment or so, then lowered his mouth to kiss her. She kissed him back to encourage him, though she nearly gagged at the familiar taste of brandy. He seemed to need it to gain courage for the assault on her fertility.

No, there would be no tenderness tonight.

He pushed her toward the bed. Obediently she climbed onto it. Out of the corner of her eye she saw him unbuttoning his breeches. Pray God they conceived this time. A baby would be a comfort. A relief, for it might end these indignities.

He lowered himself onto her. She parted her legs and willed herself to relax as he impaled her.

He needed this baby, too. They both did.

So she put her arms around him, sensing his desperation. Patiently, she endured the discomfort as he strained and grunted, moving in time with him to speed his climax, reminding herself to breathe lightly when he collapsed on top of her.

A few minutes later, he rolled over and cursed.

She felt the wetness, saw the bed marred with blood. Her woman's blood. Her courses. Almost a week early.

"Damn it all!"

She cringed as he pushed himself off the bed.

Not looking at her, he refastened his breeches. Seeing the angry tension in his frame, the jerkiness of his movements, she lay deathly still. To speak or move was to risk a virulent tongue-lashing. Lately she'd begun to imagine worse.

But thank God, this time he merely staggered out, not wasting a backward glance on her.

When she heard the door slam, she curled up into a tight ball, allowing herself the relief of a few tears before summoning Alice to help her.

Chapter Ten

*J*eremy inhaled a lungful of air spiced with the scent of freshly turned earth. His shirt clung to him in patches as he stretched. It was even warmer than yesterday, more like July than May. Beside him, Ben worked with a child's seeming indifference to the heat. Jeremy bent back down and wielded his hoe, toiling on in the vain hope that heat and exertion would obliterate what was fast becoming an obsession.

When Livvy came up beside them, fresh and ladylike in a blue sprigged gown and bonnet, lace high at her throat, gloves discreetly covering her hands, he knew he'd failed.

"It is dreadfully hot out here, isn't it?" she asked, a slight stammer in her voice.

He straightened to face her, his face burning. Custom dictated that a gentleman remain fully dressed regardless of the weather, but here he stood, a brutish oaf in his shirtsleeves, without even a cravat around his neck.

"I thought perhaps the two of you should have some lemonade on the terrace," she continued.

The breathless sound of her voice, the way she didn't seem to quite look at him, confirmed his worst fears. She was disgusted by the sight of his sweaty, uncouth self.

Rigid with mortification, he started to go past her

toward the pole where he'd strung up his discarded clothing. Then he caught her expression.

She quickly turned and began to fuss over a small tear in Ben's shirt.

But Jeremy had seen it. The look in her eyes had not been disgust. She had seemed . . . fascinated.

No, perhaps he was imagining it, he told himself as he shrugged into his waistcoat and jacket. Still, Livvy was having trouble settling on a place to rest her eyes. Her cheeks were deliciously pink as she fidgeted with the bow that held her bonnet in place.

He could no longer resist the impulse to behave rashly.

"Perhaps Ben can go ahead," he suggested. "I should like to speak to you for a few minutes."

"Of—of course," she said.

He offered her his arm as Ben trotted off. She eyed it as she might a potentially dangerous creature, then slowly laid her hand over it. The feather light touch of her gloved fingers reminded him of something . . . perhaps one of the alluring dreams he had about her.

He started off in the direction of the orchard, the longest possible path back to the house.

"Is there something particular you wish to say to me?" she said, her voice pitched a trifle higher than usual.

At least she had consented to let him touch her. He cleared his throat. "I wished to commend you again on your management of Ben. He shows a remarkable knowledge of gardening for one so young."

"Yes, Ben *is* a remarkable boy."

Her hand pressed lightly around his arm as they entered the orchard enclosure; a small sign that her defenses were weakening.

"I've seen nothing like these gardens, especially the fruit trees. Your yield must be tremendous."

"The Weald of Kent is known to be some of the most fertile land in all of England."

Her voice was calm, but a little husky. Her hand

trembled. He wished he could see her face, but she kept facing forward, hiding her expression beyond the brim of her bonnet.

"And Rosemead is a lovely home," he said casually. "I can imagine no better place for children to grow up."

Now she turned her face back to him, eyes full of vulnerable hope.

"Yes," he said, unable to hold back a grin. "I have decided to make a glowing report to the Committee."

"Thank you."

Her eyes misted with relief, but an instant later her mouth drooped.

Would she miss him?

"Of course, I shall return next week as planned," he said as they walked along the southern wall, the fruit trees luxuriantly splayed out against it. "I wish to make the most of the time I can spend with Mary."

And with you.

"Of course." Her voice was breathless again.

"Perhaps she is not ready to confide in anyone yet, but I want to do what I can to earn her trust."

"You have made progress already," she said, still hiding her face.

"I hope that I have."

He wished he could tear off that annoying bonnet.

"I feel certain that in time she will feel secure in your care."

He hated the calm resignation in her voice.

"I should like to arrange to see her more often. Perhaps you could bring Mary to the Foundling Hospital so I may see her once in a while?"

"Yes, of course. At the Hospital, with Mrs. Hill in attendance. That should not occasion any gossip. Then once Mary goes to live with you, perhaps I could visit her there as well."

There it was again: that guarded, cool friendliness in her voice, while he burned with frustration.

"Of course, but perhaps circumstances might change." The rash words leapt out of him. "Perhaps you need not be parted from her at all."

She remained silent so long he was certain he'd blundered.

"I cannot see how that could happen," she said, sounding strangled. "But I know you will be an excellent father to her."

Though she retained a tenuous grasp on his arm, she seemed to shrink into herself. He was losing her. He had to find some common ground, anything that would break through her reserve.

"You have taught me much in these past weeks," he blurted. "I cannot tell you how grateful I am for it. I think we both have particular reasons for taking interest in these children."

He felt a subtle shiver through her hand, as if he'd forged a slender thread of communion between them.

"Few men would take the pains you do to win their affection," she said quietly. "It is a pity you have not children of your own."

"It was not possible."

"What happened?"

He remained silent as they passed through an arch dripping with fragrant white hawthorn flowers and came upon raised strawberry beds. The image of Livvy and the children feasting on berries warm from the sun came to him. Then irrational anger possessed him at the thought that he might not see her again, or merely on rare, chaperoned visits to the Foundling Hospital. And he did not want to talk about Cecilia; he wanted to learn about *her*.

Lord, why had he brought up the topic of children?

"I am sorry. I did not mean to pry," she murmured.

"I am not offended." Instinctively, he laid a hand over hers, as if it might keep her by his side.

"Would it help you to speak of it?"

Her voice was soft with pity. But he didn't want her pity. He wanted . . . what *did* he want?

He wanted to know why she cloaked herself in a soiled reputation; whether there was anything that would change her decision. Whether there was any truth to the rumors about her and Lord Arlingdale. What she felt for *him*, if anything.

And to find these things out he needed her to keep talking.

"Do you truly wish to hear it?" he asked roughly.

"I do."

He clenched his jaw. Now she would see him in the same damned sentimental light as others did. But he could not hold back, not if he hoped she might yield *her* secrets. She might learn the tale anyway.

"It helps to begin at the beginning," she coaxed, as if speaking to a shy child.

And—God help him—he could not deny her.

He drew a deep breath. "A few months after we first learned my wife was in the family way, she miscarried. Dr. Denman, her accoucheur, assured us that it is not uncommon, that in all likelihood the next time the outcome would be happier. He also suggested some preventive measures."

He paused for breath, inhaling mingled scents: mint, thyme, chamomile, and others he could not identify.

"I know," she said, her voice tight and controlled. "Cold baths, a lowering regimen . . . They are also recommended to aid conception. I do not believe they are of any use."

The memory of how her eyes had glistened as she played with baby Annabel pierced him.

"I think those measures only weakened my wife. It was only after her next miscarriage that Denman decided to perform an examination." He tried to keep the bitterness from his voice. "It was then he surmised that a riding accident Cecilia suffered when she was sixteen might have left her with an injury which prevented her from carrying a child to term."

"I'm so sorry."

He scowled.

"Is there more?" She gently squeezed his arm. The tiny gesture broke something inside of him.

"I wanted us to give up," he said savagely. "I should never have listened to them. Denman said complete bed rest often proved successful in such cases, and my wife wept until—God forgive me—I agreed to try once more. Cecilia bore me a daughter, but she came . . . four months early."

A tiny creature, so delicately formed. Pale and barely longer than his hand.

"Her maid and I were the only ones there to help Cecilia."

He caught himself staring at his hand.

Livvy clasped it in both of hers. "Did your wife die then?" she asked softly.

"No. That was later. But she never regained her spirits."

"You should not blame yourself."

He stood like a stone, craving Livvy's warmth, loathing the object of pity he was becoming to her.

"I could have prevented it."

"You did what you thought best, what would make your wife happy."

"I failed."

Tears shone in Livvy's eyes. Tenderly, she began to stroke his hand.

His devastation was complete.

"Damn it, I don't want your pity! I don't want you to see me as everyone else does. They think my dedication to the foundlings most romantic. A tribute to my wife's memory and my everlasting grief."

He spat out the last words, glaring down at her.

Livvy stared up at Sir Jeremy, shivering despite the heat. He did not want her *pity*. What perverse fate made him wish for anything else? To fix his happiness on her was a clear route to disaster, for both of them.

Yet he deserved happiness.

"*I* do not wish you everlasting grief," she blurted.

He let out a sigh and his expression softened. "I'm glad."

She released his hand and turned toward the house. "I should not like to see anyone sorrowing forever."

"You have known sorrows of your own," he said, coming alongside her.

Dear God, now he hoped she would confide in him.

Her gloves felt tight and hot; her lace tucker scratched her neck, her breasts. She longed to throw off these artificial barriers; she had to remind herself that association with her would jeopardize everything Jeremy had worked for. Dear God! If a scandal ensued, Lord Bromhurst would likely remove all the children from her care.

She pulled herself together, realizing Sir Jeremy was patiently awaiting her answer.

"Nothing quite so tragic," she said coolly.

"Your husband . . . did he blame you for not bearing him a child?"

She looked straight forward, so her face was shielded by the bonnet. After all Sir Jeremy had confided in her, it felt wrong to withhold the truth of her marriage. But to arouse the protective instincts that were part of his character would be disastrous.

"He was disappointed."

"Forgive me," he said, voice lowered. "But I truly wish to know . . . were you happy with him?"

As they passed under the shade of the plane tree in the center of the garden, she lifted her chin. "I found ways to be happy *despite* him."

Suddenly Sir Jeremy planted himself before her and took her hands in his. Now she couldn't ignore the tender indignation in his eyes, the look that urged her to press herself up against his broad chest.

"Marriage is more than the begetting of children," he said gruffly. "It should be about companionship. A sharing of concerns. And dreams. It should be about . . . tenderness."

Tenderness. The word ravaged her. A kind husband, a tender lover. All she had ever wanted. And despite all the obstacles between them, he was speaking about marriage.

What a rash, noble fool.

For an instant, she wondered whether marriage would raise her back to respectability, or drag him down. No, she was playing with fire even to think about it. She had vowed never to remarry, and she could not risk losing everything again by indulging such a dream.

Almost imperceptibly, he lowered his face toward hers. She wrenched her eyes away from the heat of his gaze, only to be caught by the faint swirl of dark hair revealed by the unbuttoned neck of his shirt. His clasp tightened; despite herself she looked back up at him, seeing how he hungered to kiss her. It had been so long . . . three years . . . She felt like a starving woman.

Desire burned through her, but panic came close on its heels. Just in time, she remembered her deception. Lord Bromhurst. The children.

The children.

She jerked back out of his hold.

"No, I cannot. It is so hot," she said. "I—I am thirsty. I must go."

Without daring to look back, she bolted toward the house. After a moment, she heard his firm tread on the gravel path following her, slowly, accepting her rebuff.

And her misery was complete.

"Mary is already in the kitchen. I'll take you down to her."

Jeremy followed Livvy as she hurried out of the schoolroom. Her agitated tone reminded him that it was near the end of his time at Rosemead. Since his arrival yesterday, she'd made certain he'd no opportunity to be alone with her. Until now, when a misunderstanding had caused Mary to go down to the kitchen earlier than planned.

Would he ever manage to make things right?

"I must explain my behavior last week in the garden," he said as they approached the stairway. "I promise you I intended no insult, and I would never abuse my position as a Governor to influence you in any way."

"I know that," she replied, in falsely cheerful accents. "By all means let us speak no more of it."

She increased her pace; his frustration grew.

"Will you speak to me after I've finished with Mary?"

"Very well. You may meet me in the library when you are done."

Though her tone was polite, she sounded as enthusiastic as she might at the prospect of having a tooth pulled.

For now, all he could do was follow, suffering like a dumb brute, and try to compose himself for his upcoming time with Mary.

Yesterday he'd merely helped her with her lessons, and she'd shown definite signs of relaxing her guard when he did not press her about her singing.

Perhaps it was time to press a little further.

They reached the flagstoned kitchen, and Livvy introduced him to Cook and several kitchen maids, all of whom bobbed curtseys and eyed him curiously. Then she led him to the adjacent stillroom, where Mary awaited, wearing an apron and mixing something in a bowl on the long oak table that ran nearly the length of the room. The girl looked up and responded shyly to his greeting.

When Livvy had gone, Jeremy gazed about, beguiled by a mix of sweet, pungent and spicy scents.
Bunches of herbs and flowers hung from beams and
bottles and jars filled with cordials and preserves
gleamed from the shelves.

The place exuded the bounty and good taste of its
mistress.

"It smells so delightfully in here," he commented
to Mary, to break the silence.

"It does, doesn't it?" she echoed. "It's especially
nice when we're drying flower petals for making the
rose water and other kinds. Last month we added narcissus petals."

"What do you use it for?"

"Lady Dearing likes to use it for scent, but it's good
for washing cuts and burns, too."

So this was the source of Livvy's delightful scent.

"I shall have to frequent stillrooms more often," he
said, looking about him. "So what are we making
today?"

"Banbury cakes, sir."

"Should I wear an apron as well?"

Her shy smile glimmered briefly. "If you prefer to
watch, I won't tell Lady Dearing."

"No, I've no objection to trying, as long as you tell
me what to do. I shouldn't like to ruin anything!"

She looked as if she didn't quite dare to laugh, but
she took a larger apron off a peg and handed it to
him. He donned it, reflecting on how amused Tom
would be to see him garbed so, and rejoined Mary at
the table. The girl finished mixing the dough, then
lifted part of it out and began to add butter to it,
working it in until the mixture was soft and rich. Her
hands, so small compared to his, were capable and
confident, just as Ben's had been while pruning the
fruit trees. When not paralyzed by nervousness, Mary
had a sweet, quiet air about her.

No wonder Cecilia had become so fond of her.

Frustration plagued him. If she'd wanted to take Mary in, why had she waited until her deathbed to ask? Mary would have given her something to live for.

"Is something wrong, Sir Jeremy?"

"No, nothing," he said with a reassuring smile. "I was merely thinking of some business that has been a bit worrisome. Is there some way I can help you now?"

"In just a bit," she said, relaxing her stiff shoulders. "Now I shall roll out the dough, and you may help me cut it. If you wish, that is."

She picked up a rolling pin and pressed the dough into a large flat oblong shape. Then she picked up a saucer and pressed it down into the dough, cut out a circle and set it on a nearby baking tin. Seeing another saucer close by, Jeremy picked it up and imitated her actions.

"I'm a bit clumsy, I'm afraid," he said, as the round he placed on the tin cracked.

"I can fix it." Mary patted the round back together.

"You have quite the hand with pastry."

Her smile faded a little.

"You do not care to be praised?"

"Not . . . especially," she said, pretending to concentrate on the next round she was preparing.

"My wife was very fond of you, you know."

"Yes."

Frustration seized him. Mary, just like her guardian, seemed to want to keep him at arm's length.

"Were the other girls jealous of the attention Lady Fairhill paid you?" he persevered.

"Some of them." Mary shrugged.

"Is that why you stopped singing in the choir? Because your voice drew so much praise?"

"I just—couldn't sing anymore," she said, keeping her face down as she placed the last round of dough onto the tin. "It is time to fill the cakes."

Silently, Mary lifted the cloth from another bowl on

the table. It was clear that she would not confide in him today.

"That smells good. What is it?"

"Currants, sugar and a little rum," she said, sounding glad to be on safer subject. "Banbury cakes are usually made with brandy, but Cook says Lady Dearing can't abide the taste of it."

She spooned some of the mixture onto each of the rounds of dough they'd prepared, then began to fold over the rounds and crimp the edges to form crescents. Sweet smells filled Jeremy's nostrils.

"Lady Dearing is very fond of music, isn't she? I am sure she would be happy to give you lessons on the pianoforte or the harp."

"It's not my place to learn such things."

Again, calm resignation. He didn't like hearing it from Mary any more than from Livvy.

"Mary, I only wish you to pursue what interests you. This has nothing to do with my wife's wishes for you. I am not going to wrest you from Lady Dearing against your will."

She paused in her work, darting a quick glance at him.

"My wife only wanted me to make sure you were happy and give you what advantages in life I can."

"I'm a foundling. I can't be a grand lady."

"No, but if you decided to come live with me someday—in a few years, let us say—I would never keep you from visiting with Lady Dearing. In any case I would also be happy to provide you with a dowry."

"I don't expect to marry."

"Why not? You might meet an honest and respectable man who loves you. You would not wish to marry and have children of your own?"

She shook her head, but slowly. "I like it *here*."

"Look at me, Mary."

Reluctantly, she met his gaze.

"Do you trust me?"

After a moment, she nodded.

"Then believe me when I say I won't force you into a life you don't want. But I would like to see you now and again, and I would be delighted if someday you honored me with your confidence. If there was something amiss at the Foundling Hospital, I might be able to prevent it from harming other children."

Her lower lip quivered a little as she crimped the edge of the last cake.

"Thank you, sir. I will think about it."

He cleared his throat, pleased that she showed even such a small sign of thawing. "What do we do next?" he asked, gesturing toward the cakes.

"We must bring them to the kitchen now."

When Jeremy reached the library he was surprised to find the door closed. Puzzled, he opened it and stepped in.

He couldn't see Livvy.

"Close the door. Quickly!" her voice came from a corner of the room.

Startled, he shut the door behind him. Then he saw her atop a small ladder, reaching up to one of the bookshelves and revealing shapely ankles in pink silk stockings. She held a large net in one hand.

"Ferdie has gotten loose," she explained. "I don't want him to fly into the rest of the house."

The little yellow and black bird fluttered away from Livvy to an adjacent bookshelf.

"Oh bother!" she exclaimed. "I don't know why he is being so contrary today."

"Is there anything I can do to help?"

"No, thank you. Please remain still."

She gave out a lilting whistle, leaving Jeremy helplessly enthralled by the sight of curving pink lips. If he'd been the bird, he would have flown right into her hand.

Ferdie trilled back but remained where he was.

Livvy teetered precariously from the top of the ladder. Despite her instructions, Jeremy went to her side. She continued to exchange calls with the obstinate bird as Jeremy stationed himself beneath the ladder, close enough to catch her if she fell. Also close enough to inhale her scent, redolent of rose water. He swallowed, hopelessly allured by shapely limbs. Her curvaceous bottom was outlined by her dress as she leaned toward the bird.

He forced his gaze toward Ferdie. The bird hopped closer, just within reach. Livvy reached out with the net, her skirt swinging in Jeremy's face.

"I've got you, little rascal," she muttered.

Jeremy backed away, giving her room to descend the ladder. She reached the floor without mishap and moments later had released the bird back into its cage. Ferdie promptly flew to the top and clung to it upside down, swinging and looking pleased with himself.

"Well, that's done," she said, turning toward Jeremy with a sigh of relief.

Then she stopped, her eyes caught, no doubt, by his hungry, aching look. Hot color flared in her cheeks; the lace at her throat rose and fell. She took a hesitant step toward him. Irresistibly drawn, he began to close the gap between them.

A sharp pain stabbed through his foot. His ankle twisted, but before he could find his balance he came crashing forward . . .

Landing squarely atop Livvy.

The impact took his breath. For a moment all he could think of was the woman pinned beneath him. Sweet smells. Soft curves. Shallow breathing.

Dear God, he was crushing her!

He pushed himself up on his hands and scrambled off of her. Fear gripped him as he saw her oddly vacant expression, her continuing shallow breaths.

"Livvy! Are you all right? Did I hurt you?"

Then her eyes focused. She drew a few deep breaths, and then shook her head.

"No . . . I am not hurt," she said, sitting up. "Are you?"

"No," he said, flexing his ankle. "I am so sorry. I seem to have stumbled over"—he glanced around his feet—"an elephant."

He laughed softly, picking up the small wooden figure.

"It is I who must apologize. Robbie was here earlier playing with his Noah's ark set. I thought we had picked up all the pieces."

She chuckled, then suddenly began to laugh harder, in a sudden release of tension that was infectious. For a few minutes they both sat on the floor laughing like children.

Just as suddenly they quieted.

He stared at her. Bright color flooded her cheeks; her eyes glowed. Her tucker had come unpinned at one side, revealing soft, peachy skin he hungered to taste from her throat to the swell of her breasts.

Where a tiny brown birthmark peeked just above the line of her bodice.

Chapter Eleven

*L*ivvy blinked at Sir Jeremy's sudden movement. But he was right to get up. It was time to pretend that nothing had happened, and that they hadn't just shared a moment of tormenting awareness.

She scrambled to her feet, puzzled that he did not extend a hand to help her.

Then she saw that he was staring at her disarranged tucker.

"Oh dear, I must set myself to rights." She lifted a hand to twitch the tucker back into place, over the betraying mark, hoping his stare was just normal male interest, nothing more.

"Stop."

His voice was stone hard. She flinched as he caught her hand hovering over the edge of the lace. His free hand drifted over her birthmark.

"I've seen *this* before."

Her skin seemed to burn as he pressed a finger into the damning mark.

"Why have you been covering yourself, Livvy?" Pain and anger mingled in his voice.

He knew. It was an agony and a relief.

"You knew from the first day I came here, didn't you?" he asked hoarsely. "You knew we'd kissed at the Pantheon. That's why you've been covering yourself up with such modesty."

"I could not help it! When you arrived, you looked so very cold, so disapproving. I did not dare risk your censure." Her stomach clenched. "I didn't wish to lose the children!"

"But once you knew me better? Could you not have trusted me then?"

His shoulders were taut, his fists clenched. Anger burned in his eyes.

"I could not risk it," she pleaded. "Everything was going so well. There was no need for you to know."

"No *need*?"

The hurt in his voice shook her.

"I searched for you. Did you know that?"

Her breath stopped.

"I did," he said grimly. "For months I attended every fashionable entertainment I could. Looking for the inexperienced, *innocent* young lady I'd frightened with my clumsy advances."

She let out a ragged breath. So *that* was what he'd thought. And he'd searched for her.

Agony for what might have been had he found her mingled with her guilt. There would be no forgiveness now.

It was too late, in too many ways.

"Damn you, I worried about you!" he said, pacing the room like a caged animal. "Fool that I was, I wondered whether you had returned safely, whether the experience had shocked or harmed you in some way. I wanted to make amends."

"As you see, I managed well enough," she said stiffly. "You need not worry."

"No, you *were* harmed by it," he said, fresh rage dawning in his eyes. "Someone saw us kiss. Someone who discovered your identity and wrote about it. Am I right?"

She remained silent.

"Am I right?"

She bit her lip, then nodded.

"What gave you away? The birthmark?"

"I don't know. It may have been that someone recognized Charles, my footman. He is such a big man, and he accompanied me everywhere on that visit to London. That oaf you rescued me from—the Turk—stared at me and Charles before you knocked him down. Perhaps it was he who started the gossip, in revenge."

"I notice Charles is not here now. I suppose you have hidden him away during my visits!" Muscles rippled in his jaw. "So you lost your reputation, all through an idiotic lark! It might have been excusable for a miss just out of the schoolroom to embark on such an escapade, but how could you, a grown woman, behave so stupidly?"

"I can take care of myself. My loss of reputation does not concern me; it need not concern you, either."

"How can it not? It is my fault!"

"Do not take any heroic notions into your head, Sir Jeremy. I am quite content with my position—or lack thereof—in society and have no wish to change it."

He laughed harshly. "I don't believe you. What woman wishes to be ostracized?"

"I . . . I enjoy the freedom. People call me eccentric, but I have created my life exactly the way I wish it to be."

"Exactly?" A hard, suspicious gaze raked her. "Why *did* you go to the masquerade?"

She wrapped her arms around herself. Dear God, did he want the entire truth now? Perhaps he deserved a part of it.

She cleared her throat. "As you know, my marriage was not a happy one. After my year of mourning was complete, I thought myself free to go to London and enjoy some of its entertainments. I wanted to dance again."

"To dance? That was all you wanted?"

How could she answer? That night, she hadn't known her own reasons for going. She still was not entirely sure what she had sought. She stared down, trying to find words to explain, and her eye fell on the toy elephant Sir Jeremy had tripped over.

The children. She had to think of the children.

"That was all . . . just a lark."

"Then why did you take up with Arlingdale afterwards?"

She lowered her eyes to avoid his burning mahogany gaze. No, it would not be wise to tell him the entire story. Instead, she let out a brittle laugh. "So now you do believe the scandal sheets? Lord Arlingdale and I are *friends*. He escorts me to the opera and the theatre, but that is all."

"How can I know you are telling the truth?"

"Unless you wish to follow me about everywhere, you cannot." She lifted her eyes to his. "All you have is my assurance that when I went to London it was not with any plan of finding either a husband or a lover. Amusement was all I sought."

"I am glad to have afforded it to you then."

The raw sarcasm in his voice pierced her; for a moment she felt as evil as her reputation.

It would soothe him, no doubt, if she told him how she'd tried to find him. How she'd fed the fires of gossip by seeking out Arlingdale, only to find that the article had named him in error. How disappointed she'd been to find he was a blue-eyed man whose voice, though pleasant enough, stirred no secret chord within her.

But if she explained all this, who knew what Sir Jeremy would wish to do. And if he embroiled himself with her—the most scandalous widow in England— Lord Bromhurst would have the children away from her before she knew what had happened.

"I . . . did not mean to harm anyone," she murmured, loathing the inadequacy of her words. "I have since realized that what I did was a mistake. One I have regretted, and intend never to repeat."

He vibrated with some unnamable emotion. He took a step toward her. "Never, Livvy?"

Every nerve screamed for flight, but she held her ground. He was so close, his breath warmed her cheek.

"Never?"

His voice was rough velvet. Hunger laced with anger.

She stood her ground, battling fear. Running would only make him angrier. The pretense of indifference was her safest course.

So when his arms came around her, she passively submitted to his embrace. When his lips came down on hers, bold and greedy, she did not pull away. It would be over soon enough, she prayed.

Then fear deserted her.

For though he kissed her in avid, hungry strokes, though he held her tightly, her body responded only with delight. Her breasts tingled, her womb tightened and a whimper of pleasure rose to her throat. She fought that too.

But she was losing the struggle.

He reached a hand up to cup her breast. With her last shred of will, she leaned back and pushed her hands against his chest, using all her might. He wrenched his mouth from hers, breathing wildly.

"Have you quite finished?" she asked coldly.

His hands fell away. He staggered backward, his face twisted in a maelstrom of anger, hurt and remorse.

Livvy watched, holding her breath, listening to his harsh breathing intermingled with the twittering of finches. After a moment, he straightened up.

"My apologies," he said, face wiped clean of emotion. "I shall not force my attentions on you again."

Stifling a sob, she turned away. Her hands shook as

she tried once more to tuck the lace back into her bodice.

"I am going to the schoolroom now, to take my leave of the children," he said in a chilling, controlled tone.

She swung around. "You are not-not going to change your mind about them, are you?"

His eyes gleamed black with pain, but his voice remained stony. "What happened here is between us. I shall not act hastily where the children's welfare is concerned. For now I see no reason to alter my report to the Committee."

She bowed her head.

"They are yours. You have won."

The bitterness in his voice brought a rush of tears. She blinked them away, averting her face.

"Thank you."

Yes, she had won. At an agonizing price.

It was nearly dark when Jeremy finally rode through the gates at Fairhill Abbey. The sprawling structure lay like a twisted, dying creature on the well-kept lawn. Lights shone forlornly in several windows, leaving the rest in shadow.

His mount pricked up his ears, knowing his comfortable stall awaited, then quickened his pace, while Jeremy reflected on yesterday's meeting: the report he'd given on matters at Rosemead, Bromhurst's satisfaction that Jeremy would see Livvy no more, his own contradictory desire to ride straight back to her and seek less maddening answers than the ones she had offered him.

The devil of it was that he still longed to believe that fate had brought them together at the masquerade. That she hadn't gone there coldheartedly seeking a lover and later found that Arlingdale suited her. That her indifference to his kiss was feigned, and not because she preferred the attentions of a far more experienced lover. But he could not forget what Bromhurst had said about Arlingdale being seen escorting her into the luxurious Pulteney Hotel.

Weary of going over and over the same arguments in his head, Jeremy dismounted and handed his horse to a groom. Stiff from his long ride, he walked toward the house that offered no solace but bath and bed. But it was better than remaining under Aunt Louisa's curious nose. Better to be alone with his black mood.

"Welcome home, sir," said Grayson, opening the door to the entrance hall. "A cold supper awaits you in the library, and Haye is preparing a bath."

"Thank you, Grayson." Jeremy sighed wearily, mounting the steps.

He allowed the butler to take his coat and hat, then crossed the accursed stone floor of the hall to the library, a childhood haunt and still his favorite room in the house. Part of the original Abbey, it still seemed to echo with the muffled footsteps of monks. A bitter laugh escaped him. That made it all the more appropriate a retreat for *him*.

Velvet curtains had been drawn across the tall, Gothic-spired windows along the outer wall and a fire had been kindled in the hearth. He forced down some bread and ham and drained a tankard of ale, staring morosely into the fire, hating the quiet. There was no music here, no finch song. No laughter.

He tried picking up a book, but soon rose from his chair, overwhelmed with a sense of defeat. Entering the hall again, he caught himself skirting the cursed spot near the bottom of the steps.

He thought he had given up that habit years ago.

Grimly, he climbed the stairs. At the landing, he hesitated. To the right lay his bedchamber. To the left was the room that had been his mother's. It was the best room in the house; he'd had it redecorated for

Cecilia, hoping new furnishings would banish painful memories. That they'd make happier ones there.

What impulse pulled him there? He must be mad. There was no point in recalling anything that had happened in that dark, quiet room.

Or thinking of the nursery on the floor above.

He shrugged and turned toward bath and bed.

Jeremy woke suddenly, feeling hot, restless, strange. Then he realized he'd had another dream about her: the woman in that tattered, smeared engraving one of the chaps at Eton charged sixpence to look at. Then he realized he was no longer at Eton; it was the Christmas holidays and his first night back at Fairhill Abbey. How proud his parents had seemed at the reports they'd received on his academic progress. He liked making them proud. For a few moments they had almost seemed like a real family, like Uncle Thomas and Aunt Louisa and his jolly cousins.

He wished he could spend Christmas in London with his aunt and uncle. That was wrong, wasn't it? A boy should want to be with his own parents.

Then he heard it. They were fighting again. Now that he no longer slept in the nursery he could hear them better.

They always started up soon after he returned to Fairhill. Or did they fight when he was gone, too? He understood the words now. He'd learned some of them from the other boys. It made him embarrassed to think of his parents speaking of such things. Doing such things. And not just with each other.

Why did they have to be that way?

But he stayed huddled in his bed. Aunt Louisa had counseled him not to interfere in their arguments. It is not your duty to reconcile them, she'd reminded him over and over. He fingered the tiny scar on his temple, hearing his aunt's soothing voice in his head. He wished

*she was his mother; and that was wrong, too. His own
mother did love him; he remembered how fiercely she
had embraced him on his return.*

*He wished he could forget what he'd overheard Aunt
Louisa telling his uncle: that his parents' passions
would be their downfall.*

*Now he heard his mother's voice in the hall. She was
pleading with Papa, begging him to let her go. Jeremy
didn't like how frightened she sounded. Was Papa hurt-
ing her?*

*He rose out of his bed and stumbled in the darkness.
Somehow he found his way to the door, groped around
for the handle and turned it.*

*He'd barely come out when he saw Mama rushing
toward him from the gloom on the opposite side of the
staircase. She turned, not seeing him in the shadows.
The light from the oil lamp burning in the entrance
hall below reflected brightly off her pale nightdress before she disappeared from view down the staircase.*

*Then Papa emerged from the darkness, shouting
Mama's name and ordering her to come back. He, too,
missed seeing Jeremy in the shadows as he turned down
the staircase to follow Mama, shouting that he loved
her, not as if he did at all.*

*Then Papa cursed, and there was a dreadful
thumping noise. Mama screamed from below, and the
thumping went on and on and then stopped. But Mama
kept screaming.*

*Feeling sick, Jeremy took a few steps forward and
peered down the stairway to see his mother sprawled
across his father's body, no longer screaming but saying
"no" over and over again in a strangled-sounding
voice.*

*He stood there staring down. Papa couldn't be dead.
But he was, and Jeremy had just stood there in the
shadows watching it all like a coward.*

He should have said something.

A moment later servants came rushing to the scene.

Mama lifted her head and said it was her fault, and Jeremy knew everyone thought she'd pushed Papa down the steps.

He began to shout, telling them that he'd seen it all, that Papa had tripped going down after Mama. Everyone stared up at him as if he were a ghost and he could see they doubted his word. He kept shouting, telling them over and over what had happened, then Mrs. Grayson, the housekeeper, came up and told him to go to bed. Grayson and Papa's valet came up too, and between them they carried him to his room.

Finally, he calmed down, listening to the comings and goings and voices downstairs. Finally he slept.

When he awoke after noon the next day, feeling sick to his stomach, Aunt Louisa was there to hold a basin for him. Then she put her arms around him and he was sick again when he learned that he had his wish. He was going home with her and his uncle, because Mama was gone too. Aunt Louisa told him gently that Mama had made a mistake in her grief and taken too many drops of laudanum.

Jeremy knew better.

Chapter Twelve

"Sir Jeremy, I am delighted to introduce to you my dear young friend, Miss Wellstone. She is paying us the kindness of a visit for the next fortnight."

Jeremy bowed and smiled perfunctorily as Lady Bromhurst, in purple silk, diamonds flashing on her matronly bosom, introduced the young lady garbed in simple white muslin who sat beside her in the Bromhursts' opera box. When he'd accepted the invitation, out of politeness, he'd suspected it masked another attempt at matchmaking from Lady Bromhurst.

The orchestra commenced a disgustingly festive overture.

After exchanging the conventional courtesies, he sat down in the conveniently vacant seat next to Miss Wellstone. At least he'd plenty of practice being civil to young ladies without raising false expectations.

"You must know, dear Sir Jeremy, that Miss Wellstone is the daughter of the vicar of Maplethorpe," said Lady Bromhurst cheerfully. "The parish adjacent to ours, you know."

Perfect. Another vicar's daughter, demure and modest. Another Cecilia.

He smothered a grimace, murmuring polite words while the musicians scraped away at their instruments. *Mozart.* Did everything have to remind him of Livvy?

It was nearly a month since he'd seen her. The roses

must be in full bloom now, and still the same hard knot of suspicion and loss twisted him inside.

"Miss Wellstone has been most active in the charities practiced in her parish," said Bromhurst, in a blatant attempt to prod the conversation along. "She is most interested to learn more about your efforts regarding the branch hospital."

Vaguely aware of Miss Wellstone's expression of polite curiosity, he launched into a tedious description of all he was doing, only to be interrupted by a cry from Lady Bromhurst.

Everyone turned to look at her.

"Is something wrong, ma'am?" Miss Wellstone inquired as Lady Bromhurst snapped her fan open and began to ply it rapidly.

"Nothing, nothing at all. It is just that it is so hot here, and I had forgotten that I had my fan. Ah, that is so much better. Now I can enjoy the opera properly. I positively dote on Mozart, you know!"

Jeremy's eyes narrowed. Lady Bromhurst did not usually babble so; something else had caught her attention.

"I must thank you again for this treat," said Miss Wellstone. "To think we are going to be among the first in London to enjoy it!"

"Yes, and Catalani is in such excellent voice this Season!"

The ladies chattered on, but a moment later Miss Wellstone recalled his attention by wondering about the identity of the woman sitting in the box opposite them.

"Which one, dear?" Lady Bromhurst fanned herself uneasily. "I think that is Lady Hetherton there, in all the plumes."

"No, the beautiful lady in blue, just across from us."

Jeremy's eyes roved idly over the line of boxes. Then they snapped back to the one directly across from them.

She was there. Diamonds sparkling in her ears, on the sumptuous curves of creamy flesh bursting from the deep neckline of her sapphire blue gown. Charms she'd hidden from him under layers of lace and fabric were now boldly flaunted before the avid gaze of hundreds of males in the theatre.

Including the one who leaned toward her, the light of myriad candles illuminating hair as golden as her own, highlighting damnably perfect, chiseled features.

"It is Lady Dearing," Bromhurst said crisply to Miss Wellstone. "With the Marquess of Arlingdale."

Jeremy tore his eyes away, hoping the pair hadn't caught him staring at them.

"They make a most striking couple," said Miss Wellstone mildly, surprising Jeremy with a sidelong glance.

He forced his fists to relax.

"Well, neither is the sort of person we wish to speak of, my dear," said Lady Bromhurst, a gentle reproof in her voice.

Miss Wellstone hung her head.

"Ah, see, they are coming out, Figaro and his intended, Susanna," Lady Bromhurst announced. "We must listen carefully now."

Jeremy pretended to give his attention to the singers mincing onto the stage, but a perverse impulse caused him to glance back at the couple across the way.

Livvy and Arlingdale sat quietly, gazing down at the stage with complete propriety. His blood cooled.

She'd told him Arlingdale was her friend. Only her friend. And as for her gown, most of the fashionable ladies present wore necklines just as revealing.

And he was a damned, gullible fool to make excuses.

As the singers warbled on, flirting and scheming against one another, Jeremy hovered in an uneasy state, alternately wishing he could summon the rudeness to leave in the middle of the act, but compelled to torture himself by surreptitiously glancing at Livvy.

The first act ended, and he stoically endured the ladies' enthusiastic praise of the music, the cleverness of the plot and the glory of Madame Catalani's voice. Aware of the Bromhursts' suspicious scrutiny, he forced himself to add a few idle remarks to the conversation.

But when the next act opened with a sorrowful aria, his gaze inevitably returned to the opposite box. This time he caught Livvy staring directly at him. Even from a distance, she seemed tense. Riveted.

An instant later she lowered her gaze, and let out a visible sigh. Arlingdale shifted in his seat; his arm moved, and Jeremy guessed the marquess was grasping her hand. His bafflement deepened.

It was as if the sight of him upset her. As if she *cared*.

Bromhurst coughed, and Jeremy forced his attention back to the stage where he kept it for the rest of the second act. He had only the vaguest notion of the intrigues and follies being enacted, but clapped when the others clapped and smiled when the others laughed.

During the interval after the second act, Lady Bromhurst claimed her husband's escort to visit friends in a nearby box, leaving Jeremy alone with Miss Wellstone in a long-familiar ploy.

He was about to voice the conventional hope that she was enjoying herself when she forestalled him.

"An awkward situation, is it not?" she asked. "Please do not feel obliged to make polite conversation on my account. I can see that your interest lies elsewhere."

He stared, and suddenly he saw her. Saw a humorous smile quirk her lips, her dark eyes bright with sympathy.

"My apologies, Miss Wellstone. I am afraid I am not good company this evening. Some matters of business—"

"No, please do not feel obliged to make excuses, sir! You may trust me. At least half my father's parishioners tell me their troubles, so I am quite used to keeping confidences."

"I am certain you are. But I have nothing to confess."

"It is Lady Dearing, is it not?"

He shifted in his seat.

"Come, I saw how you looked at her."

"Am I so transparent?"

"Well, I have guessed, and perhaps our friends have, but I do not think anyone else has noticed."

With surprised respect, he regarded Miss Wellstone. He was an ingrate, no doubt. This time Lady Bromhurst had outdone herself. This young woman was intelligent and sympathetic, with a strong dash of humor, something Cecilia, despite her many virtues, had lacked. Under different circumstances he might have found her attractive.

He was hopeless.

His gaze strayed again to Livvy's box. Her large footman, Charles, appeared bearing a tray with two champagne glasses and several oranges.

"How is it that you are acquainted with her?" he dimly heard Miss Wellstone ask.

Livvy was slowly stripping the glove off one of her arms.

"I am sorry if I am prying. Papa tells me I am too curious."

"Er—ah—you wish to know how it is that I am acquainted with Lady Dearing?"

Now Livvy removed her other glove. Clenching his jaw, he turned his gaze to the Pit and saw that the better half of its male occupants were watching just as avidly.

"Do you know anything of Lord Arlingdale?"

He turned back to Miss Wellstone and cleared his throat. "Not much. He has the reputation of being a rake."

"He has the look of one," she murmured.

Damn him. Damn her.

Now Arlingdale was handing her one of the oranges, which she proceeded to peel.

"Of course you are quite his rival in looks," said Miss Wellstone consolingly. "He is golden and you are dark, but you are both quite amazingly handsome, you know."

As if it mattered.

Livvy separated a slice of the orange and fed it— *fed it*—to Arlingdale.

Murderous rage exploded in his chest.

Idiot. Gullible, naïve fool. To have cherished the hope that the couple across from them were merely *friends*.

Arlingdale leaned forward to kiss the juice off her fingers.

Pain radiated through Jeremy's jaw as he ground his teeth together.

Livvy had robbed him of everything. It wasn't the fact that she was sporting publicly with a lover that inflamed him; it was the knowledge that *he* was not that lover. At that moment, he'd have bartered not only his reputation but even his soul to be the man in that box with her. To be the man going back to the Pulteney with her; to kiss and caress every luscious, wicked bit of her; to do and try things he'd only dreamt of; to bring her to a peak of desire that matched his own.

His chest ached and he felt as if he were being strangled. He knew he wanted to strangle someone else. Livvy or Arlingdale, or both, he didn't know.

Duty kept him in his seat as the third act began. Mercifully no one in the box attempted any further conversation, leaving him free to suffer in silence.

During another anguished aria, as the Countess lamented her faithless husband, he felt Livvy's eyes boring a hole in him. When he looked deliberately at her, not bothering to hide his fury, she swept her gaze away. This time she whispered a word to Arlingdale, which the rake answered with a caressing smile.

And Jeremy wallowed in mute, brutish misery.

The third act ended, predictably, in a wedding, and the fourth began with an assignation of some sort. Jeremy had long lost track of who was trying to deceive whom. During the applause after some damned beguiling love song, he saw Livvy and Arlingdale withdraw from their box. Despite their professed fondness for the opera, they clearly could not wait any longer to seek more potent pleasure in each other's arms.

Around him, he sensed rather than heard sighs of relief from the Bromhursts. But his own pain had only begun, for while his imagination threw up tormenting images of Livvy and Arlingdale indulging their passions in her suite at the Pulteney, an insane voice within still clamored that it was untrue, that she was meant for *him*.

Deh vieni, non tardar, o gioia bella . . .

But joy was not coming for her. Never for her.

Livvy stifled a sob as she collapsed onto the seat of her town carriage.

"Livvy, Livvy," Arlingdale said soothingly.

His arm came around her shoulder in an unexpected, comforting squeeze. Feeling despicably weak, she settled onto his shoulder and let her tears flow.

"Don't cry, darling. He's not worthy of you."

"Oh, but he is."

She searched for her handkerchief. A moment later Ivor handed her his. She blew her nose and thanked him.

"Was this charade truly necessary?" he asked.

"You know it was."

"Yes, but I think the poor man is in love with you. He could not keep his eyes from us."

"He probably despises me now."

"He is jealous, no doubt," Ivor murmured. "But I doubt he despises you and if I'm not mistaken, he wants more than a mistress. You are in love with him, too, aren't you?"

Che godro senz'affano in braccio all'idol mio . . .

No, there would be no joyous embraces in the arms of her beloved.

She blew her nose again. "It doesn't make any difference. If he knew, he might try to slay dragons for me. He might be burnt."

"What a sad metaphor." A silky laugh burst from him. "You do not perhaps think this knight of yours might successfully slay the dragon of—er, gossip and slander? Or be willing to be burnt for the prize?"

"It is a silly metaphor. Slaying a dragon would be child's play by comparison. If we became lovers, it would cause a temporary scandal, but it is fashionable for gentlemen to do such things. But to make a misalliance—to expect society to welcome back an outcast—it might be even worse. It might never be forgiven."

"So you are denying yourself the chance of happiness to preserve your Sir Jeremy's sterling reputation?"

"You know there is more to it than that. He's worked so hard to raise funds for the branch hospital. Hundreds more children could be saved. How could I forgive myself if it falls through? We've come close enough to scandal already. If it cannot be averted, who knows what Bromhurst might do to restore public confidence in the institution. He may well remove Sir Jeremy from the Board of Governors. And he might . . ." More sobs crowding in her chest made it impossible to continue.

"You fear he may take the children away, too." Ivor put his arm back around her.

She nodded, tears flowing despite her best efforts.

"A puzzle indeed." He took the handkerchief from her and dried her face. "And yet I cannot help but wish you would discuss things openly with your Sir Jeremy. Between the two of you, you might find a solution."

"I dare not risk it. To jeopardize so many . . . just to pursue a romantic attachment. Perhaps he doesn't really love me. I know he is lonely. Perhaps he should just court someone like that nice young lady in the box there with him . . ."

"Come, Livvy, martyrdom doesn't become you. Think about what I've said."

Livvy remained silent for the rest of the ride. Ivor had proven an unexpectedly good friend to her, but, after all, he did not know everything.

As Bromhurst snored and the ladies listened to the final act of the opera, Jeremy suffered like a dumb beast. Dimly, he was aware of knots unraveling and the joyful reconciliation of the couples on the stage below; it was a relief when it was all over and Lady Bromhurst and Miss Wellstone raved over the melodramatic ending.

"Such sublime music, and such interesting insights into the relations between men and women." Miss Wellstone sighed.

"Most interesting," he replied mechanically.

"I particularly liked how devoted Susanna was to her Figaro. I did find myself wishing he could have trusted her throughout all those plots and stratagems."

"Er . . . yes."

"I suppose it made for a more interesting tale for Figaro to misconstrue the plot Susanna concocted to foil the Count's attempts on her virtue," she continued. "I was glad he at least went to the grove to verify the truth of his suspicions."

"He made a fool of himself by doing so."

"Yes, but it all came right in the end, didn't it? I do so enjoy a happy ending." She sighed, sounding like a featherhead, which he knew she was not. It was some sort of message.

"Well, my dears, shall we stay for the ballet, or go to the Clarendon for supper, perhaps?" asked Lady Bromhurst, smiling upon them both.

Her husband looked agreeably surprised to see him conversing with Miss Wellstone, too. Neither of the Bromhursts had any notion of what the demure but perceptive vicar's daughter was hinting at.

And just as well, for it was lunacy.

"Forgive me, ma'am." Miss Wellstone pressed a languid hand to her forehead. "This has been the most delightful treat, but I am afraid I am not yet accustomed to town hours."

Jeremy noted wryly that the healthy color still bloomed in the girl's cheeks. After exclamations of disappointment and concern, the Bromhursts gracefully agreed to take their guest home. Jeremy bowed and spoke polite words of farewell, flashing Miss Wellstone a silent message of gratitude for not prolonging his ordeal.

He had no intention, of course, of following her advice. So he told himself as he departed from their box and hurried toward the staircase, nearly knocking over a servant bearing refreshments.

To follow Livvy to the Pulteney was both risky and useless, his rational mind lectured as he plunged down the stairs and out of the theatre.

He bore down on the line of hacks, telling himself it was time to return to Russell Square. But his aunt might be awake, and he was in no fit state to speak to her. There would be no peace for him until he *knew* beyond a shadow of a doubt whether or not Livvy and Arlingdale were lovers.

Either she had lied to him at Rosemead or she was lying now.

Impatiently he flung himself into a hackney. When the driver asked directions, he hesitated a bare instant, caught between unbearable evils.

"Pulteney's Hotel. And make it quick!"

Chapter Thirteen

*J*eremy flung a handful of coins at the hackney driver and dashed from the dark street into the Pulteney. Candlelight from the massive chandeliers above blinded him, causing him to cannon into some idiot loitering near the entrance. Muttering an apology, Jeremy moved on, suddenly aware that he'd no idea which of the Pulteney's expensive rooms Livvy had hired.

In a stroke of luck he could only suppose came from Heaven itself, he recognized her maidservant—Alice, he thought her name was—disappearing down a dark corridor. He dashed after her, dimly aware of his lunacy in skulking around a hotel after a notorious widow.

This was what she had brought him to.

He followed Alice up the servants' staircase and down a luxuriously carpeted hallway, keeping a discreet distance between them, then slipping into the deep embrasure of one of the doors to watch her scratch on the door at the end.

Straining, he barely caught the sound of Livvy's voice. Though he could not hear the words, the soft tones plunged deep into his heart.

A moment later, Alice came back out and trotted back down the hall. Jeremy turned, pretending to be entering the doorway he'd hidden in, and she passed without noticing him.

The enormity of the risk he was taking slammed into him. Pain and exposure threatened, but he was so close.

Swiftly he padded down the hallway, entered the last door and closed it quietly behind him, then turned the key in its lock.

Gilded tables and chairs with delicately embroidered cushions stood before him on an elegant Aubusson carpet. Tasseled curtains were closed over long windows overlooking Green Park. The most luxurious of sitting rooms.

Empty.

And no sound came from the interior doorway that must surely lead to an equally luxurious bedchamber.

Nothing to suggest she was entertaining a lover.

His heart pounded a deafening beat as he passed through. "Livvy?" he whispered.

A large four-poster hung with rose and blue silken curtains stood empty, the snow-white coverlet pulled back.

A small sound pulled his head around.

There she was, sitting at a dressing table. All he could see was the back of a peacock-blue silk dressing gown, glorious golden hair loose down her back, a silver-handled brush in her hand.

She was alone. Entirely alone.

He had known it. He had *known* it all along.

"Alice, is that you? What is it?" Her voice sounded muffled and weary.

"Livvy."

She gasped and whirled in her seat to face him.

"Jeremy! My God, what are you doing here? Think of the scandal; if we are caught everything will be ruined!"

"Hush, Livvy."

He came toward her, enraptured by her fragrance, by soft skin glowing in the flickering candlelight. How he'd missed her over these past weeks of numb misery and vain attempts to lose himself in estate and Foundling Hospital business. His eyes devoured her beloved features: the arching eyebrows, the lusciously curved lips . . . But her cheeks were as pale as the diaphanous nightrail peeking from her half-open dressing gown. Her beautiful blue eyes . . .

"You've been crying," he said abruptly.

She averted her face. "It is not your concern," she said coldly, but a quaver in her voice betrayed her. "You should leave now," she struggled on. "Ivor— Lord Arlingdale—is going to return soon. You would not wish to—to meet him."

"You are lying."

"I'm not!"

He came another step closer. "Why are you doing this?"

Her swollen eyes closed and for an instant, her face became as serene as when she'd played that Mozart sonata.

In a moment of radiant clarity he knew. It was about the foundlings. About preserving the beautiful life she had made for herself and them. And she saw him as a threat.

He removed his *chapeau-bras* and his gloves and set them down on a commode, then removed his cloak.

"Livvy," he said, coming to stand beside her. "At every masquerade ball there is a time for unmasking. That time has come."

Livvy gripped the brush so tightly her hand hurt. *Deh vieni, non tardar, o gioia bella . . .*

She turned back around in her seat, trying to thrust the beguiling melody from her mind.

"I think I understand it all now." His voice came

softly, close behind her. "It is another of your defenses, to allow everyone to think Arlingdale is your lover."

She took a shuddering breath. It was like teetering on a knife-edge. He deserved the truth, at least part of it. But if she told too much, she would arouse all his protective instincts. They'd come so close to disaster already, but he seemed to have no idea why she had put on such a performance with Ivor at the opera. Perhaps his friends did not wish him to know.

She straightened in her seat. "You are right. Ivor is known for his skill with both sword and pistols, and while he escorts me I am free from harassment."

"How long has this gone on?"

"Since the beginning. Whoever it was that wrote that piece in *The Morning Intelligencer* thought you were Ivor; he was known to have attended masquerades before in the guise of Death, and he is much the same height as you. When I sought him out—"

"You . . . looked for me?"

The raw vulnerability in his voice shook her.

"Yes." The word burst from her. "I looked for you, and when I discovered that Ivor had blue eyes, and his voice was not as low as yours . . ."

She set down her brush and clasped her hands in her lap. How appallingly close she had come to making a most dangerous admission.

Jeremy came right behind her then; she could see him in the mirror. He took up the brush in one hand; with his other he gently lifted a strand of her hair and began to brush it. The tenderness of the gesture unlocked something within her.

"Why *did* you go to the masquerade?"

His hand warmed her neck as he gathered a strand of hair near the nape.

"When I came to London three years ago, everyone seemed to think I was looking for a new husband, or perhaps a lover. But all I planned was to attend the theatre, to shop and to renew some old acquaintances."

He continued to brush, and she gathered the courage to continue.

"When I saw the advertisement for the masquerade, I thought it would be amusing to pretend to be a different person . . . a braver one . . . just for a night. It all seemed a grand adventure: the way you rescued me from the Turk, the way you danced with me, the way you made me feel."

"How was that?"

His voice flowed through her in a soothing current.

"As if I were . . . precious to you."

The brush glided over her scalp, his hands stroking her temples, her neck . . .

"Then, when we kissed, it all became . . . real."

"Is that why you ran away?"

She nodded, letting out another shuddering sigh.

"And afterward, you met Arlingdale."

"Yes. When he learned of the mistake that had been made, and the scandal, he was most kind. I assured him that it was not his fault, that I expected nothing from him, but he offered to protect me from some of the consequences. We have discovered many common tastes, and now enjoy an uncomplicated friendship."

"And he never made a single attempt on your virtue?"

A faint thread of skepticism entered his voice.

"No. I do not know why it is, but Ivor seems to prefer coldhearted women for his mistresses. It is as if he is afraid someone will fall in love with him."

"As are you." His lowered voice resonated through her.

"This is not wise, Jeremy. You know the tale now, and I think you should leave, before we both plunge into folly."

"No. There is more I must know. After the mas-

querade, if we had found each other, if I had asked it
of you, would you have taken me as your lover?"

She closed her eyes, but it only made her more
acutely aware of his hands moving down to caress her
arms. She couldn't think. Why did he ask? Would a
lie be kinder than the truth? Everything was blurring.

"Yes."

His hands stilled.

"So now you know what a weak-willed woman I
am. You must despise me."

He was silent so long her heart began to plummet.
Then he spoke.

"Your marriage was . . . unhappy. It is only natural,
is it not, to wish to love and be loved? To touch and
be touched?"

She looked up at him, meeting eyes full of desire
and a surprising empathy.

"I would not have asked you to be my mistress,
Livvy."

She closed her eyes again. "It is useless to think of
what might have been. It's too late now."

"I love you."

"How can you? You came here thinking I was
with Ivor."

"I never did. I told myself I was a gullible fool, but
I never did believe it. I knew you were *mine*."

His hands left her shoulders. Then his breath
warmed her neck and she opened her eyes to see him
kneeling beside the chair. Putting one arm around her
shoulder, he drew her dressing gown open to reveal
her nightrail. His lips caressed the curve between her
neck and shoulder. She felt exposed, vulnerable, aching for him to continue. *To love and be loved. To
touch and be touched.*

Vieni, vieni . . .

There were reasons she should stop him, but she
could not recall them. Instead, she leaned back as he
trailed tender, hot kisses along her neck. When he

cupped her cheek in his hand, she turned her face toward his, shorn of her will, and parted her lips to welcome his kiss. Slowly, tenderly, his tongue explored; shamelessly, she kissed him back. He pulled her against him. Desire gripped her; she moaned into his mouth as his hand played over her breast, rubbing layers of flimsy cotton against her nipple.

He drew her up off the chair and into a tight embrace. The heat radiating from his black-clad body soaked through her thin nightrail. She lifted her face for more kisses, putting her arms around him, relishing the solid breadth of his chest, his heated touch as he cupped her bottom in one hand and with the other pulled her waist so close she could feel the hardness of his arousal.

A tremor shook her. She'd thought she would never want this again. She'd thought she was numb from years of enduring Walter's brusque attentions. But Jeremy's caresses had brought her back to tingling, delirious sensation, and—God help her—she wanted to try.

It might be different this time.

When he picked her up, cradling her in his arms, and began to carry her toward the bed, another tremor shook her. Now she remembered the risk they were taking. She remembered what was at stake.

Everything.

But he was already here. They could enjoy this one night—she could not deny them that—but it had to end there.

She turned her head to brush a tear against his shoulder.

He paused, right near the sumptuously draped bed, and stared down at her.

"Don't cry, Livvy," he murmured. "I love you. I want you, not just tonight, but every night and every morning of my life."

"No, don't say it," she whispered.

He clutched her more closely against him. "I must say it. I don't want you for my mistress. You deserve more. I want you for my *wife*."

"I don't wish to be married again. And the scandal . . . It is impossible."

"No, it can't be. Will you try?"

A sob burst from her. "No, no. I am yours for to-night, but there it must end."

"That is not what I want. I want you to marry me."

"No, it's madness!"

"Sanity—"

She shivered as he bent his head to kiss her again, holding her so tightly to his chest that she felt every rough breath, the hammering of his heart.

He lifted his head again. "Marry me, Livvy."

Desperately, she shook her head. "I cannot. Your reputation will not survive it. And then . . . the branch hospital, the foundlings, everything . . . will be ruined."

"We'll find a way," he insisted, and covered her mouth again, stoking her desire until her entire body hummed with it.

"There *is* no way," she gasped between kisses.

"You will not try? You are content to let it end, then, with just one night of pleasure?" He stared down at her, eyes darkened, breath ragged.

"Yes. That is all I want. It is all we can have." Desperately, she shifted in his arms, twining one hand around his neck and lifting her face to his.

But he twisted his face away. "If I did what you ask, I'd be no better than any of those loose-screws who would make you their mistress."

"No, you are not like them!"

"Then say you'll marry me."

"I can't. All I can give you is tonight."

Abruptly, he dropped her onto the bed. Her breath caught as she stared up at his ravaged features, his

powerful arms bent, big hands clasping and un-
clasping.

"Damn it, you deserve more. We both do."

He turned on his heel and walked heavily out of
the room. She lay still as death, hearing his every
movement as he gathered up his cloak, his hat and
gloves, then left, shutting the door with chilling
finality.

Then she pulled the covers over herself and curled
up tightly. Unfulfilled desire coursed through her: excruciating, painful. Gusty sobs gripped her for a time,
then ended as abruptly as they began.

She lay quietly in her lonely bed, bitter tears damp-
ening her pillow. Succumbing to desire had proven
just as disastrous at thirty-two as it had been at seventeen. That she had resisted the ultimate folly was cold
comfort. Of course, to have accepted his marriage pro-
posal would have brought a measure of joy to both of
them for a brief time, until a corrupt world eroded
everything that was sweet and dear to them both. And
this time, because she loved him, the ending would be
more painful than anything she had suffered before.

This time it might destroy her.

*As she struck the final chords of the first movement
of Mozart's sonata in C minor, Livvy smiled. It had
taken weeks, but she'd finally begun to master its
subtleties.*

*She got up and stretched, standing in a patch of win-
try sunlight. She'd always enjoyed playing even while
other young girls moaned about having to acquire this
most essential feminine accomplishment. And over the
past months, with no one to complain when she repeated the same passage a dozen times in order to
achieve perfection, no one to mock her mistakes, she
delighted in the rewards of diligent practice.*

It was the one true benefit of Dr. Croft's latest recom-

*mendation. The female constitution was irritated by ex-
cessive stimulation, apparently. The remedy was several
months of abstinence from marital relations. They'd
tried this pattern not once, but three times.*

Each time it had failed to produce the desired result.

*It had, however, brought her intervals of peace, like
now, when Walter was hunting in Leicestershire, hundreds of miles from Kent and Dearing Hall. She refused to worry about his reaction to her latest news;
she still had a whole week of solitude to enjoy.*

*She sat back down at the pianoforte, opened the
music to the adagio, and began to play again, losing
herself in the slow ripple of bass notes, the deceptively
simple melody . . .*

A crashing discord caused her to jump.

*Heart pounding painfully, she turned to see a large
fist pressed against the bass notes.*

*"Scared you, did I?" Walter stood beside her. His
eyes were wild, bloodshot, pupils dark. With drink, or
anger?*

*"You startled me, Walter," she managed to reply,
though she felt as if she were choking. "How pleasant
to see you back early."*

"Pleasant?" he repeated, leaning over her.

Yes, there was the hated smell of brandy.

*"How pleasant? Have you news for me, dearest
wife?"*

*The unholy mixture of hope and loathing in his voice
caused her to shiver; she pulled her shawl around her.*

"I am—afraid not."

*"No?" He yanked her up from her stool and seized
her arms. "Croft said you'd conceive soon. You must
be flouting his instructions!"*

*"Indeed not," she said softly, not daring to remind
him that Croft had not been sanguine about this
measure.*

*In fact, she knew Croft was uneasy over how they'd
exceeded all his recommendations.*

Walter gave her a shake. "You have not been drinking wine? Eating beef in my absence?"

"No, of course not." She'd not enjoyed such pleasures in years.

"And you've been cupped?"

"The apothecary has taken two pints from me every week." Her arm began to throb where he gripped it.

"There must be something you're doing wrong," he spat. "Good God, you've been violating Croft's order of abstinence. You've been playing me false! That must be it! Who is it, Livvy? I demand to know!"

He shook her again.

"No one. There is no one else," she said, trying not to show her fear, though surely what blood she had left had drained from her face. He might interpret fear as guilt.

"Who is it? One of the footmen? Or one of those gardeners you like to muck about with? Who, I ask you?"

"There is—no one." She trembled despite herself.

"Damn you. What is wrong with you?" His feral eyes raked over her. "What sort of woman are you? Looking as you do, I thought for sure you'd have born me three or four sons by now."

She cleared her throat. "I am sorry, Walter. I think we must face . . . the truth. I am barren."

"No! You can't be. I won't have that sniveling little brat Adolphus for my heir! I'll get a child on you yet, I swear!"

He slammed her to the floor with a suddenness that knocked the breath from her. He was upon her, grinding himself against her to arouse himself, suffocating her with brandy-soaked kisses. She gasped for air. With one hand he pressed down painfully on her rib-cage, as if she had the strength to even try to escape. With the other hand he hiked up her skirts, unbuttoned his breeches.

At least she could breathe now. She closed her eyes

*and lay still during the first painful thrusts, trying to
recall the passage she'd been learning. As her body
adapted to the familiar assault, she began to hear it in
her head: the bass notes, the simple, soaring line of
the melody . . .*

Walter cursed.

It had never happened before, but he'd softened.

*He pulled out, staring down at her in baffled fury.
He got to his knees, while she struggled to keep her
face from betraying the odd sense of triumph.*

*"Damn you, you were always a cold bitch! God, if
I'd only married a real woman!" he cursed, clumsily
rebuttoning his breeches. His voice was rough, almost
as if she'd brought him to tears.*

She forced herself to lie absolutely still.

"Damn you," he said, turning in disgust.

*For a moment, she felt relief. Only for a moment.
Without warning, he kicked her pianoforte, his boot
shattering one graceful, turned leg. The instrument teetered and crashed, wood splintering, strings humming
discordantly.*

*She scrambled to her feet, sobbing, as he headed
toward the harp in the corner.*

"No! Please, no! Not my harp!"

*She ran toward him, but too late. He'd already
grasped the elegantly carved crown, then he sobbed as
he kicked the soundboard with his foot until the wood
splintered. The broken mass of curves and strings fell
to the floor. He turned. Too late she saw his expression
through the haze of her tears. Too late she tried to run.
He caught her arms again, and this time she couldn't
stop herself from struggling.*

*"Not your harp, madam," he said through his teeth.
"Mine. It's all mine, to do with as I please. You are
mine, to do with as I please."*

*She tried to pull away as he drew back a bunched
fist, then screamed as excruciating pain shot through
her eye into her head. She dropped to the floor.*

She lay aching, blinded and gasping for breath for several moments. Walter was still there, standing over her; she could hear him panting like a winded horse. The pain receded slightly, but she kept her eyes shut, not daring to look at him. Finally, she could bear it no longer and opened them.

Through her one good eye, she could see Walter looking down at her. His face was taut with fear and horror.

"I—I'm sorry," he blurted, avoiding her gaze.

An odd detachment stole over her, as if some unknown, indomitable bit of her soul had taken over for the tear-streaked broken creature lying on the floor.

She struggled to her feet, every bone and muscle protesting. She caught her reflection in the pier glass behind Walter and stared at it for a moment, stunned. She'd known years of the lowering diet had thinned her, repeated cuppings had sapped her color. But who was this wraith with the black eye?

Thank God Papa was not alive to see it.

She turned to her husband. His eyes held remorse, but also loathing: for himself, for what he'd done. For her and the ugly feelings she had aroused in him.

Despite the pain raging through her head she saw him with amazing clarity: a powerful man with a weak mind, designed by nature to be a hard-riding, jovial country squire, surrounded by barking dogs and squalling children. A man incapable of imagining any other life and too cowardly to try.

Too cowardly to face her and what he'd become.

"You will never touch me again," she said coldly.

"No. I won't, I promise you." Air sucked in and out of his mouth as if he'd run a long distance. "I won't even come near this damned place."

Then he was gone. She swayed with exhaustion, her head throbbed and the swelling was rapidly closing her right eye.

It was over.

Chapter Fourteen

"*G*ood morning, dear! Did you enjoy the opera last night?"

Jeremy stumbled to his feet as Aunt Louisa swept into the breakfast parlor. He should have just left already, instead of making his farewells. This was going to be hellish.

"Good morning, Aunt." He cleared his throat, struggling to clear his mind enough to summon up a polite reply.

She paused on her way to the sideboard and gave him a searching look.

"Dear heavens, what is wrong?" she clucked, coming to his side. "You look dreadful!"

He knew how he looked. Splashing cold water on his face and drinking several gallons of coffee could not soften the effects of a night spent wandering London's streets and trying to make sense of what had happened.

"You have not been drinking, have you?" she asked sharply.

"Of course not. I was merely unable to sleep and went for a walk."

"You should have roused me, I would have made you a possett."

He smiled faintly. Dear Aunt Louisa. Sometimes

she forgot there were woes that could not be soothed by her coddling.

"Why could you not sleep? How was your opera party?"

"Quite pleasant," he said. "Madame, er, Catalani was said to be in excellent voice."

"Rubbish! As if you cared. There is something else, and you shall tell me all about it."

He poured himself another cup of black coffee.

"Did Lady Bromhurst's young guest come along?" she prodded. "Amelia told me she has the most charming lady visiting."

"Yes, Miss Wellstone was very agreeable."

He took a gulp of the scalding liquid.

Aunt Louisa made no reply. He looked up and to his dismay found her dabbing her eyes with her handkerchief.

He leapt up and went around the table to put an arm around her shoulders. "Dear Aunt," he murmured. "I am sorry to be such a disappointment to you."

"No, no, you are never to say so!" She blew her nose fiercely. "But Lady Bromhurst and I thought this girl would be so perfect for you! More mature, with the experience of having helped run the vicarage since her mother died, and possessing such a sunny disposition . . ."

"I am flattered you and Lady Bromhurst thought me worthy of Miss Wellstone," he said, patting the shoulder he'd cried on often enough, decades ago.

"But you won't even try to fall in love with her!" She blew her nose again. "If only you had never met that woman!"

He froze, hearing the venom in her voice.

"Who?" he asked cautiously.

"Don't be obtuse! I am speaking of that dreadful widow."

His chest constricted. "Lady Dearing? What do you know of her?"

His aunt refused to meet his eyes, instead concentrating on another wet explosion into her handkerchief.

"Has there been gossip? Tell me."

"Well, yes, there was one of those—those stupid, insinuating pieces in *The Morning Intelligencer*."

He stifled a curse. "What did it say?"

"The usual rubbish: that Lady D— must be presumed to have broken off her liaison with Lord A—, since they had not been seen in each other's company for some time." She stopped, twisting her handkerchief in her hands.

"That was not all, was it?"

"We didn't wish to tell you, dearest, but the rest of the piece hinted that she had found a new interest. A Sir J—. A gentleman well known for his charitable pursuits."

Fury shot pain through his jaw, through every weary muscle.

"And no one thought it worthwhile to tell me about this?"

"Well, dearest," said his aunt, with a sniffle, "Lord Bromhurst thought it best for you to behave as if you were unaware of the gossip. No one would dare ask you about it directly and if you behave with an air of indifference, and were seen to be pursuing—"

"If I were seen to be pursuing a young lady of character, that would help to dispel the rumors," he finished. "I see."

He downed the rest of his coffee. "I'm going to see Bromhurst and get the full story from him."

"But dearest Jeremy, before you do that, please tell me there is no truth to these rumors!"

He rose from his seat.

"There is no chance of any sort of liaison between

me and Lady Dearing," he said, each word like a blow.

She brightened. "Ah, I thought you were too sensible."

He turned away. Hopeless rage lanced through him again as he remembered how he'd kissed Livvy last night, how she'd moaned when he caressed her breast, how she'd felt in his arms. How she'd offered him a single glorious, anguished taste of the life they could have, while allowing her fear of scandal and gossip to rob them of the chance to live it.

Now he knew just how vicious rumor could be.

But what was worse was that she did not love him enough to brave it.

"Good God, Jeremy, you look like hell. What's amiss?"

Bromhurst's eyebrows bristled fiercely as Jeremy entered the study of his residence at Grosvenor Square, but he did not seem entirely surprised by the visit.

"I think you know. You should have told me about that piece in *The Morning Intelligencer*."

"Your aunt told you? God preserve us from these chattering women!"

He eyed him squarely. "*You* should have told me."

"And what would you have me say? That you're throwing your life's work away by associating with a scandalous widow? Very well, I apologize. Next time I would tell you, but I trust there will be no next time."

Jeremy's mood blackened at Bromhurst's blunt reproof. Lord, could the fate of nameless unborn children truly be affected by a stupid, pernicious bit of gossip?

"Have there been any problems? Withdrawn pledges?"

Bromhurst scowled. "Nothing so serious. But sev-

eral persons, including old Cranshaw, have asked me
if there is any truth to the rumors. I told them there
was not. I don't need to tell you not to make a liar
of me!"

"I shall not. There is no chance that I will become
Lady Dearing's lover at any time."

"I'm glad to hear it."

"I suppose your opera party last night was part of
the scheme to quell the rumors."

"Yes, and I think it may have done the trick,"
Bromhurst replied gruffly.

Jeremy rubbed his temple. "You did not . . . ask
Lady Dearing to attend for the same reason?"

"I did not. But although I saw it displeased you, I
could not help but think it fortuitous that she and
Arlingdale appeared together."

The ache in his head deepened to a throb. Had she
put on that performance with Arlingdale just to protect *him*? Did she care about his reputation and work
so much that she denied her own wishes, too?

"She is a lovely and good-hearted woman," said
Bromhurst in a softened tone. "It is natural that you
should feel an interest, and perhaps some pity for her.
But it would not do to have this go any further."

Jeremy lifted a hand to try to loosen his cravat,
feeling as if he were strangling again, denied the air he
needed to live. Being told it was poison. But perhaps
Bromhurst was right. It was driving him mad to remember how close they had come to rapture last
night, and still not to know how deeply her feelings
for him ran, whether she was merely protecting her
own way of life, or whether she rejected him for his
own sake.

He had not unmasked her, after all.

Livvy held Mary's hand tightly as they walked down
the long corridor toward the Committee Room. In a
few minutes, she would see Jeremy again.

She'd not expected to see him again so soon, just two weeks after she had turned him away at the Pulteney. But earlier in the week, Mary had announced that she had something she wished to tell all of them. The girl had specifically asked that Jeremy be present, since what she had to say might affect other children at the Hospital.

Once again the child was bringing them together. He might still be angry with her, but she was sure he would master his feelings, for Mary's sake.

A moment later, they entered the room. Livvy pressed Mary's hand again, painfully aware of Jeremy sitting beside Mrs. Hill, the matron. As he rose from his seat and bowed, she drank in the beloved sight of him: the broad chest, his easy, athletic movements, the glimmering depths of his eyes, the curve of his lips, the hint of a cleft in his chin. But there were new furrows in his brow, around his mouth. He looked as if he'd not slept well in . . . two weeks.

Neither had she.

Somehow, she managed to exchange polite greetings with Mrs. Hill and Jeremy, though his deep, velvety voice penetrated her heart sure as a knife. Strangely, there was no anger in his eyes, only regret and yearning.

She'd been forgiven. It was cold comfort.

Perhaps now he knew why she had behaved as she had that night and accepted that nothing more was possible between them.

She sat down beside Mary on the other side of the table and took Mary's hand back in hers. She'd managed to keep the children shielded from her misery this far, and Mary needed *all* of her now.

"Dearest," she said softly, "Mrs. Hill and Sir Jeremy know why we have come. Remember that each of us cares for you very much and that will not change, regardless of what you have to tell us."

Mrs. Hill and Jeremy murmured their agreement,

and Mary nodded, looking a bit pale and nervous, but oddly composed.

"Tell us from the beginning," she prompted.

Mary looked toward Mrs. Hill. "Do you remember the day I cut my hand?" she asked.

"Yes, lambkin. I sent you to Mr. Oldham—our apothecary, your ladyship—to have him bind it up."

"Mr. Oldham was not there that day," said Mary.

Mrs. Johnson's face puckered. "Oh yes, it was that feckless lad Simon Pratt." Looking from Livvy to Jeremy, she explained further. "A sixteen-year-old lad whose father, also an apothecary, had asked Mr. Oldham to take the boy on as an assistant. But Pratt proved unreliable. He was untidy, rude and careless of following Mr. Oldham's directions. We were obliged to turn him off after a month's trial period."

"He's not here anymore?" Mary asked warily.

Livvy tightened her grasp on Mary's hand, willing herself to be patient, not to blurt out hideous conjectures that, if untrue, would only frighten the girl.

Mrs. Hill merely nodded. "No, dear child. I think he went into the army or the navy since, but it's a good riddance if you ask me. We don't need anyone here who won't carry his weight."

"What did he do?" Jeremy asked. His voice was soothing, but the agonized tautness in his face proved he shared Livvy's fears.

"While he bandaged my cut, he—he said he had been watching me while I sang in the choir. And thought me a very pretty bird," said Mary, staring down at her lap.

"What happened?" Livvy spoke softly, despite the dread twisting her insides.

"He hugged me, and I tried to pull away. He . . . held me and asked me for a kiss. He said if anyone saw us or I didn't do what he wished he would tell everyone *I* had tried to kiss *him*."

Livvy bit her lip, forcing down her anger so it would

not frighten Mary. The muscles in Jeremy's jaw flexed. Mrs. Hill had reddened with outrage.

"What happened next?"

"I ran away, and he let me. But he laughed. He said he would be watching me. He kept watching me, and later he said if I didn't start doing whatever he wished he would say horrible things about me to everyone. He said everyone would believe him rather than the daughter of a—of a—"

"We can guess what he said." Livvy edged her chair closer and put her arm around Mary's shoulder. "It went no further, did it?"

Mary shook her head. "You took me to Rosemead Park with you. You were so kind . . . you don't *know* . . ."

Livvy held the girl close as Mary hid her face in her shoulder for a few moments. She began stroking her pale hair, cursing the absent Pratt, appalled that one so young would not hesitate to take advantage in such a vile manner.

"Mary," she murmured, continuing her stroking. "I have enjoyed every minute I've spent with you. You are a dear girl, and you are not to blame yourself for any of this. Do you believe me?"

Mary raised her head and nodded doubtfully.

"So that is why you did not wish to sing anymore, poor lamb," said Mrs. Hill. "You should have told me about it. I'd have had the young snake out of here in a trice."

"If any of the Governors had known about this, Pratt would have been severely punished," said Jeremy, the horror in his eyes belying the gentleness of his voice. "You do believe me, Mary?"

The girl nodded again.

"I know how difficult it must have been, but I wish you had told us sooner." Livvy patted Mary's shoulder. "No one would have believed Pratt."

Mary finally looked up. "I know it was cruel of him,

but was he not right? That my mother was a—was a—whore? What does that mean?''

Mrs. Hill reddened. Jeremy gave Livvy a direct look, silently communicating his belief that she was the right one to answer, that he trusted her to handle this properly.

"A whore is a woman who allows men to kiss her and—and touch her—for money," Livvy said. "It is wrong, but some women are reduced to it by poverty. But the fact is that most women who bring their children here are servants who have been imposed on by their masters or fellow servants."

"Indeed, Mary, your mother may have been a lady," said Mrs. Hill. "Someone paid a hundred pounds to make sure that we took you in, and left half of a very fine lace collar as a token."

"I have seen it myself," Jeremy confirmed.

Mary looked confused.

"Whatever your mother's situation," Livvy added, "she loved you enough to make sure you were brought here, to be fed and clothed and educated."

Mary looked between them all, her light blue eyes wide.

"Pratt said I was begotten in sin," she said hesitantly. "Because my parents weren't married? Is that right?"

"Whatever the circumstances of your birth," said Jeremy, "you are precious to us and in the eyes of God. Always remember that and you will make us all proud of you."

A faint color tinged the girl's face. She seemed pleased, though too embarrassed to reply.

Livvy risked a grateful look toward Jeremy. His beautiful dark eyes glowed back in shared relief.

She'd never loved him more.

Mary straightened up, disengaging herself from Livvy. "Could I—would it be possible—may I see the collar?"

"Yes, of course," said Mrs. Hill kindly. "I can take

you to the Records Room and show it to you. It will allow Sir Jeremy and Lady Dearing a chance to talk about your future."

Livvy's heart turned over; she'd not been expecting a private interview. She turned to Mary and saw the girl's gaze flicker nervously between her and Jeremy.

"Do not be afraid, Mary," he soothed. "I know the best place for you now is Rosemead Park. However, I should like to speak to Lady Dearing about the other children. I hope you have a pleasant journey home, and I look forward to our next meeting here."

Mary rose with Mrs. Hill, looking more cheerful. "Will you come to visit us again at Rosemead sometime, sir?" she asked unexpectedly.

He'd arisen to bow them out, but now he froze. Livvy hardly dared read the emotions running across his face.

"I should like to, very much." He smiled at Mary before directing a burning look at Livvy. "But it will depend on . . . circumstances."

A pang shot through her. He had not abandoned hope, which meant she might have to wound them both all over again.

As Mrs. Hill and Mary left, Livvy sat at her side of the meeting table, praying Jeremy would not stray from the safe subject of the children.

"Thank you," he said after the others had left.

Unstrung, she looked up at him.

"For everything you have done for Mary," he explained. The lines around his jaw deepened. "What a horrible experience for a child. Thank God it went no further!"

"Yes." She drew a ragged breath.

"I wish we could bring Pratt to justice somehow," he continued. "I shall talk some more with Mrs. Hill, to make sure Pratt did not impose on any of the other girls and discuss measures to prevent anything like this from happening again."

She nodded. "It would be wise."

He frowned for a few moments; she longed to say something to smooth his worry lines away.

"It troubles me that Mary was so susceptible to his harassment," he said finally. "The foundlings are often reminded of their base birth. It is meant to accustom them to a lowly station in life, but it seems to me that it may make them easy victims for scum like Pratt."

"Mary is improving every day. The more she learns that she is valued, the more she will learn to value herself."

"I hope so."

His eyes, dark with worry and longing, sought hers.

She lowered her gaze to her hands. "On our way over here she expressed an interest in learning to play the pianoforte. I think it a very good sign."

"Yes. Thank you for telling me."

His voice was low, even painstakingly gentle, as if he wished to prove to her he was not angry over her rejection.

"Perhaps it is time I rejoined Mary. We have a long drive home," she said.

"Not yet. There is something I must ask you," he said quickly, before she could even rise.

She swallowed the lump in her throat, glad to have the expanse of wood between them. "Oh Jeremy—"

"Livvy . . . did you appear at the opera with Arlingdale because of that piece in *The Morning Intelligencer*?"

She stared at him. So he'd heard the rumors.

"The truth is in your face." His eyes shuttered. "I wish you had not, but what is done is done."

"Were there any repercussions? To the Foundling Hospital, I mean?" she asked.

"Lord Bromhurst had to reassure some of our benefactors, but I believe that we have staved off the gossip. I promise you I did not know about that piece until the next morning. I am so sorry to have ranted at you as I did. I had no idea you were there on my behalf."

"It is of no consequence," she said flatly.

A sense of horror gripped Jeremy at her resigned attitude toward injustice. It was the same feeling that had been growing in him throughout all his long walks, following his seemingly futile attempts to understand what exactly lay behind her rejection.

Her face paled; her eyes grew enormous, and he realized she was looking at his hands, clenched into fists before him on the table.

He unclenched them. "I am sorry, Livvy. I am not angry with you. I am angry with circumstances. At hypocrisy and lost chances. It is wrong for you to live secluded from society, wrong to deny ourselves happiness just to appease a pack of gossips."

She would not look at him, but her mouth trembled.

"You do care for me, don't you?" he asked.

Still she would not look up. But a slow blush betrayed her. He had his answer.

"Look at me, Livvy. I think you do love me."

Then she glanced up, her eyes huge and pleading. If he needed any more proof that she was suffering as much as he was, he had it in the tears she was struggling to hold back.

"Don't you think we deserve to be happy?"

"Has not that wretched article convinced you that it is hopeless? My reputation is soiled beyond repair and will soil you as well."

"I am a champion of lost causes, remember?" he coaxed, pouring every drop of hope he had into his voice.

Her lip trembled. "But I do not wish to marry again."

"Livvy . . . my heart . . . I hope you will reconsider. I can be patient. I will be planning ways to accomplish this *without* jeopardizing the Foundling Hospital."

"I cannot think how." Her voice was small. Uncertain.

"I'll find a way. Just tell me you will think about it."

"It is wrong to think about it." Her eyes were half-closed, her breathing quickened as he leaned toward her, eagerly sensing the thread of longing that drew them together over the discreet expanse of mahogany. "But I will."

Chapter Fifteen

*W*ater droplets arcing above the fountain scattered and reflected the brilliance of the sun sailing above in a perfect, cloudless sky. A perfect July day. Or it should have been.

Livvy grimaced over her lemonade. Was it too sour, or was it just her mood?

"Lady Dee, did you hear me?"

Robbie's piping voice recalled her attention.

"I was telling you about the story Miss Burton read me."

The look in his big hazel eyes made her feel like the most selfish creature imaginable.

"I am so sorry, Robbie," she said, smiling down at him contritely. "My mind wandered off somewhere, just like a butterfly. I must catch it!"

She reached a hand into the air and made a show of snatching an invisible creature and popping it into her ear.

"There. I am ready to listen now."

Robbie giggled, but her conscience still pricked her as she tried to listen to his disjointed recounting of *The Elephant's Ball.* The other children had noticed her abstraction, too.

A week. An entire week had gone by without word from Jeremy, and she'd nearly come to the conclusion that it was wisest for them to stay apart. It was high time she accepted the fact that he had come to the same decision. Still, a perverse anger gripped her as she sat there in the sunshine with her beloved children on what should have been a glorious day.

Guilt pierced her as she realized that Robbie had paused again in his story, but before she could apologize, pandemonium broke loose.

"It is Sir Jeremy!"

"Sir Jeremy!"

"And he's leading a—a pony!"

"A pony! A pony!"

Robbie jumped out of his seat and kept bouncing as the others chattered and looked eagerly toward the stables.

Livvy turned slowly, striving to keep some semblance of dignity. There he was, on Samson, leading a piebald pony behind him, its black and white patches gleaming in the sun. A moment later the small cavalcade disappeared from view behind the stables.

"May we go meet him?" asked Philippa, her eyes bright.

"Yes! May we? Please, please, *please*!"

Helpless against their pleading, Livvy nodded. With a word to Jane to have luncheon held back, she followed the horde off the terrace and toward the stables.

A *pony*, she thought, a lump coming to her throat, maddening tears to her eyes. Most men would have brought her flowers, but Jeremy could not have hit on a better way to her heart than through the children.

He also knew she would not be able to refuse the gift.

The children had broken into a headlong run but she followed more sedately. When she had reached the stables Jeremy had already dismounted from Samson and the children were clustered around him and the pony.

"You must remember that though he is bigger than

you are, you must be very gentle with him," he said,
guiding Robbie's hand to the pony's nose.

"Ooh, he is so soft!" exclaimed Mary, stroking the
pony's neck.

Jeremy looked up to smile at Livvy over the children's heads. She melted, and despised herself for it.

"Good morning, Lady Dearing," he said politely,
but there was a glimmer in his eye that was anything
but civilized. "I trust you will not mind my having
brought a gift for the children."

She raised her eyebrows, knowing she had no choice
in the matter. "Of course not," she said, aware of the
children's eyes upon her. "What is his name?"

"Pirate," he replied, turning the pony's head so she
could clearly see the black patch around one eye. "He
comes from Lord Lewisham's stables, having carried
his lordship's sons and daughters until they all outgrew
him. I judge him to be quite steady and reliable."

"He looks good-tempered," she concurred, noting
the pony's large, kind eyes and the way his ears swiv-
eled to listen to the endearments being spoken to him
from all directions.

"May we ride him now?" asked Ben, with barely
restrained eagerness.

"If Lady Dearing agrees."

She nodded. "We can eat our luncheon afterward.
In the meantime, here is Miss Burton. I am sure she
will enjoy watching you, and I may go inside and work
on my accounts as I planned to do after we ate."

"No, no, you must stay and watch!" protested
Robbie.

She nodded, annoyance flaring at Jeremy's amused
look. Now he had the children all in a league against
her. Did he not know this was *serious*?

"He really is the kindest of men, isn't he?" whispered Jane a few minutes later, as they watched Jeremy lift Robbie into the saddle.

"Jane dear, if you continue to speak this way I shall worry you are falling in love with him!"

"Don't tease me, Livvy! You know he is here to court you. How can you look at him with such indifference?"

"There is more to it than you know."

"What I know is he's determined to have you, and you should listen to what he has to say!"

"Thank you, but please do not speak of this anymore. It would be wrong to raise the children's expectations."

"I understand," Jane whispered back. "But do at least give Sir Jeremy a chance to speak his piece."

They watched in silence as the rest of the children had their rides. Livvy's heart twisted each time she saw Jeremy help one of her children into the saddle and patiently explain the rudiments of horsemanship.

Afterward they returned to the terrace, where sandwiches, strawberries and cream awaited them. Livvy ate quietly, grateful to the children for chattering to Jeremy, annoyed with him for looking so wretchedly cheerful.

And then it was Jane's turn to betray her. Her shy governess was the first to stand up. "Well, we have had quite enough pleasure for one day," she said in her strictest voice. "We shall spend the next few hours in the schoolroom catching up with our lessons. Sir Jeremy and Lady Dearing have important business to discuss and they shall *on no account* be disturbed."

Livvy blinked. The children seemed startled into obedience and Charles, who was collecting up the dishes, smothered a grin. She didn't doubt the rest of the domestic staff would shortly be ordered to leave her and Jeremy in privacy.

Drat, he had her servants all in line, too.

She pursed her lips as he offered her his arm, blandly inviting her for a stroll in the gardens.

You should not have come here. The words stuck in

her throat. Weak-willed fool that she was, all she could do was lay her hand on his arm. "I—had not expected you to come."

"After what I said to you at the Foundling Hospital?" he said, softly indignant as he led her off the terrace, toward the gardens.

"Well, you would have had every excuse for staying away," she said, keeping her hold in his hand light. "I am still pretty certain this is not a wise idea."

"Are you sorry I came?"

She turned her head away, glad of her bonnet.

"No, don't look away. Tell me. Are you sorry?"

She couldn't resist his pleading. "No. But I should be."

He smiled as they entered the rose garden, no longer at its height, but still full of beguiling colors and perfumes. Far too romantic a spot; thank goodness Furzeley was there with Sam, the under gardener, both deadheading some of the late bloomers.

"A hot day today, my lady," said Furzeley. "A stroll in the woods would be more refreshing. If ye're tired the folly's a nice shady place to sit. I'll open the gate for you."

With astonishing nimbleness for such an aged man, he sprang ahead of them to open the side gate.

Jeremy thanked him, but Livvy fumed as she passed through the gate. If she could not depend on Furzeley, who'd given her her own little plot to muck about in as a four-year-old, to protect her virtue, she could depend on no one.

"A most admirable servant," commented Jeremy as they crossed the lawn toward the folly and the woods.

"I am sure you think so." She gave him a sideways glance.

"Perhaps they are happy to see a respectable gentleman courting you. At least I am *trying* to court you. You have been making it extremely difficult."

She bit back nervous laughter. "I thought you were so honorable."

"I am. My intentions are totally honorable, but I must employ what means I can."

She humphed.

A moment later, they passed under the open columns of the miniature temple. A stone bench stood before the tiny enclosed area used to store fishing tackle and other oddments.

As she turned to sit on the bench, she gasped. "What are you doing?"

Jeremy paused in the act of removing his coat.

"The bench is hard," he said, eyebrows raised in mock innocence. "If I set my coat on it, it will be more comfortable for you."

"That won't be necessary," she said crisply. "There are some blankets we use for picnics stored behind that door."

She rose hastily, but he forestalled her, emerging quickly with several thick carriage blankets. After he'd folded them carefully, padding the entire bench, she sat down, obscurely nettled when he took a place a few feet away from her.

"You know this is madness, don't you?" she asked, suppressing the urge to sidle closer to him.

"Madness to try to court a shrew?" He laughed.

"Madness to try to restore a pariah to society. Is there no convincing you I am a lost cause?"

He incensed her by grinning. "I told you lost causes are my specialty. If I can persuade an indifferent *haut ton* to care about foundlings, can't I at least try to change their opinion of *you*?"

He stilled the twisting of her hands by taking them in his. "Livvy, I know this won't be easy. But we do have influential friends. I believe that with their support we shall *do*."

She lowered her gaze, fighting the enchantment of his voice. "What about Ivor? No one will believe that I was not his mistress."

"I'll admit that's a sticky one. I think it's useless to try to dispel that particular rumor, but in time people will accept that you have reformed your ways. To marry *me*."

She looked up to see him smiling again. "I have not said I would."

To her annoyance, his smile broadened, drawing her gaze to his wide, deplorably kissable mouth.

"But your family—what would they say?" she asked.

"Once they know you they will love you almost as much as I do."

She bit her lip. There was no reasoning with his innocent confidence. "Adolphus and his wife would be delighted to put a spoke in our wheel."

"Would they not be relieved at not having to continue your widow's jointure?"

"Yes, but Rosemead Park is worth more than that. The way Papa arranged my marriage settlements, Rosemead goes to my husband, with additional provisions for any children I should have from any marriage. If I were to marry you—and I said if—you would be cutting out Adolphus."

"I will tolerate that *if*. For now. But let me tell you I don't believe you would allow that nincompoop to stand in your way. For now what I truly must understand is why you are so reluctant to even try."

Dear God, what a tangle of fears he was asking her to bare! Struggling for words, Livvy stared down at their twined hands for a moment.

Jeremy forced himself to wait, stroking Livvy's hands and reining in the desire to pull her luscious, fragrant self into his arms. He did not dare rush things; better to coax her slowly out of her defenses, now that he suspected the wounds she nursed behind them.

"Livvy, there is something I should tell you about."

That got her to look up, at least.

"It is nearly ancient history now, so you may not have heard the stories about my parents."

She shook her head.

"I am telling you this not to distress you, but to make you understand some things about me." He took a breath. "My childhood was not . . . the happiest. My parents, for whatever reason, felt the need to test their love for each other in an endless cycle of infidelities and reconciliations. The Abbey used to ring with their noisy arguments, which sometimes became violent. And finally one of their battles turned fatal."

She gasped, then edged closer to him in an impulsively compassionate gesture.

"It was said that my mother killed my father by pushing him down the stairs at Fairhill Abbey, but I was there. I knew the truth. They were arguing and he tripped and fell down the staircase. Later that night my mother died from an excess of laudanum."

She pulled her hands out of his hold, to grip his instead. "Oh no . . ." There was a world of shocked sympathy in her voice. "How old were you?"

"Thirteen," he replied steadily. "As I said, ancient history. But as a child, I knew things were not right, and at times my anger overpowered me. Fortunately, my uncle and aunt became my guardians, and they did much to help me master my temper."

"They sound like good people."

He nodded. "My uncle died a few years ago, but I think you will like Aunt Louisa. She's a dear thing. But what I want to say is that over time people realized I would not tread my parents' path. But more importantly, *I* realized it."

A faint line appeared between her eyebrows.

"Livvy, I'm a peaceable man. Since I grew up, I've never hurt a child or a woman. The last time I hit anyone was at the masquerade. I would never hurt *you*."

She turned her head aside, hiding behind her bonnet brim again. "I know that."

"I have done a great deal of thinking about some of our encounters, the times I've become angry or jealous. The day I tripped over that toy in the library and knocked you over. There was something alarming in your expression . . . Now I think I know what it was."

She sat very still.

"Did Dearing beat you?"

She let out a sudden breath, and gave an almost imperceptible nod. He put an arm around her, and she melted into his shoulder.

"He only did it once." Her voice was muffled.

Only once. As if that made it better. He wished Dearing were alive so he could send him back to the grave again.

Then he tamped down the useless anger. "What did your parents think? Did they put a stop to it?"

"They were not alive to see it. The servants knew, of course."

But could do nothing, for they served Dearing. And the law was little protection, unless there were major, lasting injuries and she had a concerned male relation willing to help.

"Will you tell me about it?" he asked in a low voice.

She shifted in his arms, then settled against his chest, still hiding her face. He held her close as she haltingly related the tale of her marriage to Dearing, of their final encounter, so horrible that something inside Jeremy bled to hear it.

"Walter kept his promise," she concluded. "He stayed away."

"Did you come back to Rosemead then?"

"No, I remained at Dearing Hall. I knew Walter wished me to keep up some appearance of being his

wife. I dared not go to London, or even go about
much in local circles. I could not risk giving rise to
any gossip, for fear that Walter might take other . . .
measures . . . against me."

"Good God! You did not think he would try to
divorce you for infidelity?"

"I couldn't be sure." She sighed. "He wanted children so badly, I thought he might want to remarry.
But he did not. Instead, he killed himself while out
hunting. Drunk, he put a green horse at one of the
most formidable stone walls in the Cotswolds. The
horse refused; Walter went over his head into the wall
and broke his neck."

"You cannot blame yourself for it."

"I don't."

"But others did," he said slowly.

"It is no matter," she said, shrugging in his arms.
"I was the lucky one. I mourned him for a year and
was able to begin my life anew."

No wonder she feared losing all. Being hurt again.
He stroked her arm tenderly.

"Brave Livvy," he murmured.

"No, I'm the greatest coward," she muttered.

"For fearing to enter the state of matrimony again?
After what you have endured, I'm honored you'll even
consider my offer. I can understand that you fear losing your independence. But I promise you I don't wish
to change your life. I only wish to become part of it:
to dance with you, to sit beside you in the theatre,
knowing I'm the envy of every man there, to be with
you and the children."

"Don't you wish for children of your own?"

"I did at one time. But I have an heir already, my
cousin Tom. Now all I wish for is a wife and a family."

She began to shake.

He pulled her closer. "What's wrong, Livvy?"

"Wrong? It's wrong for you to want me!" she cried.
"It's wrong for me to encourage you when a scandal

could affect the fate of so many children. It's wrong to push you away when I know how much it would hurt you, when what you speak of sounds so wonderful, almost too . . ."

"Too good to be true?" he asked, lightly cupping her chin to turn her face up to him.

She blushed; her eyes grew soft, dreamy. The prospect of success sent a thrill through him.

"When I married, I thought I loved Walter." She drew a shaky breath. "It was only a romantic girl's dream . . . and foolish desire . . . I know you are an *infinitely* better man, and my feelings for you are so different, so much stronger. But"—a shadow passed over her face—"when you touch me, I can't forget that every time I have succumbed to passion it has led to disaster."

"And you cannot believe it will ever be any different."

She nodded.

"I tell you it *will* be different. With me."

Her lip quivered. He longed to kiss her but resisted the impulse, banking his own desire.

"Will you let me prove it to you?" he murmured.

She licked her lips, and he sat like a statue, achingly aware of moistened lips, bared throat, the beautiful curve of lush breasts rising from a low neckline.

But doubt shaded his eagerness. Could he overcome the legacy of pain Dearing had left her with?

Then he heated, remembering how she'd moaned in his arms in her bedchamber at the Pulteney.

He could do this.

"I want nothing for myself, Livvy. Not yet." Tilting his face to avoid the brim of her bonnet, he brushed her lips lightly with his. "Only the pleasure of proving to you that this time, desire can bring you joy."

"This is folly," she murmured against his lips as he gave her another teasing kiss.

"What better place for it?"

"What if someone sees us?"

"No one will disturb us. You know that."

He leaned down and kissed the hollow in her throat. Her pulse beat wildly. *Yes.*

He kissed her lips again. They remained parted as he released them. Her eyes glowed.

"Let me make love to you, Livvy."

Slowly, she nodded.

Chapter Sixteen

A gurgle of laughter caught in Livvy's throat.
Jeremy paused in the act of leaning forward
to kiss her.

"*I* am supposed to be the wicked widow who leads
men astray," she explained shakily. "You are not supposed to be seducing *me*."

"I am only *trying* to seduce you." His eyes narrowed. "Are you nervous?"

"A little," she admitted.

"Well, so am I. So you will have to excuse any . . .
awkwardness."

She smiled a bit sadly as realization struck her: her
beloved, honorable Jeremy had probably not made
love to anyone before or after his wife. It didn't matter, though. He loved her; he wanted to please her. If
there was any lack, it was in her.

With Walter, she had learned to be so . . . numb.
For a moment, in her candlelit chamber at the Pulteney, she had not been afraid. Now, when it meant
so much more, she was.

Jeremy leaned forward to kiss her again. This time
his forehead collided with the brim of her bonnet.

"Some of that awkwardness?" Another nervous giggle escaped her. "I will forgive you."

He chuckled, a deep, mellow, delicious sound. His
fingers tickled her neck as he untied her bonnet

strings. He tossed the bonnet aside and pulled her to
him for a proper kiss. Shyly, she put her arms around
him, feeling the solid warmth of him through jacket
and all the layers of gentlemanly apparel.

He tasted of lemonade.

But he was wicked, teasing her with slow kisses,
finally raising a hand to cup a breast in his palm, playing his fingers lightly over her nipple. A whimper of
pleasure escaped her, finding an echo in a rumbling
groan in his chest.

Then his hand brushed gently over her shoulder to
her back. He fumbled with the small buttons of her
bodice; she sat perfectly still, barely breathing, as they
gave way one by one. Still kissing her, he pushed first
one sleeve, then the other, down her arms. Blushing,
she leaned back and helped him pull the sleeves off
over her hands, aware of his rapt scrutiny of her
breasts, rising half-exposed from shift and corset.

A moment later he'd pulled her close again, soothing her with more kisses as he struggled to loosen the
laces of her corset. Finally he pulled it down, along
with the thin fabric of her shift, then lifted a hand to
her breast again. His fingers, large but feather light,
vibrated as he stroked the rounded weight of her
breast, circled her tightening nipple. She moaned, closing her eyes, feeling the moisture well up between her
legs as he moved to her other breast, giving it the
same patient, exquisite torment, kissing her all the
while.

Dizziness stole over her as he pulled her to lean
back against his chest, then gently pressed her down
against the folded blankets. Her eyes flew open; he
smiled at her as he lifted her legs and swung them up
onto the bench.

She closed her eyes and shivered as a breeze entering the open colonnade puckered her nipples. A moment later she gasped as Jeremy's lips warmed one of
them. She put an arm around his neck, then lifted her

hand to stroke his dark curls as he continued to taste and suckle her breast, as she'd never imagined a man could do.

Then he returned to her mouth, kissing her with slow thoroughness as his hand stroked the tender skin along her side, down to the rumpled waist of her gown, past it, over the curve of her hip and down her thigh. Then he drew up the hem of her skirt, baring stocking-clad calves, gartered thighs, finally exposing her hidden curls to the light and breeze.

It was too much. She couldn't do it. Face burning with shame and defeat, she clamped her legs tightly together, fleeing into the inner core of herself where she could ignore all but the most painful sensation.

"Shhh . . . shhh. You are safe with me."

His voice washed over her, drawing her back out of herself. His hand stroked her bare hip, lulling her into breathing naturally again.

Yes, she was safe. Guarded by loyal servants, encircled by brick walls, iron gates, stone columns. Warm, loving arms.

She let out a sigh. He shifted his hand, not quite touching her, but ruffling the curls as he continued to murmur into her ear. With a cry, she turned her head, seeking his mouth again. Frantically she kissed him, putting an arm around him as he continued to tantalize her with butterfly caresses until, despite herself, she moaned and parted her legs.

He moved his hand between them, leaving it there even as she closed her legs again, shaking with desire. More hungry kisses, and she found herself relaxing again. Then he moved a finger and she burned, wondering what he would make of her wanton moisture. He let out a low groan, flicked the finger against her again. She cried out, struggling with the urge to move against it. He held his breath, then moved his finger again, and she couldn't restrain another cry of pleasure.

She held him tightly as he began to tease her in earnest, swirling one finger, then several, against her, roving around as if trying to discover the touch, the spot that would give her the greatest pleasure. And she hovered on the brink of pleasure.

La Petite Morte. The Little Death. She'd heard about it long ago, yearned for it as a rash seventeen-year-old, and finally gave up on ever experiencing such a thing, telling herself it was just a myth, or she was incapable of it . . .

Now she hungered for it even as she knew its price: a total surrender of control, not only to Jeremy, but to mysterious forces within her.

She would be helpless, under his spell.

She could not face it; as the peak came upon her, she arched and tightened, resisting it. Jeremy stilled his hand and she bit her lip, to keep from begging him to continue.

She was a coward. She couldn't. But he wanted her to enjoy this, and she did, too, at least the part of her that wasn't a coward.

She gasped at his renewed teasing strokes. "Please . . ."

"Please what?" he asked huskily.

Sorcerer!

How could she tell him what she feared when she didn't know? "Please don't let me fall off the bench," she muttered.

His rich chuckle warmed her neck. "I won't let you fall, I promise."

He claimed her mouth again, mimicking the motions of his fingers with his tongue, swirling, varying the stroke, the pressure, then dipping a finger, shockingly, inside her, while keeping his thumb over her most sensitive spot.

She moaned with each breath. Twice more she came close to what seemed to be a peak; twice more she recoiled, only to reach feverish new heights of desire.

He leaned over her, trying different touches, his breath hot on her mouth, over her breasts, the silk and linen of waistcoat and shirt softly chafing her skin, rumpled clothing and scratchy-soft wool of the blanket teasing her back and bottom, adding to the torment between her legs.

Without warning, a paroxysm gripped her body, but Jeremy held her safely on the bench until finally she lay spent and weeping, the strain and sorrow of months, perhaps years, draining away in her tears.

For a time he continued to kiss her dampened face and whisper her name in an awed voice. She drifted into a blissful place where pain did not exist as he sat beside her stroking her hair and a breeze caressed her bare flesh now and then.

Jeremy feasted his eyes on Livvy. Part of him still clamored for relief, tempted by half-closed eyes, tumbled curls, lips plump from kisses, breasts damp from suckling. But mostly he just exulted. No practiced rake, he'd managed to bring her to an intense peak of pleasure.

He wanted to run and shout and do it all over again.

Her eyes opened wider and she smiled up at him dreamily. "You look just like a child with a new toy."

"That is exactly how I feel."

Another breeze blew through. "I wish I could lock you up in my bedchamber and never let you leave," she said wistfully.

"Tempting." He grinned.

"But there is a world outside these walls."

"We can face it."

She swung her feet to the side of the bench. He reached an arm around her and helped her to sit up, tamping down a rush of pure lust at the smell of her.

"Oh dear, I *look* like a wanton woman now." Her hands shook as she reached to pull her shift and corset back into place.

"No one is coming. There is no need to rush."

He told the same thing to a wayward portion of his anatomy. He had to be patient, to take the time to soothe her doubts.

Her eyes clouded. "I am afraid it is all a dream."

"I thought you might need convincing." He gave her arm a squeeze. "Well, I brought a gift for you, too."

He felt in his waistcoat pocket and drew out the velvet pouch that had nestled there throughout his ride from London.

"Oh, Jeremy . . ."

She looked adorably flustered, blue eyes wide, hair half-down, breasts pink and exposed, staring down at the ring he held out to her: the large sapphire set like a flower among four petals of gold, adorned by pearls. A fitting tribute to her and her foundlings, he hoped.

"When you look at it, Livvy, remember how much I love you and the children. Remember it is real."

She nodded, a tear leaking down her cheek.

"Will you marry me, Livvy?"

She looked from the ring to him.

"If it is what you truly wish," she said solemnly.

"I do. I love you."

"I love you, Jeremy. God help me, I do."

And she smiled as he slid the ring onto her finger.

Chapter Seventeen

Livvy smiled wistfully as Jane embraced her later that night. If only everyone else would be as happy about the news.

"Mind you don't let anyone else know yet, especially the children. I would not wish them to be disappointed if—if anything went wrong."

"He is so in love with you," Jane retorted. "What could possibly go wrong?"

"He might not even be able to win over his relations and the Bromhursts to the match, for one."

"But he is quite a *persuasive* gentleman."

Livvy smothered a smile. "Yes, Jane. Quite persuasive."

Later that night, Livvy rested in her bed, listening to the song of a nightingale drifting across the lawns from the woods. Another charmer who made beautiful sounds to enchant his mate.

Was she enchanted?

But even as her mind warned her to prepare herself for disappointment, it drifted off into pleasanter images. She snuggled her head into her pillow, picturing Jeremy's dark curly head on the adjacent one, his arms pulling her toward him, lips, hands, his entire being ready to cherish her as he had in the folly. And the rest . . . it was going to be wonderful, too. Blushing in the dark, she hesitantly touched her breast, then the opening to her womb. He had brought her to such a peak of ecstasy in the folly, yet now, paradoxically, a space inside her ached to be filled.

He *had* enchanted her.

She was no longer a frightened, hiding creature. She was a woman determined to have the man she loved.

Jeremy watched Aunt Louisa, Tom and Charlotte as they gaped at him from their respective seats in drawing room. Their stunned expressions were pretty much what he had expected after announcing his engagement to Livvy. At least two entire minutes passed before his aunt broke the silence.

"If you are teasing us, Jeremy, I must say it is a most unpleasant joke."

"I am not joking."

Aunt Louisa's face hardened, but her eyes were bright with restrained tears. "But why, Jeremy? It is so sudden. It must be an infatuation. You should reconsider, take some time to think about it before you tie yourself up with such a—a lady," she ended nervously, having caught his thunderous expression.

"I know this seems sudden, but I promise you I am certain of my feelings."

"You may think you are in love, but remember that your parents were supposed to have made a love match."

He bit back a sharp reply.

Now Tom was avoiding his gaze; this was going to difficult.

Unexpectedly, Charlotte came to his aid. "Lady Dearing has been most kind to those poor children. That shows a motherly spirit, does it not?"

"Yes, that is a part of my love for her," he said, looking gratefully in her direction. "If you could see how gently she deals with them, Aunt, you would know she is a woman of character. You will like her so much once you know her."

"But—but she is Arlingdale's *mistress*."

Charlotte looked startled; Tom slunk down in his chair.

"Do you think I'm fool enough to court another man's mistress?" Jeremy demanded. "Arlingdale is her friend; the rest is gossip."

Aunt Louisa opened her mouth, then shut it again. Her eyes were troubled.

"Perhaps if I tell you everything you will understand," he suggested.

Reluctantly, she nodded. But by the time he'd finished telling them about Livvy's first marriage and the masquerade and its aftermath, omitting only the more intimate details, Aunt Louisa's expression had softened. Jeremy caught Charlotte dabbing her eyes with her handkerchief. Tom looked troubled.

"All I ask now is that you invite her here to dine, so you may all meet her and judge for yourselves," he finished.

Aunt Louisa tried to scowl. "Perhaps it is all as you have recounted. But considering her reputation, all I can say is it is going to be very, very difficult."

"But if Jeremy loves her, I think we should do all we can to help her," said Charlotte.

"Mama, I think Charlotte is right," Tom echoed. "It's going to be dashed difficult, but . . . well, perhaps this is what Jeremy needs."

His aunt looked suspiciously at the other two, then cleared her throat. "Very well, I shall give her my support. *If*, when she comes to visit us, I find she is worthy of Jeremy."

It took him a moment to take in her words.

"Thank you, ma'am," he said meekly.

"I said *if*."

"I know," he replied. "And I love you for it."

"Have you gone mad?" Bromhurst glared from across the drawing room at Grosvenor Square.

Jeremy returned his gaze steadily.

Lady Bromhurst glanced from him to her husband and back again, a frown marring her patrician features.

"I do not wish to be rude," she said, with a majestic calm in direct contrast to her husband's bristling expression. "But what a shocking announcement! And so sudden, too."

"Not as sudden as you think. I have loved Olivia Dearing for at least three years."

The Bromhursts stared at him, eyebrows raised. Good. Keeping them off balance would keep them listening.

"*I* was the one who kissed her at the masquerade that destroyed her reputation. We suspect that a drunken boor who was pursuing her sold the story to *The Morning Intelligencer.*"

"If she went to a public masquerade, she must have known the risks," Bromhurst blustered. "You can't marry the woman just because you were involved in that old scandal!"

"Only think of the talk it will cause," exclaimed Lady Bromhurst.

"Damn it, Jeremy, think of the children," her husband added.

"Have you forgotten what she has done for four of them?"

"Sorry, lad. I don't forget. Lady Dearing is an admirable woman, in many ways." He paused, aware of his wife glaring at him. "That is why I have discreetly allowed her to care for those children. But to condone your marriage is entirely a different matter. Your reputation and your fortune make you a most eligible catch in the eyes of every hopeful young lady of the *ton* and her parents. If you marry Lady Dearing, it will be seen as a shocking misalliance. Jealous persons will say that she has corrupted not only your morals but your judgment. We will lose all support for the branch hospital."

"It is by no means a foregone conclusion."

"And how can we get over the fact that she is Arlingdale's mistress?" asked Lady Bromhurst. "His *mistress*, for heaven's sake. You saw her yourself, at the opera."

"*The Morning Intelligencer* mistakenly linked their names, but I know for certain she is *not* his mistress."

Bromhurst began to rub his nose, a clear sign he felt distressed.

"Might it not be possible to set it about that she has reformed her ways to marry me?" Jeremy suggested.

"Nonsense. I cannot support such a mad tale." Lady Bromhurst raised her chin.

Jeremy massaged an aching forehead, reminding himself he hadn't expected this to be easy.

He turned a beseeching gaze toward Lady Bromhurst and poured his heart into his next speech. "Please, all I ask of you now is that you meet her and speak to her. Once you know her, I think you will see for yourselves how she has been wronged."

Her ladyship's face softened. "Well, perhaps it might be possible to arrange some sort of meeting."

"No!" Bromhurst interrupted. "It is completely out of the question. There will be no meeting."

Jeremy stared for a moment, surprised by his friend's vehemence. Then rage welled up in him.

"I understand perfectly," he said, rising to his feet. "All my personal merits, all my efforts are as nothing to you. My usefulness to the Hospital lies only in how I am perceived: the romantically inconsolable widower devoted to the cause of helpless infants. And in order to maintain the established order of things, I must remain inconsolable."

"Please sit down," pleaded Lady Bromhurst, eyes darting between him and her husband. "You know we only wish for your happiness."

"Yes, but only with another like Cecilia," he snapped, staying on his feet. "Not with a woman who by her independent nature threatens that same established order."

"Jeremy, don't you understand what will be said?" said Bromhurst, his face contorted with pity.

"What the hell do you mean?"

"If you marry her, people will begin to watch you both, expecting your marriage to be just like your parents'."

Shock immobilized him for a moment.

"You don't think our detractors won't pounce on the chance to revive that old scandal?" Bromhurst added grimly.

"Yes, Jeremy. Cannot you see how impossible it is?" his wife added.

"No." He looked them each in the eye. "I will not bow to malicious gossip. And I won't accept the entire burden of a society that allows children to be abandoned, where they are made to suffer for the sins of their fathers."

Lady Bromhurst made a small sound of distress, but her husband sat like a statue.

"You know I would do anything for the Hospital. If you'll let me, I'll keep working on its behalf and make every effort to find a way to preserve its good name. But I won't abandon Livvy."

For a moment, Jeremy hoped Bromhurst would relent. But he shook his head, the denial in his face striking Jeremy like a blow.

"You leave me no choice," Bromhurst said with a coldness belied by the unaccustomed shaking of his hands. "If you persist in your obsession with this woman, I will have no recourse but to ask you to resign from the Board of Governors."

Jeremy stared at his friend for a nightmarish moment. He'd not thought it would come to this, but he could hesitate no longer.

"Good-bye then." He bowed deeply to her ladyship and strode out of the room.

Lady Bromhurst cried out after him. "Sir Jeremy! Please don't go!"

A rustling sound indicated she was following him through the corridor down to the entrance hall.

"Jeremy!" she begged.

Jeremy accepted his hat from an astonished footman.

"Jeremy, wait."

Bromhurst's voice boomed through the hall.

Jeremy thrust the hat on his head while the footman hastily retreated.

"You don't know what you're getting into, lad." Bromhurst's voice broke. "But if this is so important to you, then—then we'll see what may be done."

Jeremy raised his eyes from the head of his walking stick. He had never seen such a bereft look on his friend's face, but he sensed Bromhurst still hoped that further developments would weaken his resolve to marry Livvy. It didn't matter, he told himself fiercely. This was a start.

A breeze brought the scent of the gardens through the drawing room's open French doors. Livvy stared down at the pianoforte, having lost count of the times she'd begun the rondo she was attempting to learn. She smiled, chiding herself for a lovesick idiot, and looked down at the ring winking on her finger. She'd worn it only in secret until yesterday, when she'd forgotten to remove it before going to church. She'd explained to the children that it was a gift from Sir Jeremy, which they'd accepted without question.

Sophronia had looked quite sick at seeing it.

Perhaps there was no need to hide it anymore. Things were going well.

Deciding to give up on the pianoforte, she crossed the room to the small table beside the sofa. She picked up the folded letter she'd carried around like a fool since it had been brought several hours ago.

Dearest Livvy, was written in a large, confident masculine hand. For a moment she merely basked in the greeting, imagining his voice saying the words.

> *I have good news. Aunt Louisa wishes you to come dine at Russell Square on Wednesday. Charlotte and Tom are most anxious to meet you.*

Most anxious! She suppressed nervous laughter over his wording. She could read between the lines. Still, he had convinced them to give her a trial. No mean accomplishment, she was sure.

> *I have also prevailed upon Lord and Lady Bromhurst to attend, so that you may become better acquainted with her ladyship. While it was not easy to persuade them, I believe they will stand our friends.*

At least he knew enough not to pretend Lord Bromhurst was pleased. She could imagine the poor man's dilemma.

She skimmed over details of time and travel: he was going to spend a few days on estate matters at Fairhill Abbey before returning to London for his weekly meeting and the dinner party on Wednesday.

> *I long to see you again, and bid you remain brave and cheerful. Happiness will be ours. Your devoted Jeremy.*

She folded the letter again and set it down. There was nothing more to do now but wait for Wednesday and prepare herself to face his relations and the Bromhursts with confidence and dignity.

On impulse, she strode over to the harp, a tune by

Dibdin tugging at her memory. As she began to play, the words came back to her.

> *Go, and on my truth relying,*
> *Comfort to your cares applying,*
> *Bid each doubt and sorrow flying,*
> *Leave to peace and love your breast.*

Comforted, she improvised on the refrain before moving on to the second verse.

> *Go, and may the pow'rs that hear us*
> *Still as kind protectors near us*
> *Through our troubles safely steer us*
> *To a port of joy and rest.*

As she plucked the final chords, she could not help smiling at the thought of seeing Jeremy again soon. Perhaps they could even steal some time alone . . .

A loud clapping from the French doors made her start.

"Charming. Quite charming," drawled a male voice.

Dear God. Sir Digby Pettleworth. What was *he* doing here?

"Good morning, Sir Digby," she said icily. "I trust you intend only a short visit. Else I shall have to summon Charles to escort you to the door. You do remember Charles, my footman?"

"Of course I do."

His manner was far too calm, considering the violent manner of his ejection from Rosemead three years ago. Livvy bit her lip. Sir Digby Pettleworth was not a brave man. If he showed no fear of Charles there might be an unpleasant reason for it.

"What brings you here?" she ventured.

"Ah, I thought you would wish to know! In fact, I have every hope that today you will not spurn my expressions of admiration as you did three years ago."

He sauntered into the room. She remained seated at the harp, noting that he had put on flesh and now sported a gaudy diamond in his cravat.

"And why would you think that?"

Whether it was her aloof manner, or a desire to prolong the moment, he halted.

"Why, not long ago I learned that you have ended your long-standing liaison with Arlingdale and are seeking a new protector."

"Ah, you have read that piece in *The Morning Intelligencer*. I would advise you not to heed what is written there too closely."

He smirked. "My information is more direct than that."

How she hated the self-satisfied popinjay with his diamond pin, his sallow complexion and his potbelly. But he had a dangerously spiteful tongue. He'd used it against Harriet Debenham once; he would not hesitate to use it on her.

"If you wish to tell me something, I will listen," she said, digging her nails into her palms.

"I will tell you how I know you have broken with Arlingdale. I was there, at the Pulteney, the night *Le Nozze de Figaro* premiered at the King's Theatre," he replied, speaking each word with relish. "I saw quite a different gentleman follow your maidservant up the back stairway."

She felt sick, but she lowered her eyes so he would not see it.

"I know the man who visited your room that night," he continued with a delighted wink. "And, my darling lady, it was *not* Arlingdale."

Chapter Eighteen

"*I*t disappoints one to know that such an upright and moral gentleman should be subject to the same base urges as lesser men," Sir Digby mused, envy lacing the mock regret in his voice.

Livvy clasped her hands tightly in her lap, suppressing the angry retort that rose to her lips. She instantly comprehended the situation. Sir Digby was not merely seeking revenge for her earlier rejection; he was jealous of Jeremy and wanted to topple him from the position of respect he now held.

He was an insect. But it was wise not to antagonize a wasp.

"W-what gentleman are you speaking of?" she asked, intentionally allowing a nervous tremor into her voice.

"Why, Sir Jeremy Fairhill, of course."

"You must have been mistaken."

"No, I could not be. Perhaps you were not aware that for some time now I have been a member of the Foundling Hospital's General Committee? I see Sir Jeremy every Wednesday. I could not possibly be mistaken."

She allowed some of her dismay to show. "I will admit Sir Jeremy visited me. He only wished to assure himself, for the good of my children, that I was not consorting with Lord Arlingdale."

"Who do you think would believe that?"

"Anyone who knows Sir Jeremy would believe it."

Annoyance crackled from his eyes. She bit her lip, wishing she had not triggered his envy.

"Then his reputation must be safe," Sir Digby continued, composing his features. "Nevertheless, I cannot in good conscience keep the Committee in ignorance of his doings. It will be my unpleasant duty to bring it up at the next meeting."

"But—but that would cause such a stir."

"It is terrible to contemplate." Sir Digby shook his head. "Who knows? They might decide they can no longer place their trust in one who threatens the institution's good name."

She looked down, hiding her fury, hoping he would take it for despair. She needed time to decide what to do.

He took a step toward her. Another breeze brought a whiff of the vile pomade he used on his hair.

"And as for the woman who led him astray . . . well, they could hardly be expected to entrust her with the care of our poor young innocents."

If he had a soul, what a sad, repulsive thing it was!

She mastered the urge to call Charles and have the slimy creature cast down the steps. She needed time to get word to Jeremy; this was a matter they needed to address together.

"But surely the Governors would do neither of those terrible things," she said plaintively.

"If the Committee does not act, I might feel obliged to publish my findings. In the public interest, of course."

She felt sick. To report such gossip—it was unthinkable behavior for a gentleman. Yet the threat had come so easily to his lips . . .

"I should hate to be driven to such extremes," he continued. "My dear old father-in-law would be so shocked and disappointed. He thinks the world of Sir

Jeremy; one hates to think what he might do in the bitterness of his disappointment. Or of all the Cits who would follow his example."

Jealousy dripped from his voice, but Livvy knew he spoke the truth. Tobias Cranshaw was indeed one of the Hospital's most influential benefactors.

"A dreadful outcome, don't you think, my darling?"

She kept her eyes down so he would not see the hatred in them. "Yes . . . most dreadful."

"One that should be avoided at any cost."

"But—what do you mean?" she asked, feigning ignorance.

"I could ensure that Sir Jeremy's brief indiscretion remains a secret. And that those dear little children remain in your loving care."

She was unsurprised by the lascivious light in his eyes. Perhaps she could use his swaggering confidence against him.

"And in return? Surely you cannot be suggesting . . ." She stared up at him, wide-eyed.

"In return you shall allow me to be your friend. Your advocate on the General Committee. Your protector."

As if she were fool enough to trust him! The vindictive scum would not stop with making her his mistress; if she allowed it, he'd bilk her of her jointure, strip her of everything: independence, dignity, even the children.

He took another step forward and put a hand on her shoulder. Her skin crawled.

"I—I shall have to summon Charles if you continue, sir!"

"Do not dare!" he said, more roughly than before.

Something in his voice stung her like a foul memory, but at least he removed his hand from her shoulder.

"If you summon that damned footman, it will be all the worse for you and your precious Sir Jeremy," he growled. "Tell me. Do we have an understanding?"

He slid his hand back onto her shoulder. This time she endured it.

"You must give me some time . . . I cannot think . . . it is all so complicated . . ." She looked up, trying to look desperate. "Please, give me a week and I will give you your answer."

A week to get word to Jeremy and find a way to deal with this snake.

Laughing, he released her shoulder and walked toward the door to the corridor. "A week? No, my darling. I wish to have your pledge of cooperation." He shut it. "Now."

She thought furiously. Though flabby, he was a big man, possibly strong enough to overpower her. There were still the open French doors . . . but fleeing would not help.

"Oh dear," she blurted, inspiration striking her. "I cannot—what I mean is—the French lady, you know . . ."

He goggled at her for a moment.

"My monthly visitor," she explained meekly.

"You are lying!"

"No, indeed I am not!"

A look of fastidious horror spread over his features, and she went limp with relief. He believed her. Perhaps her ploy would gain her some time.

"When *will* you be ready to cooperate?" he demanded.

"By Saturday," she said, stretching her lie as far as she dared.

"Very well then, you shall engage your usual suite of rooms at the Pulteney. I shall meet you there at ten o'clock in the evening on Saturday."

She nodded, lowering her head.

"I shall look forward to it. But in the meantime, I hope to see further proof of your compliance."

Her heart sank. "You—you do?"

"I would be very disappointed if you ran with this tale to Sir Jeremy, for both your sakes."

He stared down at her hand. It was useless to hide her ring now. It seemed he knew everything already.

"What do you wish me to do?" she asked.

After a pause, he replied. "You shall end your disastrous liaison with Sir Jeremy. You shall meet him at the Foundling Hospital this Wednesday after the weekly meeting and tell him in person. A pity you cannot cry off in a letter, but I do not think he will believe it."

She kept her gaze averted, calculating quickly. A day and a half. Enough time to get word to Jeremy. Not enough time for him to reply or come to her assistance.

"No tricks, please," said Sir Digby in a bored tone. "You shall compose a letter to him under my direction. Now."

Obediently, she went to her writing table. Sir Digby stood over her, a hand on her shoulder, and dictated the short letter, merely requesting Jeremy to meet her on the Hospital grounds after the meeting. When she'd finished sealing and directing the letter, Sir Digby took it from her.

"I shall hire a messenger to ensure its timely delivery," he said, smiling. "If I hear that you have made any additional communications to Sir Jeremy, or that there has been any sort of slipup, I shall be obliged to publish my information. Perhaps I should also tell you that I have a friend who knows the entire story. He will not hesitate to make it public should anything happen to me."

Another enemy? A sense of helplessness stole over her. She and Jeremy had talked of winning the support of decent people: his relations, his friends. They'd been so naïve. They'd never considered the dregs of society like Sir Digby, or the mischief they could wreak with their depraved whisperings.

"I understand." She allowed her head and shoulders to droop, to hide her frustrated anger.

"I shall be looking forward to Saturday," he gloated.

He turned and left. She straightened up and took a few turns around the room. She felt ill. There was no time to speak to Jeremy before Wednesday, and she needed a plan.

She sat down, willing herself to think. Sir Digby's weaknesses were simple; he craved good living and gossip, and feared poverty and physical violence. Offering him anything—her self or her money—would only lead to more trouble. Was there a way she could threaten him without causing a scandal?

He also had an unknown ally.

She got up again and paced, holding back tears of desperation. Something was eluding her.

Do not dare!

His angry voice echoed in her mind. It was after she'd threatened to call Charles that Sir Digby's veneer of politeness had cracked. His raised voice reminded her of something. She stopped pacing and tried to imagine Sir Digby's voice amplified and slurred with drink.

She shook with anger as it came to her. Now she knew why he hated her so much, and why he was so ready to publish damaging gossip. He must have done so before, probably more than once. He had ruined her reputation, and now he threatened not only her and Jeremy, but the Foundling Hospital itself. And she would stop him, though the cost might be high.

Sir Digby Pettleworth was the Turk.

"Follow me, my lady."

Livvy followed the supercilious butler through the Bromhursts' quietly elegant residence in Grosvenor Square. He conducted her to the library and left her there, promising to convey a message to his mistress. By not taking her directly to the Lady Bromhurst's drawing room, he was probably passing a judgment on her social standing. Or perhaps she was just early.

She had not paced about more than a few minutes when a fashionably dressed, matronly woman appeared in the doorway.

"Lady Dearing?" the lady asked, eyebrows lifted over clever gray eyes that held curiosity but no hint of welcome.

Livvy curtsied.

"I am Lady Bromhurst," the lady announced. "What is the meaning of this visit?"

Livvy squared her shoulders. "In truth I wish to speak to Lord Bromhurst on a matter regarding the Foundling Hospital, but I thought it more proper to inquire for you first."

The lady scrutinized her critically for a moment.

"You are pale," she said, her voice just degrees above freezing. "I trust you are not ill."

"Thank you, I am quite well. But there is a problem I must discuss with Lord Bromhurst. I hope you will be kind enough to arrange for us to speak."

Another quick scrutiny, and Lady Bromhurst nodded. "Very well, I shall see if my husband has finished his breakfast."

Livvy paced again. Lady Bromhurst's chilly demeanor was just what she expected. However, she seemed a sensible woman, perhaps, once one got to know her, as kind as her husband.

A few minutes later, both the Bromhursts entered the room, wary expressions on both their faces.

"This is a surprise, Lady Dearing," said Lord Bromhurst. "I had thought we were dining together at Russell Square tomorrow."

"I had to come. I have news which affects all of us. Jeremy is at Fairhill. I could not get word to him in time, so I hope that you will be able to help me."

"Help you?" Lord Bromhurst echoed, his eyebrows

twitching fiercely. "This sounds serious. By all means let us sit down so you may tell us what's amiss."

"Do you wish me to leave?" Lady Bromhurst asked primly.

Livvy glanced between her hosts.

"No, my dear," Bromhurst returned. He turned to Livvy. "You may trust my wife to be discreet."

She nodded. "Thank you, but I should also like to be sure no one else hears what I have to say."

Lady Bromhurst closed the door. "Are you satisfied?" she asked, as if Livvy were behaving in a needlessly theatrical fashion.

She nodded and they seated themselves.

"What a wretched business," Bromhurst fumed, once she'd put him in possession of the facts. "I knew no good could come of this!"

"Blaming me will do no good." Livvy raised her chin. "We need to decide what to do about Sir Digby."

Bromhurst frowned.

"You do not expect Lady Dearing to comply with this—this *creature's* demands?" asked Lady Bromhurst indignantly, with a look of unexpected sympathy toward Livvy.

"Of course not." His mouth twisted wryly. "I wish we had not come to such a pass, but you were right to come to us. You have not told Jeremy anything, have you?"

"No. All he has is the letter I mentioned."

Bromhurst remained silent for a few more moments. "I think I know what may be done to put an end to Sir Digby's schemes," he said, with grim satisfaction.

"You do?" she and Lady Bromhurst asked almost in unison.

Bromhurst looked at Livvy compassionately. "Sir Digby will be stopped, but you must understand that I cannot afford to risk more such problems. You must make an end to it, Lady Dearing."

"You cannot mean—you do not wish me to cry off?"

"Yes, that is what I mean."

"How can you say that?" she protested. "After all Jeremy has suffered with his first wife . . . Is there no way? Does his happiness mean nothing to you?"

Lady Bromhurst made a small choking sound.

"His happiness is why I wish I'd never allowed him to go to Rosemead Park," said Bromhurst. "I should have known he'd try to make a noble fool of himself over you! It's hopeless, my dear. I'm sorry to say . . . but quite hopeless."

"How can you be so sure? Jeremy is not a fool; he is well versed in the art of persuasion. If he believes we can overcome this, why can you not help us?"

"Forgive me, I don't mean to be unkind. But if Jeremy did spend a night with you, or even made you his mistress, people would gossip but many would view it as a regrettable but understandable peccadillo."

"Hmmph."

Livvy turned her head and saw Lady Bromhurst glaring at her husband.

"However," Lord Bromhurst continued, his face reddening a little. "If Jeremy took you as his wife it would be seen as a serious lapse of judgment by every sensible man who currently contributes to the support of the Hospital. It would be a disaster. I am most sorry, my dear, but you must give him up or I shall have to take measures to prevent further scandal."

His words knifed through her, confirming the fears she'd set aside in the glow of Jeremy's lovemaking. Yes, perhaps he was a noble, adorable fool . . . Without others to share his vision, it was hopeless. And the children would suffer. Hundreds of nameless unborn children. And the four at Rosemead who meant everything to her.

"I see," she said, letting out a ragged breath. She would cry later, when there was no one to see it. "I shall give him up, but you must promise me that I can keep my children. You must set in motion whatever is required to make them my legal wards."

Lord Bromhurst rubbed his nose thoughtfully. But Lady Bromhurst's face crumpled. Unexpectedly, she rose from her seat and put a hand on Livvy's shoulder.

"You must do at least that much for her," she told her husband fiercely.

Livvy turned her gaze to Lord Bromhurst.

He heaved a sigh. "I do not know if it has ever been done. By royal charter all the foundlings are wards of the Foundling Hospital. We return children to parents who reclaim them, and when they are old enough, we send them to masters with written apprenticeship agreements. I do not know if it will be possible to arrange for an official transfer of guardianship."

Despite herself, Livvy recognized his distress. He *was* a good man, doing his best in a wretched predicament.

"Then promise me you will try."

"I promise. And while I am president the children shall not be removed from your care."

Lady Bromhurst returned to her seat, still frowning.

"You must forgive me for having railed at you earlier," said Lord Bromhurst more softly. "You are not at fault in this wretched situation and neither is Jeremy. The fault lies squarely with Sir Digby, and I promise you I shall bring him to justice."

"But do you remember what I told you, that Sir Digby has a friend who is privy to all these secrets?"

"I shall discover who it is and deal with him as well. It is my hope that I can do so without involving Jeremy."

"And I will keep my appointment with Jeremy tomorrow, just as Sir Digby expects."

"What will you tell him?" asked Lord Bromhurst, scowling again to hide his emotions.

"The truth. Part of it." She drew in a painful breath.

"I shall tell him that I do not believe we will be able to overcome the prejudices against our marriage. I shall not tell him that we spoke today."

"Thank you."

"I am not protecting you from his anger for your own sake," she said coldly. "I have the children to comfort me; Jeremy will suffer the most. He will need his friends and family to console him. I hope you will do so."

"We will do our best, my dear," said Lady Bromhurst, her face working in the effort to restrain tears.

"Of course we will," said her husband, with a weak attempt to sound hearty. "Jeremy will do. As will you, Lady Dearing. You are made of resilient stuff."

"I wish you success in dealing with Sir Digby, then," she replied, making no attempt to return his smile. "Is there anything else you require of me?"

"No. Make no further communications. Your arrangement is for Saturday at ten o'clock, at Pulteney's hotel. Have I got it right?"

She nodded. "Perhaps you will do me the kindness of letting me know when you have resolved the matter. In the meantime, if you should need to reach me I am staying at Grillon's tonight. I find I have conceived a distaste for Pulteney's hotel."

She rose to leave.

"Are you certain you are well enough to go?" asked Lady Bromhurst, rising along with her husband.

"As your husband said, I am made of resilient stuff, ma'am," she said, turning to go. "I shall do."

Livvy's head throbbed, but the odd, hollow calm that always followed a night of crying sustained her as she stood alone on the field surrounding the Foundling Hospital, awaiting Jeremy.

It seemed the wait was endless. Had Sir Digby managed to cause trouble after all? Fear that more trouble was to come churned inside her.

Then she saw Jeremy striding across the lawn, his gaze focused on her.

Before he'd come within twenty feet, worry had already hardened his face.

She couldn't bear it.

"What is it, Livvy?" he asked when he reached her side.

Her throat tightened.

"What happened?" His velvety eyes were full of concern. "Why are we meeting here, now?"

"I . . . shall not be at Russell Square this evening." The words came out as if a stranger had uttered them.

"What?"

"What I mean to say is that I cannot marry you."

He bent forward suddenly, as if she had punched him. "Cannot? What is this?" His voice softened. "Has someone been troubling you, Livvy? Tell me, then we'll decide what to do about it. Together."

His gentleness ripped her apart.

"There is nothing we can do," she said flatly. "This is my own decision. I am sorry I allowed you to persuade me, back at the folly, but on consideration I have realized it is hopeless."

He let out a ragged breath. "How can you say it is hopeless? I have spoken to my family and the Bromhursts; they are willing to meet you."

"I am sorry to cause so much . . . trouble . . . and disruption. But I think it is unfair to ask everyone to support our marriage when it can end only in disappointment."

"No!" he shouted. "It will *not* end in disappointment. Livvy, I know you have little reason to expect any sort of justice, but believe me, this time it will be different."

She removed her ring and held it out to him, wishing her hand did not shake so much.

"You cannot give up before we've even begun." His voice broke.

Dear God. Jeremy.

"I am so sorry. Please, take your ring back. It was a lovely thought, but I cannot accept it."

He ignored her outstretched hand. "This is madness," he snarled.

"To continue would be mad."

"Is it wrong to want to be happy? Keep the damned ring. We can postpone the dinner party until you change your mind."

Anger smoldered in his voice; pain contorted his face. Memories tormented her: how he'd made love to her in the folly, all his hopes and plans . . . and this was his reward for making the mistake of loving her.

She reminded herself of the stakes.

His reputation.

The Foundling Hospital, just across the field from them.

The children.

"I will not change my mind."

"Then I'll keep it for you until you do."

He swept the ring from her palm and thrust it into his pocket. She lowered her gaze, thinking he would leave, but instead he grasped her hands. She sensed him struggling with the urge to pull her into his arms. Her heart beat painfully, reminding her that she was still alive, that she could still suffer.

"Let me go, Jeremy. It is over."

"How can it be? I love you!"

"It is over."

"Are you such a coward that you prefer to hide safely at Rosemead rather than reach for the greater happiness that is offered to you? To both of us?"

Fury crackled through his voice, but he gripped her hands desperately.

She choked back tears. "It is best we part. Let me go. Please."

"Damn it, Livvy, don't do this."

She shook her head.

"Go then!" he said, dropping her hands. "Go back into hiding and tell yourself it's for the best, damn you. Damn you!"

She turned and ran then, tears blinding her all the way to her carriage.

Chapter Nineteen

"*W*hatever is the matter, Jeremy?"

He paused on the stairway, staring up at Aunt Louisa.

"Livvy is not coming this evening," he said dully.

"Not coming?" she echoed, staring at him as he ascended to the landing. "Has there been some sort of mistake about the date?"

"No. She met me at the Foundling Hospital to break off our engagement."

His aunt gazed up at him for a moment, and he could almost hear the words in his mind. *It is for the best, dearest.* At least she didn't say them.

All she did was come forward, arms outstretched. "Oh, my dear boy . . ."

He forced himself to tolerate the embrace. Her surprise at least proved one thing: that she'd had nothing to do with Livvy's change of heart.

"I was so afraid she would hurt you, dearest," she said, stepping back and peering up at him nervously. "Do you wish to tell me what happened?"

"No. I'm returning to Fairhill."

"Won't you at least spend the evening with us?"

"No."

"I will send word to the Bromhursts. Don't worry about anything, dearest, but return to us as soon as you may."

She brushed away a tear.

He gave her a reassuring hug before going on to his room, though for the first time in his life he could not accept her sympathy. He only longed for Samson, the solitary open road and the numbing effects of long, wearying exercise.

"Well done," said Livvy heartily, as Ben completed a passage from Mother Hubbard.

He closed the book, beaming at her praise. His vulnerable smile warmed her bruised heart.

"Let us work on your sums now. Fetch your slate, please."

As Ben crossed the schoolroom to get his slate and chalk, Livvy looked toward Robbie, happily engaged in drawing what must be his hundredth rendition of Pirate. Although he sometimes exaggerated the number of the pony's legs, his drawings radiated his exuberant energy. It made her smile just to look at them.

But her pain was too raw; it had been only two days since she'd betrayed Jeremy to save herself and the children. Today, tears still followed close upon smiles.

She brushed one away, trying to clear her vision. Philippa and Jane had their heads together over a mathematical tome that she'd brought back from London, exploring the glories of ellipses and parabolas together. She noted Jane's intent frown and Philippa's look of delighted absorption and brushed away another tear. Ben was coming back to her with his slate.

After she'd prepared several sums for him to work on, she sat back, ready to help if he needed it. The sound of scales being practiced on the pianoforte drifted up from the drawing room below. Already, Mary's deft fingers were acquiring a new skill. And yesterday evening, she'd even joined them in singing a silly ballad.

Livvy blinked back another tear. The children were thriving, and she knew she had made the right choice for them. None were ready for a return to the Foundling Hospital. Their place was with her, and hers with them. She doubted she would ever visit London again; her world was contracting once more to the limits of Rosemead's wall, and perhaps it was for the best. She would *do*, as she'd told the Bromhursts.

But guilt and longing filled her nights. They would be easier to bear, she thought, if she were not so deadly certain that she'd broken Jeremy's heart along with her own.

"Are you quite finished, sir?"

Jeremy nodded. Grayson picked up the tray containing his half-eaten dinner.

"Is everything quite all right, sir?"

"Of course," he replied absently.

Grayson's head shook as he moved stiffly out of the room.

No doubt the servants thought him mad. For the past few days, he'd closeted himself in the library, taking all his meals there and spending the rest of his time handling the new list of potential benefactors Bromhurst had handed him on Wednesday, only seeking his bedchamber when thoroughly exhausted. Even then he awoke early from restless dreams, aching with desire for Livvy, unable to comprehend or even accept her rejection. For a woman who'd already shown such courage to falter . . . he had not expected it.

Perhaps she had been wronged so many times that she truly had lost heart.

He picked up the list Bromhurst had given him and copied out the next name and direction. Doggedly, he wrote out yet another neat copy of his standard solicitation letter, folded and sealed it.

He took up the list again, but it faded before his eyes as he thought again of Livvy at the Foundling Hospital, holding back tears. She'd twisted a knife in her own heart as well as his. Why?

He forced himself to write and sign yet another letter, but as he laid it upon the growing pile on his desk, a sense of futility stole over him. Was he truly doing this for the children? Or for himself, to fill the emptiness of his life with something that had a semblance of meaning?

He closed his eyes. He had only to think of the children at Rosemead, to remember that without the Foundling Hospital they might be dead, to know that his work had meaning.

God, he missed them, too. They might even be missing him.

Why had she done this to all of them?

All he could think was that her fears outweighed her love. That her wounds ran too deep for his healing. Helplessly, he raged at her dead husband, the nameless viper who had blackened her reputation, her worthless nephew. And finally, at her.

He raged at himself for not finding a way to make things right.

He fought the urge to sweep paper, pen and ink pot off the desk in one grand, stupid, melodramatic gesture. Instead, he rose to follow impulses that had haunted him for months now.

Carrying his candle, he left the room, heading toward the entrance hall. He crossed the cold stone floor, climbed the steps and turned left, toward the corner room traditionally occupied by the mistress of the household.

He reached the door and briefly leaned his forehead against the dark wood. In the hush and gloom it was easy to remember the smell of his mother's perfume, the angry voices. But they were gone now.

As was Cecilia.

He thrust the door open and looked in. Though the furnishings were shrouded in protective coverings and the wallpaper had faded a bit, all else was exactly as it had been when he'd had the suite redecorated prior to his marriage. His dead wife had left no mark on this room, though this was where they had consummated their marriage, where she had given birth and watched their tiny daughter die, where she had slipped away from life a few years later.

There was nothing here for him; no clue to the maze that was his life.

He turned and closed the door quietly, then made his way to the third floor. To the nursery.

The wavering circle of light from his candle illuminated faded carpet and more furniture in covers. All was as it had been; they had never discussed what to do with the room's contents, allowing it to fade slowly, visited only by servants.

He roamed around, picking up the rattle he'd rushed to buy as soon as he'd learned Cecilia was in the family way. There, on a shelf lay the other toys: the lamb on wheels, the Noah's ark, so like the one Robbie enjoyed. The rocking horse, still standing in the corner, its painted eyes staring into nothingness. He gave the thing a single push, and it continued to rock for a while, an illusion of life in a place where there was none.

He should have persuaded Cecilia to sell these things, or give them away. Better yet, they should have brought Mary home, along with a few other children to form the family nature had denied them. But it was not the *done* thing. Governors sometimes hired children in their teens to work on their estates; no one took in younger ones to raise as their own.

The only one to do such a thing was Livvy.

He pushed away thoughts of hedgehogs and Banbury cakes and stumbled toward the hearth. Something above it caught his eye. He lifted the candle and went closer. It was a framed sampler that Cecilia had brought with her upon her marriage. He set his candle on the mantel and unhooked the picture from the wall. Holding it close, he examined the twining flowers and birds, the typical pious schoolgirl verse, all worked in tiny, exquisitely neat stitches.

> *My Fathers in Heaven and Earth below,*
> *Rightful paths to me do show.*
> *In humble and obedient ways,*
> *I will honor them for all my days.*
> —Cecilia Norris, July 12, 1796

She'd been . . . ten when she worked this. The same age as Mary was now. He reread the verses. *Humble and obedient.*

Only twice had Cecilia ever asked anything of him. After her second miscarriage. And on her deathbed.

He slammed the sanctimonious lines against the wall.

The sampler fell to the floor in a mangled heap of wood and fabric. He stared down at it, his anger fading to remorse. It was all he had of Cecilia, the one object that resonated with her restrained, gentle character. He ought to preserve it, in her memory.

He bent down to the wreckage. The frame was splintered beyond repair, but the sampler itself was undamaged. As he removed it from the frame, something fluttered out from the space between the sampler and its backing. As the pale, delicate thing drifted to the floor, he stared, disbelief turning to shock, shock bringing a resurgence of anger.

At last he began to understand.

Chapter Twenty

"*G*ood God! How can you sit there and tell me what you did was for the best?" Jeremy leaned furiously over the desk in Bromhurst's study.

"I could not afford to risk any further scandal," Bromhurst muttered. "But how did you guess?"

"I knew there was only one reason Livvy would have thrown away our chance for happiness: her children."

And once he had come to that realization, a terrible weight had lifted from his chest. Now Bromhurst had confirmed it; Livvy had jilted him only under coercion from Sir Digby. Hope simmered just beneath his anger; he turned his focus back to his one-time friend.

"And I knew there was just one person who had the power to coerce her into crying off."

Bromhurst's mouth twisted. "I stand by my actions. It was the best compromise I could think of, once Sir Digby started his mischief."

"Livvy came to you for help, and you threatened her with the loss of her children. You call that a compromise? You call yourself a friend?"

"Don't you see that if there had been any other way, anything else I could have done, I would have?"

"No, damn you! I don't see! How could you treat her so? If you knew all that she has suffered already . . . You *do* know!" he exclaimed, seeing the guilty redness on Bromhurst's face.

Bromhurst's hands shook but he met Jeremy's gaze levelly.

"It was my duty to assess her character and her motives before allowing her to take one of our children home with her. I am not a heartless man; I have done what I could for her, within the limits of my responsibilities to the Hospital."

"You did what you could?" Jeremy leaned back over the desk. "You knew that Dearing beat her? And you still did this to her? Damn you!"

The rustle of skirts behind him caused him to turn around. Lady Bromhurst stood behind him, anxious lines in her face belying her dignified manner.

He turned and bowed with exaggerated politeness. "My apologies for shouting. I promise you I will not hit your husband, no matter how sorely tempted I am to do so."

"Very proper," she said, inclining her head. "But I agree that you have every right to feel angry with Bromhurst."

"Amelia! What are you saying?" her husband cried.

She gave him a disdainful look. "I told you we should have informed him of what was happening. Now that I have heard poor Lady Dearing's story I feel even more certain that we behaved very wrongly. Have you at least told Sir Jeremy what you have planned for tonight?"

"I had not gotten to that," Bromhurst muttered. "I still think he should stay out of it. Matters are well in hand."

"Well in hand, when two fine people are made miserable by it?" She sniffed. "I am disappointed in you. I thought you more clever than that, but perhaps age is addling your wits."

"And you are becoming foolishly sentimental!" He

scowled. "But Jeremy does not need to hear us arguing, my love."

"Don't *my love* me! Don't even think of saying such words if you can't find it in your heart to help dear Sir Jeremy and his Livvy."

Stunned, Jeremy watched Lady Bromhurst bully her husband into submission.

"Calm yourself, Amelia," begged Lord Bromhurst. "If you and Louisa Fairhill can find a way to mend Lady Dearing's reputation, well, perhaps Jeremy and I can put our heads together to solve our problems with Sir Digby Pettleworth."

"Ah, now you are being reasonable." She bestowed a tolerant smile on her husband and nodded to Jeremy. "I think I must pay a visit to Louisa now. I shall leave the two of you together to plan a proper comeuppance for Sir Digby."

She sailed out of the room, leaving Jeremy and Bromhurst to look at each other warily.

"Women," Bromhurst grumbled. "First she tells me it's hopeless, and now she blames me for believing her." He let out a nervous bellow of laughter.

Jeremy did not smile.

"Lad, you have to forgive me. It's a wretched mess, but I was thinking of the children. I can't say it will turn out right, either. But I promise you I'll try."

Jeremy sat back in his seat, not immune to Bromhurst's obvious remorse. And he needed the man's help.

"Thank you. Now tell me what you have planned."

From his position just inside the door of the corner suite at the Pulteney, Jeremy glanced at the clock on the mantel. By the single branch of candles he saw it was nearly ten o'clock. He doubted Sir Digby would be late.

He continued to listen closely, hoping to discern the

sound of approaching footsteps above the beat of rain against the windows. Finally, he heard someone in the hallway. A moment later, the door handle turned.

"Hello! Where are you?" Sir Digby's voice quavered. "Are you in the bedchamber, darling?"

Sir Digby closed the door behind him. When he came face to face with Jeremy, he screamed like a woman.

In a single, swift movement, Jeremy seized his neck with one black-gloved hand and covered his mouth with the other.

He hoped the rainstorm had muffled the coward's shriek.

"If you scream again, I'll snap your neck," he said in a loud whisper, disguising his voice. "Nod your head if you promise to keep quiet."

Sir Digby's eyes bulged, but he nodded.

Jeremy thrust him toward a chair in the middle of the room. Sir Digby fell into it, trembling and massaging his neck.

"Damn you, Arlingdale! What are you going to do to me?"

He grinned, allowing his teeth to show through the mouth hole of his mask.

"Ask you a few questions," he hissed.

"I'll—I'll tell you whatever you wish to know. Please don't hurt me!"

Donning the guise of Death again had been a master stroke.

"Do you think you do not deserve to suffer?"

"I meant no harm. Lady Dearing agreed to meet me here, you know, and—"

"Of her own free will?"

"I—I was obliged to use some persuasion, but—"

"You threatened her with the removal of her children, did you not?"

Sir Digby cowered. Jeremy leaned over the chair and repeated his question, still using a stage whisper.

"Y-yes, I did. B-but I thought she was no longer your mistress. I thought she'd got that high and mighty Fairhill on her hook."

"It so happens that I believe she and Sir Jeremy would make a very fine match of it." He straightened back up.

"You—you do?"

"Lady Dearing was never my mistress."

"N-no? My apologies, Arlingdale, but you cannot blame me for believing what seemed to be common knowledge . . . can you? You're not going to call me out, are you?"

Jeremy bared his teeth again. "Perhaps. Perhaps not. Or perhaps I shall leave that honor to Sir Jeremy. I wonder which of us would enjoy it most?"

At that moment a crack of thunder sounded. Lightning flashed, penetrating even the drawn curtains.

Sir Digby shivered violently. Jeremy hoped he hadn't terrified him into palpitations. At least not before he had finished the interrogation.

"You—you aren't Arlingdale, are you? Who are you?" Sir Digby breathed.

"Quiet."

Sir Digby shrank back in the chair.

"You have confessed to threatening Lady Dearing into this assignation. Do you also confess that at the same time you coerced her into crying off from her engagement to Sir Jeremy Fairhill?"

Sir Digby nodded.

"Say it."

"Very well, I confess. It was for the good of the Foundling Hospital! I could not bear the thought of the scandal, the damage to Sir Jeremy's good name—"

This time an upraised hand was enough to stop him.

"You are becoming a bore."

Jeremy allowed the fat dandy a moment to squirm before continuing.

Thunder sounded again. Jeremy waited for it to sub-

side before moving on to his next question. "Did you
not try to force your attentions upon a lady at a masquerade three years ago?"

"I—I did."

"And when she refused to comply with your wishes,
did you sell damaging information about her to *The
Morning Intelligencer*?"

"Yes." The word was barely a squeak.

"And have you continued this vile trade in gossip
since then, even publishing a piece that could have
damaged the credibility of one of the Governors of the
Foundling Hospital and threatening to do it again?"

Sir Digby gulped, then nodded.

Jeremy leaned back over him.

"Yes, yes, I admit it! Will you let me leave now?"

"I have one more question. You have claimed to
have a friend who is party to all these secrets. You
will now reveal that friend's identity."

"M-must I?"

"If you wish to avoid giving me the pleasure of floor-
ing you as I did three years ago at the masquerade."

Sir Digby shrank back in his seat.

"I might not stop there." Jeremy yanked him up by
his cravat and held on to his throat.

"Oh, very well, damn you! It is Dearing—the present Lord Dearing, her nephew."

Jeremy stared down at the miserable creature. It
should have been so obvious: members of the same
dandy set, both with expensive habits . . .

"How much did Dearing pay you to cause trouble
for his aunt?" He gave the fop a shake.

"F-f-five thousand pounds."

Fury surged through him. Dearing would pay for
this, and for anything else he'd done to Livvy.

But now it was time to make an end of Sir Digby.

"Very well, I am finished now, except for one
thing."

He tore the diamond pin from the sorry creature's cravat.

"Thank you for your donation to the Foundling Hospital," he said aloud, grinning.

"Damn you, Fairhill! I should have known it was—" He gagged as Jeremy began to haul him toward the door of the bedchamber.

"Don't worry, I won't soil my hands on you much longer," Jeremy said soothingly. "You will soon have other things to worry about. Come meet some friends of mine."

He dragged Sir Digby into the bedchamber. There Bromhurst and Cranshaw stepped forward to meet them, menacing expressions on both their faces.

And Sir Digby Pettleworth's fate was sealed.

Holding Ben's hand on one side and Mary's on the other, Livvy walked toward the gate of the churchyard. Jane followed behind with Robbie and Philippa, all of them picking their way carefully down the gravel path, trying to avoid puddles left by the previous night's heavy rains.

They'd spent more than their usual time chatting with the kindly vicar and his wife. Livvy wanted to delay long enough to make sure Adolphus and Sophronia were gone. Just yesterday, they'd renewed their attempts to convince her to leave the country, complaining about suffering new and stinging comments about their inability to control her actions. She wanted to hear no more of it.

But there they were, still talking to other churchgoers just past the gate. For a moment Adolphus's gaze met Livvy's. Then he turned away again. She slowed, then decided to brazen it out and walk past them and their older son, who had drummed his heels against his seat for at least half the service.

But when they reached the narrow gate little Walter

was there. He blocked their path, legs planted apart, arms raised, and a challenging look in his eyes.

Livvy sighed. She rather wished she had the raising of the poor boy; Adolphus and Sophronia were doing their best to spoil him.

"Please let us pass, Walter," she said pleasantly, fixing the lad's gaze with her own.

"Why should I?" Walter sneered. "Why should I step aside for a bunch of bastards? B-b-b-bastards!"

Mary cringed; Ben gripped Livvy's hand tightly, no doubt burning with his inability to make a satisfactory retort.

"It's all right, dears." She looked back at Walter. "You should step aside, because it is the courteous thing to do."

He stood his ground. "Mama says you're a Jeze—a Jeze—a Jezebel!"

The insult came as no surprise to Livvy. It would have been laughable were it not so sad. She noticed that Adolphus and Sophronia—along with half the parishioners of Cherrydean—were looking their way, but with no apparent intent to restrain their son.

"I see I shall have to move you myself." She released the children's hands and stepped forward, hoping Walter would back down.

"I think not!" He dug a toe into the mud and gravel and kicked up, spraying her with rocks and gravel.

She stared down at splotches on her skirt, startled, then appalled. Ben rushed past her. Before she could stop him, he'd knocked Walter down.

"Mama! Papa! He hit me!" Walter bawled, sitting on his backside in the mud as Ben stood over him, fists clenched.

"Come back here, Ben," Livvy ordered sharply and pulled Ben away from the other boy.

Adolphus came running to the gate. "What is the meaning of this?" he demanded. "Are you hurt, my boy?"

"That bastard nearly killed me, Papa," the boy

whined, allowing his father to help him up from the dirt.

With relief, Livvy saw that apart from mud coating his backside, the boy was unharmed. Glancing up, she saw the onlookers hastily covering their mouths to hide shocked amusement at the sight.

"Oh my darling, what did they do to you?" Sophronia exclaimed, running up to join them. "Are you hurt very badly?"

"He is not hurt at all, Sophronia," Livvy said.

Adolphus straightened up; his eyes blazed with righteous indignation. He reddened as someone in the crowd muffled a giggle. After a brief, haughty look at the villagers, he turned back to Livvy.

"You will all answer for this," he said in a weighty tone.

"Nonsense!" she replied. "Walter kicked the gravel up at us, and Ben retaliated. I suggest we all go home and punish them in our own ways."

"It must have been an accident," Adolphus retorted. "Walter would never do something so ungentlemanly."

Livvy raised an eyebrow.

"Indeed, these—these *children* of yours go beyond all tolerance," said Sophronia. "Adolphus, you must deal with this properly since *she* will not."

"Indeed, I will, my love. You will be hearing from me, Aunt," he said in ominous accents.

"You are ridiculous. What are you going to do, call me out? Or Ben?" She shrugged. "Do as you must. We are going home. Children, come along please."

She reached for the children's hands again, and held them in a comforting grip as they passed the Dearings. Though she could not see what Adolphus and Sophronia could make of such a paltry brouhaha, she did not like the expressions on their faces.

They looked oddly triumphant, as if they had been waiting for just such an incident.

During the carriage ride home, Livvy did her best to balance between admonishing Ben for his lapse of control and reassuring all the children that nothing awful would come of the incident.

On their return to Rosemead, however, she sent a groom with an urgent note to the Debenhams. Perhaps she was being overanxious, but she did not want to be unprepared should Adolphus try to do more than fling angry words. Much as she disliked asking for help, she was no fool. Julian, being not only a man but a viscount and the wealthiest landowner in the district, not only could but would use his influence to help if her nephew tried to stir up trouble.

After she'd dashed off the note, she rejoined the children in the schoolroom. Seeing Ben still looking shaken, she sent him into the gardens. Even if he did a bit of work there, she decided it would be better for his soul than to adhere too strictly to the restriction against Sunday labor.

She had just retired to the drawing room, hoping for a quiet moment to recover her spirits, when Thurlow announced Adolphus, followed just minutes later by Mr. Selford, the magistrate.

Livvy's stomach clenched as she saw the almost maniacal light in Adolphus's eyes, but she greeted the two men politely. Once they'd sat down, Adolphus launched into a highly slanted version of the incident, denouncing Ben's character and insisting the magistrate take him into custody. With a measure of relief, she saw that Mr. Selford, a sensible man, was looking a bit impatient with the matter, though clearly unwilling to offend someone of her nephew's position.

Finally Adolphus paused to draw breath, and she jumped into the breach. "Mr. Selford, you must excuse Lord Dearing," she said, smiling. "His affection for his son has clearly led him to exaggerate what was a minor fracas between boys. No harm was done, and Walter did behave in a rather provoking manner. My nephew neglected to mention that his son kicked mud onto my dress. Not that this excuses Ben's behavior—as I have already told him! But I think it would be a grave mistake to refine too much on the matter."

Mr. Selford cleared his throat and looked at Adolphus. "My lord, I must say that there is little I can do in such a case. The lad is too young to be charged, and the offense was not severe. It is not as if it were a case of murder! Since no harm was done . . ."

"No harm? Why, my poor son is prostrate now, with his Mama in constant attendance!" Adolphus protested, but his voice wavered.

"Poor boy," Livvy interjected quickly. "I am sorry his nerves were so easily overset. But dear nephew, you must realize that pressing the matter further will only make a laughingstock of you and young Walter. Everyone will think him a namby-pamby, milquetoast creature."

Adolphus reddened as her words sank in. She knew it was a sore point with him, that he had always been painfully embarrassed by Walter's low opinion of his athleticism.

But she also guessed that Sophronia was behind this, and that she would make Adolphus's existence a living hell if he failed.

"You can do *nothing*?" he asked desperately, turning back to Mr. Selford.

"I could speak to the lad," Mr. Selford offered.

"You say you will merely *speak* to him?" Adolphus sputtered. "The boy is a menace, a firebrand. He has no place in a respectable parish such as ours!"

Livvy curled her hands until the nails dug into her palms, but she maintained a serene countenance. "Mr. Selford, you are well aware that in all the time he has been here, Ben has never harmed anyone. Nevertheless I think it an excellent idea for you to speak to him, and impress upon him the importance of self-control."

She rose and walked out of the room at a decorous pace. After directing Thurlow to send for Ben, she returned to the library to find Adolphus still holding forth on all the horrible consequences that would ensue if Ben were permitted to continue to live in the parish.

As she entered, both men stood up.

"Adolphus, you are really making a great to-do about nothing," she said calmly, taking her seat again. "I advise you to go home and have some chamomile tea. It is amazingly soothing to the nerves."

As he sat back down, he looked from her to the long-suffering magistrate and back again. Then his small eyes lit up. "If the boy cannot be charged, then a complaint must be lodged with the Governors of the Foundling Hospital!" he announced.

Livvy's nails dug into her palms again. To destroy her credibility with the Foundling Hospital was a clever ploy. But after all she had given up, Lord Bromhurst owed her his support.

Again, she controlled her countenance. "Lord Bromhurst will uphold me. He is not the sort of man to refine too much on such a paltry incident."

Adolphus stared into her face for a moment, scowling. His eyelid began to twitch again as she returned his gaze steadily.

"Furthermore, if there are any complaints from local landowners," she said, looking toward the magistrate, "I believe Lord Debenham will help you reassure them."

Mr. Selford's brow cleared, but Adolphus's face contorted. His entire body radiated fury at having been thwarted once more.

A cough sounded from the doorway. "My lady," said Thurlow. "Charles looked all over the garden but he was unable to find Ben."

She stared at him for a moment, new worries tightening her chest, then turned back to the others. "I told Ben to go into the garden and think over what he had done. I suspect he has gone further, into the woods. It may be some time before he can be found. Mr. Selford, may I offer you some refreshment while you wait? Of course, if you have more pressing business, I should not like to keep you."

"Well, yes, I do have some other matters I need to attend to," said the magistrate, his brow clearing. "I can very well speak to Ben tomorrow."

He rose, but Adolphus remained seated, his expression suddenly intent.

"Do you wish us to search for the lad?" Thurlow inquired.

Livvy shook her head, trying to look nonchalant. "No, there is no need. If he does not come back within another hour, I shall look for him myself. I know the children's favorite hiding places."

Mr. Selford bowed and took his leave then. Adolphus followed, stony-faced.

Livvy allowed Thurlow to see them out, sinking back into her chair. She ought to feel relieved, and yet she did not. Was she just weary of having yet another battle to fight? For clearly this was another attempt to wrest the children from her. Even Adolphus knew they were the core of her world; without them, she might as well do as he wished and live in Greece.

She rose from her chair, weariness giving way to the anxiety at the thought of Ben. The garden walls did not obstruct a view of the drive; perhaps Ben had seen Adolphus and the magistrate arrive. Well, perhaps he was just hiding in one of his usual places.

She headed toward the French doors, intending to search for Ben, when indecision caught her. She recalled the odd, desperate gleam in Adolphus's eyes as he left, and the conviction grew on her that he had not given up the fight.

Perhaps he was going ahead with his resolve to

cause trouble for her with the General Committee at the Foundling Hospital. She still thought Lord Bromhurst would stand her friend, but she had better warn him. Adolphus might even now be preparing to go to London, or to send a messenger to the Foundling Hospital with his complaint.

Again, she hesitated on the threshold, torn between the desire to comfort Ben and the need to send a message to Lord Bromhurst. Hastily, she sat down at her desk and penned the note. It took a mere ten minutes, and another ten to arrange for it to be dispatched to London, but once she'd done so, she hurried out toward the gardens.

Her first thought had been that Ben had gone to the hermit's cave again, but perhaps Charles had missed his hiding place. She hurried through the gardens, checking under arches, in odd corners, until she reached the orchard. When she entered the toolhouse, she breathed a sigh of relief. Ben was sitting, head on his knees, in a far corner, almost completely hidden behind a wheelbarrow.

She walked up to him softly, almost wondering if he was asleep. But once she had reached him, he raised his head, revealing a dirty, tear-streaked face. Conscious of a boy's pride, she decided not to comment on it but instead got down to sit on the floor beside him.

"You chose a rather uncomfortable spot for thinking," she said with a slight smile. "But quiet."

"I s-s-saw Lord D-d- . . . Dearing, and—and . . ."

"Yes, Mr. Selford came along. But they are both gone now, and I think it is time you came back to the house."

His face contorted with the effort of hiding his feelings. "I'm s-so *sorry* . . ."

She patted his shoulder. Recently he'd outgrown— or pretended to outgrow—the desire for hugs. She sensed the tension in his lanky body, and her heart

ached for him. For all her children, really. The stigma
of their birth would follow them throughout their
lives, and she would not always be able to protect
them. Somehow, she had to help Ben and the others
learn to deal with such insults without either getting
into deeper trouble or coming to believe they deserved them.

"Walter *was* very provoking," she said with a slight
smile. "But next time something like this happens, you
will be wiser, won't you?"

He nodded, and she withdrew her hand from his
shoulder. "We will talk more of this later. Shall we
return to the house now?"

He nodded again.

They scrambled to their feet and Livvy looked up
at high windows on the west side of the toolhouse.
The sun was not yet low enough to enter; it was earlier
than she'd thought.

An instant later something smacked into one of the
windows, causing the glass to shatter. For a moment
she thought it might be a bird. Then she saw that
some hard, flaming object had struck the shelf on the
opposite wall, near the entrance, where Furzeley kept
bags of seed and also sacks and flasks of the powders
and oils he used to treat diseased or infested plants.

Almost instantly, the contents of the shelf caught
fire.

Chapter Twenty-one

"And then her ladyship went out to look for the lad."

Thurlow came to the end of his recital just as Jeremy was reaching the end of his patience.

"I'm going to look for them both," he said, heading out of the library through the French doors.

"Very good, sir."

The butler's approving tone only added to Jeremy's remorse as he stepped onto the terrace. His blood boiled when he thought of that sad creature, Dearing, attempting to bully her. But she'd managed to stand her own, his Livvy!

He strode across the terrace, eager to pull her into his arms again. Surely she would understand and forgive him for his harsh words when they'd parted. It would be harder to convince her that he'd cleared the major obstacles against their marriage, but he would do it.

At the edge of the terrace, he glanced across the neat enclosures spread out below. The orchard . . . Somehow he felt Ben would be there, perhaps hiding behind one of his beloved fruit trees, or in the toolhouse.

As Jeremy raked his eyes across the scene, a chill came over him.

He hadn't mistaken it. A small plume of smoke rose

in the distance, from the direction of the orchard. Perhaps Furzeley was burning some garden debris.

But it was Sunday. The servants' day off.

Distant screams pierced the silence.

It was Livvy.

"Thurlow! There's a fire! Send help!" he bellowed back across the terrace.

Fear clutched his heart as he hurtled down the steps and into the gardens.

Livvy screamed with all her might.

She held Ben close as they huddled in the far corner of the toolhouse, praying someone would hear her. Orange flames grew in the opposite corner, near the door. Now they were spreading to the next shelf. Smoke billowed toward the ceiling.

There was no time to wait for help.

She glanced around. The windows were too high for her to boost Ben out. It was forty feet to the doorway, but they could manage it. They had to.

She stripped off her gloves and handed one to Ben.

"Ben, listen to me," she said over the low crackle of the fire. "We're going to make for the door. If we have to go through smoke, put this over your nose and mouth. Do you understand?"

He nodded, eyes wide with terror.

"Be careful of the glass!" With an arm around his shoulders, she set off along the opposite wall from the fire. The blaze continued to spread; heat radiated from the burning wall. Flames licked the potting table.

It collapsed just as they passed the glass beneath the broken window. Several smoking pots came crashing down. Livvy held Ben back as one rolled just ahead of them. Then she ran on.

All the shelves on the opposite wall were now in flames, lacing the smoke with acrid smells of burnt lime and tobacco water.

The cloud of smoke above them spread.

Holding Ben's shoulders, she hurried forward in a crouch, telling herself all would be well. The floor was slate; it would not burn. There was a clear path to the doorway.

Now the heat came from both sides; the shelves on the adjacent wall were burning, too. She shrieked as a rake fell from its peg into their path. But the wooden handle had not caught yet; she stumbled over it, pulling Ben along with her.

Terror gripped her as she saw the doorway ablaze. The heat was stifling; popping sounds came from the windows as the glass began to distend and shatter. Black smoke descended toward them.

"Get down!" she shouted over the crackling roar. "Hold onto my foot!"

She pulled her skirts up around her waist, fell to the floor and began to crawl, Ben touching her ankle as he followed. The slate was hard and hot. She could no longer see the doorway clearly. She began to pray.

Let the doorway be close. Let us survive this. Let me see Jeremy again.

She crawled on, eyes streaming. The stifling heat intensified and the cloud of black smoke pressed down on them; she lowered herself to a creep.

"Ben!" she screamed, panicking when she did not feel his grasp.

She started to turn around, then his hand gripped her ankle again. She pressed on.

Let me see Jeremy again. Give me a chance to tell him the truth and see if together we can make things right.

"Livvy!"

Jeremy. His beloved voice sounded faintly, unbelievably, over the roaring of the fire.

He couldn't be here. She crept a few feet more, praying she had not lost her mind and they were still heading in the right direction.

Jeremy shouted again, his voice barely cutting through the noise and blackness.

Smoke filled the building.

"Cover your face!" she cried to Ben.

Lifting her skirt to cover her own nose and mouth, she plunged into the black wall ahead of her, trying to hold her breath, hearing Jeremy's voice ever closer. She crept a few more seconds, gasped, and then emerged suddenly, choking and coughing, into the sunlight.

Through streaming eyes she saw Jeremy flying down the gravel path toward her. She turned and sent thanks heavenward as she saw Ben emerge from the smoke, coughing but unhurt. An instant later, Jeremy was there, helping them up. Putting an arm around each of them, he began to drag them away.

The fire roared louder. She glanced behind her and saw that the roof had caught. Sparks flew from the burning woodwork; smoke poured out though the shattered windows.

She stumbled, looked down and let out a hoarse scream.

Jeremy stared down at the flaming hem of Livvy's gown for a horrified instant, then shoved her to the ground. Falling to his knees beside her, he pulled the burning fabric to one side of her. Pain seared his hands as he beat and crushed the flames into the damp ground.

"We've got to get further away!" he shouted.

He pulled her back up, then dragged her and Ben a few dozen yards from the blaze. A crowd of servants ran toward them, bearing buckets.

Jeremy lowered Ben and Livvy onto a grassy patch next to the path, then dropped down with them, relieved to find both were breathing easily. Thank God they hadn't been caught in the smoke for too long.

But Livvy's dazed expression alarmed him.

"Were you burnt, Livvy?"

"No. But . . . I don't understand . . ." She stared up at him and began to shake.

"Hush, Livvy." Despite the stinging of his hands, he pulled her and Ben into his arms and held them tightly as both trembled in a delayed reaction to their ordeal. "You're safe, thank God. Livvy . . . Ben . . ." Then he stiffened, fighting an appalling thought. *"Ben."*

The boy raised his head, his expression distraught.

"No, it was *not* Ben!" Livvy raised her head quickly. She put an arm around the lad before looking back at Jeremy, her eyes regaining their focus. "Ben didn't set the fire; we have to find out who did!"

He tamped down useless rage as the likely culprit occurred to him. "What exactly happened?"

"Ben was hiding in the toolhouse. He was upset because—"

"Yes, Thurlow explained it to me. Go on."

"Do you think there could be a connection?" She shivered.

"Don't worry," he said, rubbing her arm. "We'll solve this; just tell me what you saw."

As she related what had happened, he held her close, trying to reconstruct the crime. A rock or brick, wrapped in oily rags, lit and cast through the window . . . He arose and shouted for Charles, the burly footman, who had taken charge of the servants working to douse everything surrounding the toolhouse to contain the spread of the fire. As Jeremy sent him off with orders to take half the servants to search the surrounding area, Miss Burton hurried into the orchard with a basket on her arm.

"Is anyone hurt?" she cried as she neared.

"I don't think so." Livvy glanced up from where she still sat, an arm around Ben. "Except . . . Oh dear God, Jeremy . . . Show me your hands!"

He held them behind him. "There are more important matters to deal with."

Giving him a stern look, she rose to her feet. But she turned to the governess first. "Jane, did you bring the rose water and the Turner's cerate?"

"Yes, and bandages and scissors."

"Well then, leave me the basket and take Ben to the house." She gave Ben a quick hug and a kiss on the cheek. "Don't worry about anything, dear. None of this is your fault and we are all safe."

"Should you not go back too?" Jeremy asked.

"No. I am perfectly recovered, and I wish to see this through." As the boy walked off with Miss Burton, Livvy fixed him with another fierce look. "Now show me those hands!"

Her stringent command released any lingering fears for her well-being. Grinning, he gave her his hands. She grasped them and turned up his palms. Angry red burns covered most of his right palm and fingers; the left was not so bad.

"Good God! How long did you plan to hide this?" she scolded him, dropping his hands and bending down for the basket Miss Burton had left.

She guided him to the closest bench, clucking over him in a most satisfying manner, then bade him sit down while she rummaged through the basket.

"Now you must sit still; this may sting a little," she warned him.

She poured some of the rose water over his burns. He grimaced. "Now I'm going to smell of roses."

"It will help keep off infection."

"You remind me of Aunt Louisa," he teased, spirits soaring as she carefully dried his hands.

"I hope she did not allow you to neglect such injuries," she snapped.

It was almost worth the pain to have her fuss over him so lovingly, he thought, as she spread ointment on his burns and bandaged them loosely in gauze.

"There. Later I'll give you a decoction of bark for the pain, but I think you will do."

"With you to care for me, I haven't a doubt I will."

She edged closer to him, her soot-and-tear-stained face breaking into a smile that lit his heart. Ignoring the agony of his hands, he pulled her into his arms and kissed her hungrily, first on the forehead, then her cheek, then claiming her mouth in a sweet burst of mingled relief and desire.

She looked up some time later, eyes glistening. "Jeremy, while Ben and I were crawling out of that fire, I vowed to myself that if I survived I would meet with you and tell you how sorry I was to have hurt you so terribly."

"It is *I* who should be sorry, for calling you a coward. I should have realized the sort of coercion used on you."

"But what of Lord Bromhurst? Sir Digby?"

"It's all settled. It's a long story which I'll tell you later. But now, just know that I am here, and that I am not going to leave you again. Not ever."

After another kiss, he cleared his throat. "Now we need to bring someone to justice."

He had just arisen from the bench when a masculine voice echoed across the orchard.

"Livvy! Fairhill! What the devil is going on here?"

Debenham ran up to them, his blue eyes wide with shock as he took in the sight of the burning toolhouse, Livvy's smoky appearance, Jeremy's bandaged hands.

"Good to see you, Debenham," Jeremy replied. "We may need your help."

He had nearly finished explaining the situation when Debenham pointed in the direction of the back gate.

"I think we have our culprit," he said.

Charles came through the gate towing Lord Dearing along with him, while Furzeley brought up the rear brandishing a pitchfork.

"I found him in the woods," Charles told them impassively.

"And I found this just outside the gate," said Furzeley, holding up a tinderbox.

"I have no idea where the tinderbox came from!" Dearing blurted, struggling to escape the big footman's grasp. "I saw the smoke from the road and was coming to see what was the matter."

"He was running the other way, ma'am," said Charles.

"Thank you, Charles," said Jeremy. "Now you and Furzeley may leave us to deal with this creature."

Reluctantly, Charles let go of Dearing, whose eyelid twitched wildly as he goggled at Jeremy and Debenham, seeing no possibility of escape.

"Well?" asked Jeremy, once the servants had withdrawn.

"Don't look at me that way!" Dearing cried. "Do you think I—I, a gentleman—could have set a fire, when my aunt has been harboring a firebrand in this very house?"

"Damn you, Adolphus!" Livvy cried furiously, leaving Jeremy's side to glare at her nephew. "So it was to implicate Ben that you did this. Oh, you are unspeakable, to involve an innocent child in your schemes! May you burn in hell for this!"

"I didn't set the fire! You have no proof!"

"How do you explain that glove?" Debenham pointed to the blackened glove the idiot still wore.

"It was only a toolhouse, after all! I meant no harm!"

White-hot rage possessed Jeremy. He found both his hands around Dearing's neck, the excruciating pain from his burns only adding to his fury.

"Damn you, you heard their cries for help!" he snarled. "And you ran away, you miserable coward, leaving your aunt and a child to die!"

Dearing burbled incoherent protests.

"Perhaps you should allow him to breathe, Fairhill," Debenham suggested. "Not that I really care. He deserves strangulation, but his dead body would prove difficult to explain to the magistrate."

Jeremy loosened his grip.

Dearing took a few gasping breaths before speaking. "You won't press charges! Think of the scandal!"

"You will not escape the consequences for what might have been murder."

"But—but no one died. And none of it would have happened if she hadn't taken in those little bas—"

Jeremy's hand on his throat silenced him.

"They are children of the Foundling Hospital. We take care of our own."

"The circumstances are against you," Debenham said pointedly to Dearing. "A case could be made that you coveted this estate enough to murder your aunt."

"I didn't wish to murder her! Only to—"

"To drive her away?" Jeremy finished. "But who can be sure of your motives? Just how do your finances stand, Dearing? You are well known for your expensive tastes; will anyone doubt that you wished to come into a comfortable property sooner rather than later?"

Dearing cringed.

Reluctantly, Jeremy released his neck. "I'll leave you two choices. Stand trial. We will brave the gossip; we have plenty of practice, after all. Or leave the country."

"If I run away everyone will think I tried to kill her. Damn it, I see how they look at me in the district, all politeness, but underneath all vile rebellion! They're all in league with her. I'd never feel safe to return."

"Exactly. So which is it to be?"

"Dear God, the scandal of a trial . . ." The pathetic creature glanced around imploringly. When no one showed any signs of softening, desperation clouded his face. "Where shall I go? What shall I do?"

"My cousin's husband has an estate in Jamaica," suggested Debenham. "Perhaps they could use a clerk there. I could arrange it, if you think it will help get rid of him."

"Thank you, Julian," said Livvy. "It might do."

"Jamaica? If disease doesn't kill me, the climate will!" Dearing protested.

"Perhaps you would prefer to stand trial?" Jeremy asked.

Dearing's shoulders slumped.

"Then that is settled," Debenham said cheerfully, grasping the creature's arm. "If you wish, I'll arrange matters from here."

"Thank you," said Jeremy. "But there is just one more thing I must do."

He strolled up to Dearing and plucked the diamond pin from his cravat. "For the foundlings."

"Bravo!" Debenham grinned. "Now I'll leave you to discuss more . . . interesting matters."

Jeremy heaved a sigh of relief as he watched them go. Then he glanced down at Livvy and smiled.

They did indeed have more interesting matters to discuss.

Chapter Twenty-two

*L*ivvy swayed. Jeremy's smile made her feel weak, giddy, as light as a balloon ascending from Hyde Park. Irresponsible, as if she were living in a dream. But when he pulled her back into his arms, she held him off with her hands against his chest.

"Still worrying, Livvy?"

The expression in his eyes was so tender she almost forgot what she wanted to say.

Resisting the temptation to just sag into his warm embrace, she looked toward the toolhouse. The roof had caved in, though the brick walls stood and smoke continued to drift eastward over the woods. The sight was a potent reminder of how the world could intrude on their happiness.

"I see you still need some convincing," he said. "Shall we find a pleasanter place to talk?"

She took his arm and began to walk with him, still feeling light-headed. "How did you discover what happened?"

"I confronted Lord Bromhurst about it. When he told me what had happened, I joined in with his plan for foiling Sir Digby's scheme."

"What did you do?"

"We kept the assignation at the Pulteney. Sir Digby

was a bit perturbed. I think my costume may have had something to do with it."

"Oh my . . . the costume from the masquerade?" A giddy laugh escaped her as they entered the herb garden. "He must have thought the devil himself had come to claim him. What I would have given to see that!"

"It *was* quite effective." He grinned. "I wrung a complete confession out of him, including an admission that your nephew had paid him to cause trouble between us."

"Adolphus paid Sir Digby?"

"Yes. He must have guessed about our engagement."

"Oh, that is my fault. Sophronia saw the ring!"

"You shouldn't have had to hide it," he retorted grimly.

"And then, not content with breaking up our engagement, they looked for a way to take the children from me. They must have known it was the only thing that could drive me from England." She shivered. "I never would have guessed it of a puling creature like Adolphus."

"What matters now is that none of those scoundrels will menace us again." He slid an arm around her waist.

"But what of Sir Digby?" she asked as they passed under an arch into the flower garden.

"Tobias Cranshaw, his father-in-law, hid in the bedchamber and heard everything. He has been disappointed in Sir Digby for a long time, and wishes he had never allowed his daughter to marry an idle dandy with such expensive habits. He has sent Sir Digby and his daughter to live on Sir Digby's estate in Yorkshire, requiring them to seek his permission if they wish to come to London."

"Sir Digby could not have been happy about that."

"It was that or a debtor's prison. Cranshaw has also

threatened to cut them off without a penny if Sir Digby ever tries to profit from malicious gossip again. But I have not yet told you the best of it."

"What is it?"

He guided her to a bench and they sat down together, surrounded by beds of purple candytuft, tall blue larkspur, nodding Canterbury bells.

"Cranshaw was very moved by your story," he said, putting an arm around her. "How you took in the foundlings, everything you have endured at Sir Digby's hands. The long and short of it is that he has promised to use all his influence in the City—and it is vast—to make sure that support for the Foundling Hospital continues to flourish despite any gossip about *us*."

"That *is* good news." She sighed. The scent of carnations filled her nostrils.

"If you are still worrying about what others will think, let me tell you that you now have the most earnest support from Lady Bromhurst and my aunt. They are already hatching schemes for how to present our story to the *ton*. Lady Bromhurst says she will speak to Countess Lieven. If we can enlist *her* support, your position in society will be assured. And of course, today's events should prove useful . . ."

"How?"

He got a faraway look for a moment. "Yes, of course. Olivia Dearing, the brave heroine who saved a helpless foundling from certain death in a hideous fire, and—"

"Rubbish! I was terrified."

"Livvy, you *are* a heroine, and everyone shall know it. Do you have any other arguments for me now?"

"None at all," she said meekly, leaning against him. "It is just so difficult to believe."

"It *has* been a devilish week. There is so much I learned, so much I still want to tell you."

For a moment he gazed out at nothing in particular;

it was then that Livvy saw the change in his face. A new peace, as if he'd come through some sort of ordeal and was the stronger for it.

Then he smiled, patting his waistcoat pocket. "But that can wait. Now I think I must prove to you that this is all real."

He leaned over for another tender kiss, then clumsily reached into his waistcoat pocket with his left hand.

"I should like to try this again," he said, pulling out a velvet pouch and removing her ring from it.

"Will you marry me, Livvy?"

She smiled. "You cannot stop me!"

He carefully slid the ring back onto her finger. She turned her hand and the ring sparkled, as if it had captured the spirit of every favorite blue flower: bluebell, lobelia, larkspur, Canterbury bell.

"Then let us not wait any longer. Marry me today."

She jerked her head up. "*Today*?"

"There's no need to wait. And I don't want to." He patted his waistcoat pocket, looking insufferably pleased with himself. "The Archbishop was kind enough to provide us with a special license."

Shock kept her immobilized for a moment. Then he took her hands lightly in his. She stared down at his bandages.

"You don't wish to wait, do you?"

"No, but what will your family think of such a hasty wedding?"

"They will not be offended, I *promise* you." Amusement glimmered in his eyes, along with something more potent.

"And the children . . . they must be terribly frightened, especially Ben. It would be such an enormous change for them. But perhaps they will welcome it."

"Then let us go and find out." The look in his eyes intensified, as if, despite her dirty face and burnt gown, she were the most desirable thing he'd ever seen. An answering warmth flushed her body; all she could do was nod.

They went together into the house, his arm indecorously around her waist. No doubt the servants were already anticipating a new master, she reflected as they climbed the steps up the terrace.

Twenty minutes later, after she'd changed out of her burnt gown and restored her appearance, they entered the schoolroom. Mrs. Thurlow sat in one corner, reading to Robbie who was perched on her lap. Jane sat at the table with the older children, Ben close beside her.

The children raised their heads to stare anxiously at her and Sir Jeremy.

"Lady Dee! Sir Jeremy!" Robbie hurled himself out of the housekeeper's lap and ran to Livvy. "There's a fire, Lady Dee! Did you know?"

"We know," she said, hugging him tightly. "But it is burning itself out. We are safe."

The other children crowded around her and Jeremy. She reached out and hugged them all as best she could.

"Could the house burn too?" Robbie piped.

"No, it will not. We are all safe now."

"But how *did* the fire start?" asked Philippa.

Livvy frowned, wondering how much to tell the children. Ben at least had probably guessed.

"It was set by someone who will no longer trouble any of you," Jeremy said.

"I will speak to each of you about it later, if you wish," Livvy added. "But for now, just know we are all safe. Now please sit down. I have some exciting news for you."

The children took their places around the table. Mrs. Thurlow and Jane stood nearby, wearing expectant smiles.

"What I wish to tell you is that Sir Jeremy has asked me to marry him, and I have agreed."

Mrs. Thurlow and Jane broke out in earnest wishes for their happiness. A moment later, Philippa added hers, followed by the others, but the children looked sober.

"Will Sir Jeremy come to live with us?" asked Robbie, voicing the question Livvy suspected the others feared to ask.

"I should be delighted to live here with all of you," Jeremy answered promptly. "I also have a house called Fairhill Abbey, in Hampshire. We may go there sometimes, but Rosemead Park will always be my favorite place."

The children beamed. Livvy's heart swelled with gratitude.

"Will you stay with us tonight?" Robbie asked naïvely.

Jeremy stifled a grin. "Would you like me to?"

The children all nodded.

"But it would not be proper for me to stay here without being married to her ladyship. I wonder how such a problem might be solved?" He winked in her direction.

"Would it be possible for you to marry today?" Mary asked gravely.

His face perfectly solemn except for deep creases in each cheek, Jeremy nodded. "That sounds like a capital idea." He turned to Livvy, wicked lights in the depths of his eyes. "Do you think your vicar will oblige us?"

"He will be delighted to do so," she said breathlessly. "I'll have a message sent to the vicarage."

"Well then," said Mrs. Thurlow. "I must get to Cook. You must allow her time to bake a cake, at least!"

The children burst out in crows of delight.

Livvy rejoined Jeremy in the library over an hour later, having bathed and changed into a rose-colored silk gown chosen for her by the girls, who'd taken great pleasure in helping Alice fuss over her hair and jewelry.

He arose, smiling, from the wing chair. His carriage and valet had arrived some time earlier from Cherry-dean where they'd been awaiting his summons, so he was now impeccably dressed in a dark blue evening coat, his cravat carefully tied, his face cleanly shaved, his hair still slightly damp.

The breath caught in her throat at the sight of him: her husband-to-be, with the mahogany eyes, the velvet voice, all power and gentleness. Gloves hiding his bandages. Her knight!

With a joyful cry, she hurled herself into his waiting arms and lifted her face to be kissed.

"I forgot to thank you for saving my life," she said huskily, some time later.

He pulled her even closer. "Livvy, if you knew how I felt, seeing the smoke, hearing you scream . . . I ran as fast as I could, but my legs felt like *lead*. I thought I would never get there in time. A few burns are a small price to pay for having you safe in my arms now."

She sighed, leaning against the warmth of his chest. "How *are* your hands?"

"Not bad. Haye had to help me more than he usually does." He shook his head regretfully, but his eyes gleamed. "I am afraid I might be a bit clumsy undressing you this evening."

"Wicked man! Perhaps *I* should do all the undressing tonight."

"I should like that." He grinned.

Her cheeks heated, just as he must have intended. *Wicked, wicked man!*

He cleared his throat. "I asked Thurlow to summon the vicar for about five o'clock. Let us sit down; there's something I must tell you."

Blinking at his altered tone, she followed him to the sofa.

"What is it?" she asked, nestling against him.

"It concerns Cecilia. Some things I learned about her this week."

She sucked in a breath.

"When you broke off our engagement last week, I returned to Fairhill, like a wounded beast—"

"Oh, Jeremy—"

Fondly, he pressed a gloved finger against her lips. "I wandered around that hateful place, trying to make sense of things. Perhaps in some corner of my mind I already realized that children—the ones we could not have and the ones from the Hospital—were the heart of the matter, for I found myself in the nursery. There I found a sampler Cecilia had worked when she was a girl. The sanctimonious verse on it seemed to epitomize everything that had been wrong about our marriage."

She gasped.

"Did you think, like everyone else, that ours was the perfect union?" His mouth twisted. "It was calm and peaceful certainly, and Cecilia was the most dutiful of wives. But I never really knew her. Perhaps the only time she expressed herself with true candor was on her deathbed, when she begged me to care for Mary. Now I know why."

"Dear God . . . you can't mean . . ."

"I discovered the truth when I hurled that sampler against the wall. It broke apart, and out fluttered half of a lace collar. I could not mistake it; it was an exact match to the one at the Foundling Hospital. I questioned Cecilia's father and finally learned the truth.

"When she was sixteen, Cecilia was seduced by a soldier from a regiment stationed in her village. My guess is that she fell in love with him and he'd taken advantage. I'll never know for certain. In any case, she was sent away to have her child in secret. A servant delivered Mary to the Hospital with the hundred pound fee."

He frowned. "Her father was too proud to admit he was palming off what he would have considered damaged goods on me, and I, in my ignorance, believed her story about having had a riding accident in her youth. But Mary's birth left Cecilia with more than a broken maidenhead."

"No . . ."

"Denman said that sometimes women who have had a difficult first birth are so injured they cannot carry another child. Now I know why Cecilia seemed to blame herself for her miscarriages. Her father, who is a harsh, unforgiving man, must have forbidden her to tell me. I wish she had. Her guilt cankered every moment of our marriage."

He lowered his gaze, and memories beset her. How he'd made love to her in the folly with such eagerness . . . his delighted look after he had brought her to rapture . . .

"Jeremy." She paused, wondering if she dared ask. But he had bared so many wounds to her already. She took a deep breath, and the words started coming in a torrent. "Jeremy, before my wedding night my aunt warned me that the marital act would be an ordeal. She said it was best done as quickly as possible, in darkness and silence. I did not believe her. No matter how wretched things were with Walter, I still believed something better was possible. But I know there are women who do not."

His face was still shadowed. Bitterness leached out in his voice. "I married Cecilia because she was good and virtuous; I thought that with her I could enjoy the pleasures of the marriage bed without risk of repeating the dramas that made Fairhill Abbey such a hellish place in my parents' day. But early in our marriage, when I tried some of the things I'd heard women liked, it was clear Cecilia found my efforts to please her disgusting. She never complained, but I knew she preferred . . . darkness and silence, as you said. I resigned myself to it. When our hopes for conceiving a child were finally dashed, it was a relief to both of us."

A spurt of indignation mingled with her pity for his dead Cecilia. Though wounded, could she not have realized that Jeremy would treat her with kindness and understanding? And to be married to such a dear, beautiful man, and not take advantage of his desire to please her . . .

She put her arms around Jeremy and hugged him fiercely. "I wish she had been honest with you. Instead, she punished you as well as herself, by not allowing you to make things right."

"I cannot blame her too much; she could not help her upbringing." He cleared his throat. "Do you think we should tell Mary?"

"Not yet, I think. But when she is older, I think she will like to know the truth."

He kissed her cheek. "She could not ask for a better mother."

"Or a better father, now."

She sighed.

"What is it, Livvy?"

"I do still wish I could—"

"Bear us a child? Don't let it trouble you. We have each other, and four children already."

"Yes, I know. We are blessed."

"More like four hundred, actually," he murmured. "If you count those at the Foundling Hospital!"

She didn't know whether to laugh or weep, but he put an end to her dilemma with a long, smoldering kiss.

A loud cough interrupted them.

Thurlow stood in the doorway, his eyes twinkling.

"Sir. Ma'am. The vicar has arrived."

Chapter Twenty-three

*T*he evening sun slanted in through the French doors of the drawing room, deepening the colors of the flowers spilling out of every vase: larkspur, carnations, snapdragons, pinks. Livvy stood beside Jeremy, serenely aware of the well-wishers surrounding them.

To one side stood Jane and the vicar's wife, beaming. On the other, near Jeremy, stood his relations who had arrived not a quarter of an hour before: his short, plump Aunt Louisa, smiling and dabbing her eyes with a handkerchief at the same time, his cousin Thomas, tall and dark like Jeremy, head fondly bent over that of his pretty, fair-haired wife Charlotte, whose belly proclaimed her to be very much in the family way.

All listened quietly as the vicar enumerated the purposes of holy matrimony.

"First, it was ordained for the procreation of children, to be brought up in the fear and nurture of the Lord . . ."

Philippa and Mary looked solemn and adorable in their best gowns, ribbons in their hair. Ben stood quietly, his stance an imitation of Jeremy's, his eyes still shining from the compliments he'd received on his flower arrangements. Robbie was picking his nose.

Livvy turned her head slightly and gave him a stern

look. Instantly, he pulled the finger out of his nose and assumed the mien of an angel.

She turned her attention back to the vicar, who continued to enumerate the reasons for matrimony.

". . . mutual society, help, and comfort . . ."

A lump came to her throat as she glanced toward Jeremy, admiring the broad, noble forehead, the determined lines of mouth and jaw.

A moment later the vicar asked, perfunctorily, about impediments, and went on to prompt Jeremy in making his vows.

"Jeremy Edward Fairhill, wilt thou have this woman to be thy wedded wife, to live together after God's ordinance in the holy estate of matrimony? Wilt thou love her, comfort her, honor, and keep her in sickness and in health, and, forsaking all others, keep thee only unto her, as long as ye both shall live?"

"I will," he replied, turning down at her, eyes bright with love and a deep awareness of the vow he was making.

The vicar turned to her.

"Olivia Anne Dearing . . ."

She listened carefully to the words she'd given scant attention at the foolish age of seventeen, much like the ones the vicar had directed to Jeremy. She also heard the differences. *Obey him. Serve him.* And a glow spread through her, for here was one man she could trust with such promises.

"I will," she said, in a voice that rang throughout the room.

As Jeremy took her hand tenderly in his bandaged and gloved one and they pledged their troth to each other as prompted by the vicar, her joy deepened. Finally, he slipped a gold band on her finger, and his voice struck the same deep chord within her as it had on their first meeting.

"With this Ring I thee wed, with my Body I thee worship . . ."

*   *   *

Livvy set the candle down on the nightstand as Jeremy shut the door of her bedchamber. *Their* bedchamber now.

As he came to her, she feasted her eyes on him: her handsome husband, who'd worked so hard and waited so patiently for this day, this moment.

She vowed he'd be properly rewarded.

"Nervous, Livvy?"

The dear man! He was still worrying about *her*.

She shook her head, put her arms around him and lifted her face for a kiss that tasted of cake and champagne.

A moment later, she slid out of his arms.

"What is wrong? What are you doing?"

"Unmasking," she said, flashing him a wicked smile as she went to light the branch of candles on her nightstand.

She did the same with the candles on her commode, until the light flickered over the birds and flowers painted on the walls, the exotic bed hangings, the eccentric mix of furniture, the bowls of freshly cut pinks that filled the room with their spicy-sweet fragrance.

"I always thought your bedchamber would be paradise." Jeremy took her back into his arms. "I did not know it would look like it, too. It suits you."

She kissed him, then broke free again to sit down by her dressing table. Quickly, she removed her pearl necklet and earrings and set them into her open jewel case. Then she began to unpin her hair.

"Let me help."

She looked up at Jeremy with a saucy smile, and shook her hair out onto her shoulders. "Did we not agree that *I* was going to do all the undressing tonight?"

"I was joking."

"I was not, and I would be backward in my duties as a wife if I permitted you to injure your hands!"

He looked adorably aroused and confused all at once.

"Jeremy . . . my love. There's no need to treat me like a Dresden shepherdess anymore. I left those fears behind the day you made love to me in the folly. Now you see me as I am: a brazen, wanton woman. Are you shocked?"

"I shall accustom myself," he said gruffly.

"Tonight, let me seduce *you*."

"Is that what you truly wish?" He sounded strangled.

"Yes. Let me undress you and touch you and make love to you. *Please*."

He released a ragged breath. "A man would have to be mad to refuse such an offer."

She chuckled, then bent over to remove her slippers. Her hair fell over her shoulders but—she realized from Jeremy's sudden intake of breath—did not block a most indecorous view of her breasts.

Delightedly, she drew up the hem of her gown on one side to untie her garter, then slid the stocking off that leg. Jeremy leaned back against the high edge of the bed, eyes riveted on her as she removed the other stocking.

She arched to unfasten the mother-of-pearl buttons on the back of her gown, then stood up, allowing it to swish to the floor. She removed her petticoat, undid her stay laces, deliciously aware of his rapt gaze, until finally she stood, clad only in her shift.

"Livvy . . ."

She smiled at having rendered her eloquent husband speechless.

Shrugging, she allowed the shift to float to the floor.

Jeremy's gaze devoured her from head to toe, then returned to her face.

She licked her lips. "What do you see, Jeremy?"

"I see *you*, Livvy. The most beautiful, desirable and the very bravest woman I know."

She put her arms around him, and he pressed a searing kiss to her lips. Her body tingled, pressed against the wool and silk of his coat and waistcoat. She withdrew to remove them, one by one, relishing his frenzied expression.

"I rather enjoy being your valet," she jested softly.

He let out a low chuckle. "I shall have to dismiss Haye."

She knelt at his feet, ignoring his protests, and removed his shoes and socks, delighting in the size of his feet, the hard angles, the muscles of ankles and calves. She rose up and unbuttoned his shirtsleeves, careful of his bandages, then untied his cravat and pulled it away. He swallowed, his Adam's apple catching her eye as she undid the buttons at his neck.

Now he was as he was when she'd admired him in the garden.

She tugged his shirt free from his pantaloons and drew it up slowly with one hand, passing the other lightly over his ribs, chest and shoulder and stopping to kiss his chest. He groaned, his entire body tightening.

She pulled the shirt over his head and he continued to lean motionless against the bed, his bandaged hands on either side of him, watching her like a starving man.

"I've been longing to do this, you know," she said. "Ever since I saw you working in the garden the first time. Do you know I watched you from that very window?"

He shook his head. "I would have thought you would find me . . . crude . . . and repulsive."

She laughed, tracing the bulge of muscles from his upper arms down to his wrists. "Yes, I was so repulsed that I could not help but come into the garden the next day for a closer look."

"Yes, that was the day . . ." He paused, as she

flicked a finger over his chest. "That was the day I began to hope."

She stroked the light growth of hair down the center of his chest, then traced its ridges and contours. He closed his eyes, allowing her to touch and admire every muscle, and moving not one of them. Rigid with desire but holding back so she could safely explore him.

She decided she'd tormented him enough.

She pressed herself up against him, savoring the smoothness of his warm skin over the hardness of his muscles, then lowered her hands to the buttons on either side of his pantaloons.

His hand stilled hers.

"Livvy . . . I don't know if I can bear much more."

"Did I do wrong?"

"No! But I have wanted you for so long. This first time, if you touch me, it will be over . . . too soon."

A bold and shocking idea came to her. "Do you mean—is there something I could do for you? Like what you did at the folly?"

"I'd never ask such a thing!"

"Let me try. *Please.* I want to," she whispered.

He let out a rough breath, then picked her up and lifted her onto the bed. Together, they removed the rest of his clothing, and she took a moment to drink in the sight of him, beautiful and vulnerable in his arousal.

She reached her hand down and touched him. He let out a deep groan, then lay still, staring up at the top of the bed canopy with a tortured look. She touched him again, savoring the velvet hardness of him, then stroking the length of him. She kissed him again and worked both hands over him, stroking and circling, more muffled groans proving the power of her unpracticed touches. Soon he jerked, crying her name, and filled her hands with his seed.

She watched as he lay for a few moments, eyes closed, face blissfully serene. When his eyes opened she smiled down at him.

"Now *I* feel as if I have a new toy."

He grinned mysteriously. "It is my turn now."

She lay back, wondering. He gazed at her for a heartbeat before kissing her. Then he trailed kisses down her neck to linger at the hollow of her throat, just long enough for her to yearn to be touched elsewhere. Then he kissed her breasts in turn, causing her to gasp in mouthfuls of pink-scented air. When she could bear it no longer, he shifted and surprised her by kissing her navel. A moment later he moved down the bed. Surely he wasn't going to? . . .

Then he did. The gauze of his bandages brushed her thighs as he opened her up and kissed her. She flushed and her body arched in protest as she sensed a climax coming; it was too soon.

He lifted his head; she gave out a beseeching moan, and he lowered his mouth to her again. She continued to resist as he held her open, tickling the insides of her thighs with his dark curls, his hot breath on her. Each feathery touch, each deeper kiss brought her higher until she twisted and cried out, caught in an updraft of exquisite pleasure.

She floated for a while, barely aware of Jeremy shifting on the bed to lie beside her again.

"*That* was brazen," she murmured, when she could speak.

He laughed. "I have been longing to do that—and many other things I've only heard about—for months now."

He put an arm around her again, and his bandages rasped lightly against her skin.

"I had nearly forgotten!" she said contritely. "Do your hands pain you very much?"

"What hands?"

Amusement lurked in his eyes, and something else. Hunger, and a question.

Smiling, she opened to him. Carrying his weight on his elbows, he lowered himself carefully over her. With a soft cry, she lifted her hips, put her arms around him and pulled him in. And he was there, filling her, and it was just what she had yearned for, since the night after his lovemaking in the folly. This closeness. This bond.

She twined her legs around his. He lowered his face to kiss her, withdrew and returned with unnecessary gentleness. She kept time with his slow movements, her hunger building until she could bear it no more. Then, boldly, she moved her hands down to cup taut buttocks and pull him deeper.

He paused, eyes dark with surprise and arousal. Murmuring words of entreaty, she pulled him in for another harder thrust. His breath grew louder, his thrusts more powerful, and she met each one, moaning, no longer in reassurance but out of longing for the new peak building within her.

She closed her eyes. Her womb tightened and she cried out as her body pulsed around him. He let out another groan, and she opened her eyes to see his face contorted with rapture.

They clung together for a moment, then he rolled to one side. He pulled her close and she rested in a sweet nook she found in his shoulder. A tear escaped her eye to splash onto his chest.

"What is it, Livvy?" he whispered, tightening his arm around her. "Are you all right?"

"Yes, yes. It is just that—it was just how I imagined it would be when . . . when I was seventeen. No, even *better*."

"I'm so glad." He let out a shuddering sigh. "So do you believe this is real now?"

"Not at all."

He shifted to look at her, narrowing his eyes.

She gave him an impish grin. "You will just have to prove it to me again in the morning."

His laughter rumbled through the bedchamber. "Do you truly believe I can wait so long?"

Epilogue

August 1813

*T*he Archbishop concluded a benedictory prayer and dug a bit of ceremonial dirt from the area marked out for the branch hospital's foundation.

A cheer went up. Jeremy kept a restraining hand on Robbie's shoulder to keep the scamp from rushing out with his own little spade. A moment later, the Archbishop invited the assembled Governors, benefactors and their families to join in, and Jeremy released Robbie. The boy darted off to the excavation area with the other children.

"Well my friends, it's a day of triumph for both of you," said Bromhurst, emerging from the crowd to beam at him and Livvy.

"For all of us," Jeremy replied quietly, smiling down at his wife.

She had an odd, faraway look as she stared out at the field where their children were happily digging. Aunt Louisa, Tom and Charlotte had joined them, holding little Nicholas's hands. Although the babe could not walk yet, he seemed to enjoy toddling between his parents in the sunshine. A few feet away the Debenhams kept a close eye on Annabel.

But Jeremy suspected Livvy was picturing what he did: the several hundred children who would be playing on these fields once the commodious new building was ready to house them.

"Lady Dee! Lady Dee! We want you to come dig with us!"

Robbie's voice came piping over the hum of conversation around them.

"Excuse me, I think I shall join the children," she said.

"Are you certain you feel up to it?"

"I promise you I'll only pretend."

She smiled up at him; he drank in the sight of her bright eyes, her rosy complexion, the lush swell of her belly. She'd awoken bursting with energy, but he couldn't help worrying that she would overexert herself.

"I'll go with you, then."

"Could you stay a bit?" asked Bromhurst. "I've something to tell you, and it won't take but a few minutes."

So he pressed a kiss to Livvy's cheek and let her go.

"I never thought things would turn out so well," said Bromhurst, smiling after her. "But I've never been so happy to have been wrong."

Jeremy returned the smile. He knew his friend harbored lingering regret for his actions of a year ago. Although they'd long since mended the rift, a reminder today felt right.

Bromhurst cleared his throat. "I have some good news."

"Yes?"

"Cranshaw has just told me he is altering his will. Pettleworth and his wife are to receive an annuity sufficient to support them in comfort, but the bulk of Cranshaw's fortune shall go to the Foundling Hospital."

"That *is* good news."

"You and Livvy can take much of the credit."

Jeremy smiled, recalling how, during the early

months of their marriage, she had charmed Cranshaw and the others. There had been a burst of gossip, inevitably, but Cranshaw's support in the City and the romanticized tales Lady Bromhurst and Lady Debenham had spread of their marriage and Livvy's heroic behavior during the fire, had ultimately resulted in an increase in donations.

Jeremy's eyes narrowed as he detected a shadow crossing Livvy's features. For a moment, her face seemed unusually blank, then she smiled down at Robbie again. Perhaps the sun had gotten into her eyes.

"To think you'll be seeing your own babe soon!" said Bromhurst. "When was it that dear Livvy expects to be confined?"

"In about two weeks, according to Knighton."

Livvy seemed perfectly well now, again making a show of digging with the children. Perhaps he was foolish to worry so much about her upcoming confinement.

He watched her, remembering the time when unlooked for joy had stolen up on them, when her courses were late, first by days, then by weeks, and a slight morning queasiness confirmed that she was in the family way.

Dr. Knighton had a glib explanation; marriage to a kinder husband had had a harmonizing effect on Livvy's constitution. Whether or not he shared Jeremy's radical opinion or not, the popular accoucheur could not afford to even suggest that Dearing had somehow been incapable of fathering a child.

Whatever the case, Livvy had remained serenely happy throughout her pregnancy, sweetly refusing to follow anything but her own inclination regarding diet and activity, while he had worried incessantly.

Jeremy's stomach clenched. Livvy had turned his way, and there was an odd expression on her face: part doubt, part excitement. No. It could not be.

"Are you feeling tired?" he asked, hurrying to meet her.

"I think—I am nearly certain my pains have begun!"

"But Knighton said it would not happen for another two weeks!"

"He never claimed his predictions were exact."

"What is going on here?" Lady Bromhurst asked, hurrying up. "Livvy, have your pains begun?"

"I think so."

"I knew we should not have come!" he exclaimed. "We should have stayed in Russell Square, within reach of Knighton. It is my fault! I should have—"

Livvy placed a hand on his arm. "Don't worry, my love. I am sure everything will be well."

"How can I not worry? What are we to do? It's a full hour and a half drive back to London from this godforsaken place. Three hours before Knighton could possibly come here!"

"Calm yourself, Jeremy," ordered Lady Bromhurst, then looked toward her husband. "Bromhurst was in just such a state when our first came, but he can assure you that it took ages. If you leave now you may very well reach London in time for Dr. Knighton to attend Livvy."

"What? Submit her to the bouncing and swaying of a carriage for all that time?" Visions of having to deliver the baby by the roadside tormented him.

"No, I would rather not go so far," said Livvy. "Jeremy, I think we should go back to that village we passed—South Houghton, was it?—and see if perhaps a surgeon or a midwife could be summoned."

Aunt Louisa bustled up to them, Nicholas wrapped around her hip. "What is happening?" she asked excitedly. "Has Livvy's time come?"

"Yes, we think so. We are going back to South Houghton now."

"Well, what are you gaping and standing about for?

Get Livvy to the carriage, and don't worry about the children. We will take care of them."

Pains seized Livvy twice before they reached the village. Jeremy was relieved to find the Red Lion a clean and comfortable hostelry, and the landlords more than willing to dispatch stable boys to the surgeon and midwife. Just after he'd seated Livvy in a chair in the best chamber, more carriages were heard below. Minutes later, in burst his aunt, Charlotte, Lady Bromhurst and Lady Debenham, all chattering excitedly. He did not know whether to be annoyed or relieved.

"Is there anything you need, Livvy?" Lady Debenham asked, while the other ladies inspected the room.

"I—oh . . ." Livvy broke off, gripping the arms of the chair.

They all watched with bated breath until she relaxed again.

"A fierce one, was it?" asked Lady Bromhurst. "You should not worry, dear. It is a sign things will go quickly."

"Quickly! There is no one here—not Knighton, not that blasted surgeon, nor even the midwife!" he protested.

"Jeremy dearest," said his aunt sternly. "Since you persist in frightening Livvy, we must ask you to leave!"

He bowed his head, appalled that he might have made things worse with his worries. But if he left, and something terrible happened . . . this might be his last chance to see Livvy.

Her cheerful voice penetrated his misery.

"No, I want Jeremy *here*," she insisted to the other ladies.

He glanced down to see her gazing up at him with loving concern, as if *he* were the one suffering those horrible pangs.

After a spirited exchange between Livvy and his

aunt, Jeremy was permitted to stay, though the ladies' following reminiscences of their respective ordeals made him not a whit more comfortable. But Livvy seemed glad they were here.

A few minutes later, she moaned, her face contorting with pain.

"Is there nothing that can slow this?" he begged.

The ladies turned to look at him as if he were demented.

Minutes later, mercifully, the landlady entered, followed by another woman of middle age and tidy appearance.

"Dr. Perry was not at home, m'lady," she said. "This is Mrs. Hodge."

Jeremy eyed the midwife dubiously. She seemed competent and respectable, but still . . . what if something went terribly wrong? Then he noticed Livvy smiling at the woman, and decided it was no use saying anything. Mrs. Hodge seemed to be their only hope.

Lady Debenham and Lady Bromhurst excused themselves a moment later, then Mrs. Hodge asked him to help Livvy onto the bed so she could check the progress of her labor. Having done so, and given Livvy a kiss on the forehead, he went to a corner of the room away from his aunt and Charlotte, feeling lumpish, morose and completely useless.

Livvy submitted to Mrs. Hodge's gentle examination, uneasily aware of Jeremy brooding in the corner. He worried so much; perhaps memories of his tiny daughter's birth made it difficult for him to believe in a happy outcome. She wished there was a way she could reassure him. Though more dreadful than anything she could have imagined, her pains felt natural. Purposeful.

"It won't be long now, my lady," said Mrs. Hodge. "Are you quite comfortable?"

"I should like to sit up," she said.

"Let me plump your pillows," said Charlotte, rushing up to help her. "If only we had a proper birthing bed for you. I so wish you could have used the one where Nicholas was born!"

"It was so kind of you to offer, Charlotte."

"Well, this bed should do," said Mrs. Hodge. "Most of my mothers get through the business in my chair, but I did not think you would fancy it, being Quality."

Another pain beset her, starting as they all had with a tightening of her belly, but then progressing to a constriction so hard it seemed to tear her apart inside. Her vision and hearing shattered; for a moment, she was alone with her pain.

"A bad one, m'lady?"

The midwife's kind voice brought her back to the room.

She nodded weakly.

"It's a good sign. It means the baby will come soon."

She glanced back toward Jeremy. He looked so miserable that she was tempted to ask him to leave, but if she did, he would undoubtedly continue to imagine the worst. And she wanted him near.

"I don't want to lie down," she said decisively. "I want my husband to hold me."

Mrs. Hodge looked at her for a moment, then nodded. "Very well, m'lady."

A few minutes later, it was arranged. Jeremy sat at the edge of the bed, Livvy in front of him, his arms securely around her, while the midwife sat on a low stool before them.

Another blinding, tearing pain seized her, but this time she felt Jeremy's arms around her, heard his beloved voice murmuring encouragement throughout.

"Thank you; that was better," she said as the pain subsided, allowing her head to sag against his shoulder, and smiled. Though nature had her body in its grip, there were still some things she could control.

She spread her hands out. "Come here, please . . . Aunt Louisa . . . Charlotte."

They came forward, each taking one of her hands. Soon, another pain hit her, so sudden, so fierce that she cried out. Afterward, she began to shiver.

"Forgive me, darling." Jeremy warmed her with his body. "I want never to see you in such pain again!"

The other women laughed, then Livvy joined in. Her birth waters flowed. Mrs. Hodge smiled.

"Another good sign?" Jeremy moaned.

"I think it is nearly over, darling," she murmured over her shoulder as she braced herself for the next pang. It was finally coming: the moment she'd longed for. It felt right to meet it in Jeremy's arms, surrounded by his family.

Then she cried out, as a new sort of pain wracked her.

"You can push now, m'lady."

Obeying Mrs. Hodge's prompting, Livvy pushed with all her might, groaning all the while. It seemed to help. During the next pain, she worked even harder, then gave a cry of excitement. She'd felt the baby move.

"Well done. I see the head now."

"Brave Livvy." Jeremy kissed her cheek. "And they call women the weaker sex."

"Bosh!" said Aunt Louisa.

Livvy rested back against his chest, listening to the women's laughter and mustering her strength. The next pang came quickly; she strained and groaned; her pain and her power became one. The baby moved again, inch by inch, then more quickly until suddenly the pressure ceased.

"I have him. A fine boy!" exclaimed Mrs. Hodge.

Livvy sagged, then stared down at the wet infant in the midwife's hands. The sudden silence was broken seconds later when he began to cry. Her eyes misted with relief at the lusty, indignant peals.

"A boy! How clever of you, Livvy," said Aunt Louisa, peering down at him.

"Such dark eyes—just like Jeremy's," said Charlotte. "And will you tell us now what you have decided to name him?"

"William," Livvy breathed. "After my Papa."

A short while later, she rested on the bed, clean and dressed in the landlady's nightrail, watching Aunt Louisa and Charlotte avidly as they finished swaddling her son, who had quieted while being bathed. Jeremy had moved to a corner, rapt in contemplation of his son.

"May I have him now?" she begged.

Tears trickled from the corners of her eyes as Aunt Louisa handed her son to her. He felt so sturdy, so comfortable in her arms. His skin was a nice pink, and his eyes . . .

She smiled toward Jeremy. "He *does* have your eyes."

He nodded nervously, then William began to squirm and turn his head.

"He's hungry!" she exclaimed. Eagerly, she pulled down one side of the nightrail.

A few minutes later, with the midwife's help, she had William vigorously suckling at her breast. Quietly, everyone but Jeremy filed out of the room.

Looking up, she saw him still standing in the corner, with an odd, stunned look on his face as he gazed at her and William.

"Come and join us," she said softly.

He tiptoed across the room and climbed gingerly onto the bed beside her.

Then a chorus of hurrahs sounded from below, and they both started. Even William let go of her breast.

"It seems everyone has heard the news," she said, smiling. "It sounds as if the entire Board of Governors and their families are down there in that parlor!"

Jeremy nodded absently, his gaze on William. She

lifted her son up, patted his back, then put him to her other breast, but after a few sucks he seemed more interested in looking about, his eyes wide if unfocused.

"Do you wish to hold him, Jeremy?"

"If—you think I should. I've never held a baby so young, not even Nicholas."

"Here. Meet your Papa," she said, handing her son over.

Jeremy took the child and stared down in silence for a moment. His expression relaxed; anxiety gave way to awe. "He looks so . . . *big* . . . and healthy."

A tear sprang to her eye, but she wiped it quickly, preferring to watch as William squirmed inside his blankets.

"He seems to enjoy kicking as well as he did inside me," she said, chuckling. "I am not sure he likes to be swaddled."

A small fist emerged from the swaddling clothes. Still looking awed, Jeremy stroked the palm with his forefinger. His eyes widened as William opened his hand only to close it around his finger.

"He's strong, too," he added, beginning to sound smug.

She tilted her head up to give Jeremy a kiss, shocking to find a single salty tear sliding down his cheek.

"Indeed he is," she said softly. "Indeed he is."

Author's Note

This story drew me into many new areas of research, fascinating and sometimes disturbing.

Among the latter was the study of English property law regarding married women. Although a husband had the right to income from any property a woman brought into a marriage, it *was* possible for a caring father to make provision for her and her children through marriage settlements. These settlements could ensure the husband could not "kiss or kick" her into signing the property over to him so he could gamble it away; at the same time they could restrict her right to sell or devise the property to an heir of her choosing. In Livvy's case, her father settled Rosemead Park on her and her children. The reversion clause that caused the property to go to her last husband and his heirs would have been highly unusual, but Livvy's father wanted to ensure she would be in a good position to remarry if she were widowed and childless.

Readers might ask why characters in this story did not resort to adoption. The answer is that legal adoption did not exist in England at that time (the Adoption of Children Act was passed only in 1926). Although people could and sometimes did take in children to raise as their own (Jane Austen's brother Edward Austen Knight was "adopted" by wealthy and childless relatives), only legitimate blood heirs could

inherit titles or entailed land. Most people did not
think of adopting orphans or foundlings in the way
they might today.

The foundlings in this story come from an institution that really existed: London's Foundling Hospital,
which was established in 1739 through the efforts of
Captain Thomas Coram, a deeply compassionate man
who was horrified by the plight of abandoned children
dead and dying on the streets of London. I have tried
to be faithful to all the details of the foundlings' care
at the Hospital which I culled from an excellent book
on the subject, *Coram's Children*, by Ruth K.
McClure.

The sad statistics for the numbers of babies turned
away from the Hospital and the appalling infant mor-
tality rate in London's poorhouses are both factual.
Opposition to the Foundling Hospital was widespread.
Many believed that foundlings, who were usually of
illegitimate birth, deserved to suffer for the sins of
their parents and argued that providing a refuge for
bastards encouraged promiscuity. However, many
were not so heartless. A group of Lady Petitioners,
including eight duchesses, eight countesses and five
baronesses, was influential in helping Coram obtain
the royal charter to open the Foundling Hospital.
Throughout its history, the Governors of the Hospital,
a diverse group including peers, businessmen, professional men and clergymen, did their best to provide
the foundlings with decent care and education that
would prepare them for useful and productive lives.

Although I was able to discover some names of
Governors and Hospital staff during the Regency, history has recorded little more about them. Hence, all
the specific individuals and incidents related to the
Foundling Hospital are my own invention and have
no relation to real persons or incidents. There was no
branch hospital during the Regency. During this time,
moral reform societies began to proliferate and sup-

port for the Foundling Hospital faded. However, it continued to operate until the 1920s, and the charity Coram Family still exists to serve the needs of vulnerable and disadvantaged children.

Much of my information about pregnancy and childbirth during the Regency period comes from a fascinating book by Judith Schneid Lewis, *In the Family Way*. Invariably, any difficulties with procreation were attributed to an imbalance in the woman's constitution. Recommended corrective measures included: cold baths, sea bathing, bloodletting, abstinence from sex, and a "lowering regimen" that restricted "heating foods" such as meat, cheese and wine and recommended "cooling foods" such as vegetables and fruits.

On a happier note, my research shows that many husbands did indeed attend their wives in the birthing chamber, and that many aristocratic women, encouraged by their physicians, nursed their children rather than hire wet nurses. In any case, Livvy is an eccentric and strong-willed woman and would not have had it any other way!